Still Life in a Red Dress

COMING SOON

From Dennis Jung and
Martin Brown Publishers

Eye Of God

Morning of the World

Still Life in a Red Dress © 2012 Dennis Jung.

This novel is entirely a work of fiction. Though it may contain references to products, places or people, living or dead, these references are merely to add realism to the product of the author's imagination. Any reference within this work to people living or dead is purely coincidental.

Published by Martin Brown Publishers, LLC
1138 South Webster Street
Kokomo, Indiana 46902
www.mbpubs.com

ISBN: 978-1-937070-15-1

To Kathleen for her patience and support, and to Nora Astorga for the inspiration that allowed me to tell this story.

DENNIS JUNG

became interested in writing after receiving encouragement
from friends who read his letters relating his travels in Asia and
the Pacific. His use of visual imagery and his strong sense of
place are what make his novels as much an escape to a geo-
graphical location as the mental landscape of his characters.
Tapping into a background in anthropology, he weaves into his
stories a sense of the mystical and the universal in the human
experience - the drama and the conflicts that consume us all,
regardless of culture. Mr. Jung lives in Santa Fe, New Mexico.

Still Life in a Red Dress

by

Dennis Jung

And we call for the great stimulants of the exhausted ones--
Artifice, Brutality, and Innocence.

--Joni Mitchell

"Every soul shall have a taste of death."
-The Quran, Sura III:185

1

PART ONE
Western Darfur, Sudan
October 2008

The thread of one's life, if one is fortunate, is circuitous and endlessly surprising, replete with tragedy and triumph, virtue and sin. Yet if one's heart is pure, it leads straight as an arrow to the point of completion.

Sonny nudged the bandana back over his nose with the back of his hand, his splayed fingers sticky with blood and grit. He turned and looked back at his companion. Khatir, his turban half-unraveled and dragging in the sand, strained under the weight of the last two bodies. A pair of vultures nipped at the young Dinka's heels, their wings spread as they hopped from leg to leg, squawking, and mocking him. Khatir, anxious to be done, cursed and kicked at his tormentors without breaking stride. A permanent scowl had set in on his broad, dark face. Sonny watched him for a moment longer, and then let his gaze fall back on the bodies piled haphazardly at his feet.

Nineteen of them. Twenty-one counting the two Khatir would add. The chances were good there had been more of them when they left their village. From the tribal scars and their clothing, he guessed that they were also Dinka. He could only guess how

Khatir felt about burning his dead kinsmen, an elaborate burial being the more traditional means of earthly departure amongst his tribe. Any sentiment on the part of the young African was obscured by stoicism and the fact that neither he nor Sonny shared much of a common language, their only discourse a crude mixture of Sonny's rudimentary Arabic and Khatir's refugee camp French. Hence, they stumbled through their workday communicating with little more than shrugs and flicks of the eye.

He started to reach into his shirt for his cigarettes when he remembered his hands. Squatting, he took a handful of the coarse sand and rubbed it over his hands and between his fingers. The blood came away like old paint, part flakes and part gummy. As he scrubbed, he stared at the face of a young woman sprawled at the edge of the pile, her arms pinned unnaturally at her side. It was difficult to guess her age; a side effect of deprivation. In this part of hell, adolescent girls masqueraded as old crones; their fly speckled eyes sunken and distant.

Unlike most of the others, her face and throat appeared unblemished. He felt tempted to turn her over and look, but he knew all too well what he might find. Several of the women had been disemboweled, their intestines looped over the scrubby undergrowth like some grotesque banquet for the vultures. Wedged beneath her was a small, skeletal child and what appeared to be another woman. The battered, bloodied face made it difficult to tell.

The thread of one's life. He swatted at the flies as he glanced up at the white hot sky and thought again of the prayer card nailed to the tent pole beside his cot.

"And if one's heart is pure," he murmured. "Always the hard part. "He looked back down at the corpses and rose to his feet.

And the point of completion? It had come around much too soon for these poor souls. Although for some of them, not soon enough, he guessed. And the setting for their demise a scant two miles from The Doctors Without Borders camp which promised at least temporary salvation.

He thought again of the prayer card and the young boy at the

2

Nairobi Airport who had handed it to him.

"I have message for you, *bwana*. You say this prayer every day and God help you. Yes? Only give me five shillings. Five shillings, *bwana*. Okay, four."

He had slipped the boy several greasy bills and stuffed the tattered card into his pocket and forgotten about it. It was only after he arrived at the camp and began unpacking his meager belongings that he bothered to read it. Something in its sentiment appealed to his burgeoning willingness to embrace possibility. The slip of paper became part cosmic lottery ticket, part mantra. Reciting it aloud became a ritual he performed every morning, followed in short order by a resolute stroll to the crude latrine just outside his hut.

His co-workers marveled at how he had survived four months in the camp before contracting the digestive malady that befell most of them in their first week. Part of it was luck, part of it conditioning. He liked to believe that half a lifetime spent in the tropics and a stint in a Spanish prison had bestowed upon him near perfect intestinal invulnerability.

Afterwards, with an empty gut and an open mind, Sonny offered the prayer as his intention for the day ahead. To open his heart. No matter what. To kindness and hope, or death and despair - the latter being far more common. In the end, it always seemed to come down to the same two choices - serenity or delusion. It bothered him to no end that most days he had difficulty telling the difference. And his point of completion? This current misadventure made him ponder the possibility that he might well have reached it.

He lit his cigarette, his face bent away from the hot wind, and studied the pile of bodies a moment longer. What had the Buddha said? Life is suffering. Lately life did indeed seem like one big shit eating contest. If so, these people obviously had, at the very least, tied for first place. Their kharma was simply to move on to the next life. Better luck next time. What else could he think? Lately, his half-ass Buddhist fatalism seemed to be his only explanation for the hopeless mayhem that he witnessed on a daily basis. Fatalism and some deluded sense of penance. Maybe burning the dead and ministering to the near dead was his point of completion, if not his penance.

He took two quick drags of the cigarette and flicked it over his shoulder before picking up the two Jerri-cans of petrol. They had found the corpses that morning as they were returning from a re-supply run to the U.N. airfield. Twenty-one of them, scattered along the roadway like litter. They had to stop and remove a half-dozen or so in order for the trucks to continue down the rutted track. Henri, the head driver, had wanted to leave them, but Sonny had volunteered Khatir to help him drag the bodies off the road and dispose of them. Don't wait for us, he had told the Frenchman. He heard Khatir object, but Henri had only shrugged and nodded. The camp, a mile or two away, would be an easy walk, even in the heat of the day. Besides it would give Sonny time to think. Empty his mind of the bedlam and confusion of the camp.

He circled the pyre, sloshing the gasoline over the bodies, then tossed the empty cans to the side of the road before nodding to Khatir who stood poised, lighter in hand, awaiting Sonny's signal to light the strip of bloody rag he held primly at arm's length. Without waiting, Sonny turned and started up the road, pausing only to retrieve his day pack from beneath a rock where he had stowed it to discourage the marauding vultures. He heard the whoosh of the gasoline igniting, and a moment later the sound of Khatir's sandals slapping the hard packed dirt road.

Neither of them had any interest in observing their handiwork for the smoke was bound to attract attention. At best, maybe only a band of curious rag pickers, at worst the same predators whose work they had just disposed of. Gauging from the mutilation, he guessed the perpetrators to be *janjaweed*, the Arab militia responsible for most of the depredations that plagued Darfur. Or renegade SPLA rebels. Possibly even a Nuer raiding party. Take your pick. He only hoped they were long gone by now.

"*Monsieur.*"

Sonny glanced over his shoulder. Khatir had stopped and

was staring at something behind them. Without breaking stride, Sonny turned and walked backwards, squinting at the shimmering mirage of the road as it disappeared into the washed out line that fused the desolate terrain and the white monochrome of the sky. It took him a moment to make out what his companion had seen. A lone vehicle, the ubiquitous white Land Rover from its silhouette, had stopped a couple hundred yards or so down the road. Sonny slowed and shaded his eyes from the glare. After a moment, a single figure seemed to separate itself from the vehicle. Khatir muttered something unintelligible.

As they watched, the Land Rover appeared to swing around and head off in the opposite direction. Even from this distance, Sonny could sense something of the disgorged passenger's ambivalence. After a few seconds, he could see that the person had started to walk down the road towards them.

Khatir glanced at Sonny, his jaundiced eyes and the row of scars on his forehead the only features visible beneath the swath of his crimson headdress. There was curiosity registered there, but also unease. His gaze seemed to say it might prove foolish to wait for this stranger, but then again it was not his people's way to abandon someone in the desert. Sonny studied the advancing figure a moment longer, unsure of his own inclination. He turned in a slow circle, his gaze pausing on the flinty, eroded hills that encircled them before settling again on the shimmering silhouette on the road. What could it hurt to wait? Maybe plenty if they weren't alone. He glanced over at the pillar of greasy, gray smoke curling up from the pyre. Maybe someone from the camp would see the smoke and come for them. Then again, maybe not.

"Khawaja," Khatir said.

"A white man. Yeah, sure."

Who else would be crazy enough to abandon the security, false as it was, of a Land Rover and set out on foot alone in this country? Ill advised at best, dangerous and stupid at the worst. A right on estimation of his own current circumstance, he thought as he reached into his daypack for his water bottle. He took a swallow, and handed it to Khatir. The water tasted of chlorine and the tea he had filled it with earlier that day.

"*Khawaja*, yeah? Then I guess we better wait."

Khatir stared at the bottle a moment before raising his eyes to meet Sonny's. His gaze revealed nothing. Not gratitude, not amusement, only silent consideration. It frustrated Sonny to no end not to be able to communicate with the young man standing beside him. He wondered what Khatir thought of this hellish world, or felt about Sonny and the other *khawaja* crazy enough to join him here. Regardless of what they shared, the gulf separating Sonny and his fellow refugees seemed to loom larger by the day.

As he waited, he thought of the prayer card. The thread of ones life. Be it accidental, predetermined, or intentional. A chance encounter in the waiting lounge at Charles De Gaulle airport had led him here. How much of this, the grisly task they had just completed, the end of these lives might be predetermined? That left only intention - his path to completion.

As the distance closed, Sonny could now make out the approaching figure. It appeared to be a woman from the gait; tall, and burdened by a large duffel bag. It suddenly occurred to him that they could have possibly forgotten to pick up a new volunteer at the airstrip. No one at the camp had mentioned anything.

The two men waited in silence, Khatir nervously scanning the horizon while Sonny rummaged through his shirt pockets for the last of his cigarettes. He had started to smoke again while in prison, a habit that had only grown worse in the camp. Now only half a pack remained of the carton he had begged off one of the nurses. He had resigned himself to quitting, rationing them carefully in the hope they would last until he left. Today he was already three over his limit. He removed a couple from the crumpled pack of Gitanes, cupped his hand around his lighter, and lit them both before handing one to Khatir.

As they smoked, they watched the woman approach. She wore a pair of khaki colored camouflage pants, a long sleeved chambray work shirt, oversized sunglasses and a baseball cap pulled tightly down over her head. She stopped ten meters before them, dropped her duffel bag in the sand and lifted her hat, revealing a thick mane of coarse red hair. He could see some of her features now; a high forehead, a wide mouth. The rest of her face was concealed by the sunglasses. Her skin tone was reminiscent of an early summer tan. She stared at them a moment before glancing at the funeral pyre. The spectacle of a pile of burning bodies didn't seem to faze her in the least.

"*Bonjour. Le camp? Est-ce loin?*" she asked.

Her voice sounded hoarse, as if she hadn't had a drink in a long time. Before Sonny could reply she swung a large camera from behind her shoulder and in one smooth motion began photographing the pyre, the whirring click of her speed loader breaking the desert's silence.

"I should've guessed," he muttered under his breath. "How come they left you?"

She glanced at Sonny before looking back into her viewfinder. She moved to her left and leaned forward, scanning for the best angle.

"An American. Great," she said as she squatted on her heels, refocused and took another series of shots. "I'm not sure why they left. I got the impression a pile of burning bodies didn't suit their interests. That or I didn't pay them near enough." She looked at him and shrugged. "It is only a few miles to the camp, right? Just over those hills they said."

"About that."

She stared through the viewfinder for another moment before slipping the camera over her shoulder and walking over to them. Freed of the heavy duffel, she had a cat like stride, her figure lithe and fluid in its movement.

Sonny nodded at the duffel bag she left lying in the sand. "You gonna bring that?"

"It's heavy. And it's full of supplies. Antibiotics and stuff. Least you could do," she said, lifting her sunglasses.

He took a final drag from the cigarette and flicked it over his shoulder, his eyes never leaving hers. Another prima dona journalist was his first thought. But she did have nice eyes. Deep set with a thin delta of wrinkles at the corners, the irises copper colored in the midday light. Her dusky skin tone looked natural, something ethnic. He allowed himself a smile as he recalled the expression an uncle from East Texas was overly fond of using when referring to someone of mixed blood, especially a woman. High yellow. The phrase always seemed to conjure up something pleasantly carnal.

She appeared older than first impression – just either side of fifty. It had been a while since he had seen an attractive woman. The few women aid workers had little inclination or time to spend on their appearances, much less their hygiene.

She lifted the camera again and fired a volley first at Khatir and then at Sonny who held up his hand to block her shot. She lowered the Nikon and stared at Sonny for a moment.

"I've seen you somewhere before," she said, offering a smile.

"Not likely."

She lifted her shirt tail to wipe her face. "No. I don't forget a face. Give me a minute, and it'll come to me. Maybe..."

Khatir grunted in alarm, and before Sonny could even react, Khatir started to run.

Sonny glanced around to see what had startled him.

"What is it?" the woman asked.

Sonny didn't reply but continued to scan the horizon. Then, out of the corner of his eye, he saw them. Fifteen, maybe twenty riders breached the low rise of hill to their left. Most rode camels, a few others astride horses.

"Ah, hell."

He glanced back at Khatir who sprinted towards a solitary stand of stunted acacia trees and jumbled brush.

"Who are they?" she asked.

8

"What's your name?"

She stared back at him, her eyes registering nothing more than mild curiosity.

"Harper."

"Harper. We're in a bad situation here. One we're going to have to be real smart about. Understand?" he said, glancing back at Khatir who was scurrying on all fours into the clump of dried brush. Several of the riders had already split off and galloped toward the brush.

"They're *janjaweed*, right?" she asked, her voice still oddly devoid of concern.

"Give me the camera." Before she could react, he lifted it off her neck and tossed it into a nearby bush. "What else do you have in the bag?"

"I told you. Some medicines. Food. Personal stuff."

"No more cameras?"

"No. My spare got stolen. Why?"

"All you've got to say is we're doctors, okay? *Médecins Sans Frontieres*. Canadians. You got it? Nothing else."

Sonny glanced once more over his shoulder and saw that some of the outriders had surrounded Khatir's hiding place. Harper moved to his side, and they both turned to face the other riders who now reined in their horses and camels around them in a whirlwind of dust, creaking saddles, and heaving animals. Sonny could smell the leather mixed with sweat and dung. They all wore the prerequisite *jallabiya*-white robes and headdress, several of which appeared smeared with blood. Most of them carried AK-47s, the rest, an assortment of machine pistols and generic assault rifles. All of them wore at their waist the long curved swords favored by the raiders.

For a long moment, no one spoke or moved. Finally, three of the riders swung down from their horses and walked towards them. Their leader, his status obvious by his posture and the deference of his companions, appeared quite young, no older than perhaps his early twenties. He stopped in front of Sonny and studied him for a moment before turning his attention to Harper. The young Arab was handsome, fine featured with gray, intelligent eyes. Only his tea-stained, maloccluded teeth marred his appearance.

"*As-Salaam Alaykum*," Sonny said.

Without taking his eyes from Harper, the Arab barked an order and his two lieutenants shoved Sonny onto his knees.

"*Médecins Sans Frontieres.* Doctors Without Borders. We are doctors," Harper said, her voice quavering.

The Arab laughed and reached over and flicked Harper's cap off her head, then reached for her sunglasses. Harper raised her hand to stop him, then thought better of it and allowed him to take them. He examined them briefly before handing them to one of his companions. Several of the other men had started to go through Harper's duffle bag, scattering the contents into the sand. Suddenly, a torrent of shouts and jeers erupted from the others as they pointed to something.

Turning, Sonny saw that their companions had set fire to the brush where Khatir had sought refuge. A moment later he heard Khatir scream.

"Don't look," Sonny said to Harper.

One of the men behind Sonny slapped him in the back of his neck with a riding quirt.

As the Dinka's screams grew louder and more intense, Harper hung her head and winced. The young Arab yanked her by her hair, twisting her face, forcing her to watch as Khatir scrambled out of the conflagration, his clothes ablaze.

"*Abid! Abid!*" his tormentors yelled as they tried to drive Khatir back into the flames with their whips. Instead, he ran, stumbling and shrieking, the raiders hounding him with their quirts and swords. Unable to watch, Sonny stared at the ground in front of him. The camels, upset by Khatir's cries of agony, began to bellow as in protest. After what seemed an eternity, the screams stopped and the camels again fell silent.

"You fucking bastard," Harper muttered under her breath.

"Hey," Sonny said, shifting his body to get the young Arab's attention. "We're Canadians. French Canadians. *Parlez-vous Francais? Firinzi.*"

The sting of the quirt on the back of his head knocked him down on all fours. He struggled to his knees but was kicked back down. Harper started to say something, then yelped in pain as the quirt come down across her back, not once but twice, before she fell beside him.

"*Malesh,*" the Arab said, laughing as he placed his boot on Harper's back, pinning her to the ground. Reaching down, he ripped the neck of her shirt.

Malesh. Sonny remembered the phrase from prison. It was a favorite expression of one of his Arab cellmates. Roughly translated it meant 'Too bad.' Sonny twisted his face to look up at the Arab.

"Hey! You speak English? *Hael ingilizi?*"

The Arab looked at Sonny and sneered. "*Ingiliz.* I speak. I learn in Khartoum," he said, breaking into a boastful smile.

"The Koran forbids you to harm women. Yes? You cannot harm a woman."

"Woman? This is whore! *Kelb en-Nasrani.* Christian dogs!"

"We are doctors. *Medecins Sans Frontieres.* Your government in Khartoum does not want you to harm us. Do you understand?"

The Arab glared at Sonny, and started to reach again for Harper's shirt.

"Hey, you goddamn idiot. Think about it," Sonny yelled, struggling to his feet.

One of the men behind Sonny kicked him in the ribs, knocking him back down. Before he could get up, several of their captors began striking him with their quirts. He curled up in an effort to protect his face as two of them grabbed his leg and began dragging him away. Through his hands, he saw three of the others lean over Harper and begin tugging at her pants. She cursed and kicked at them, which only intensified their efforts to subdue her. Sonny tried to scramble towards her but each time the Arabs pulled him back, punishing him with their quirts. As he tried once again to get to his knees, he was kicked and shoved onto his stomach, his face half buried in the sand. Through the dust and swirling robes, he glimpsed Harper holding onto her pants with one hand and slugging one of her tormentors with the other. One of them slapped her hard across the face, and ripped off what remained of her shirt.

Sonny tried again to struggle to his feet, but someone stepped on his back, forcing him back down. An instant later he felt what he could only assume was the barrel of a gun pressed against the back of his head. He felt a sudden wave of nausea. It was over. He would be dead at any moment. He could hardly believe it would end like this. Yet part of him accepted it, was even relieved. Kharma. His only regret was the woman. She would be just another innocent bystander paying for his mistakes.

"Kuf!"

Whatever their leader had shouted, it stopped the assault. The boot stayed planted on Sonny's back a moment longer before his assailant stepped way. Sonny lifted his head and looked up at the young Arab. The young man offered him a look of amusement, then abruptly turned and swaggered over to one of the camels. Sonny watched as he removed what appeared to be a battered radio from a saddlebag, an old Vietnam era PRC-25, guessing from its shape and size.

Harper, clutching her shirt in front of her, scrambled to Sonny's side. He could feel her trembling.

"Listen to me," Sonny whispered. "If I tell you to run, you run. Don't think, just go."

She stared at him as if unsure of what he meant. He could see an emptiness in her eyes, a distance that he sensed was the ultimate defense mechanism.

"There's no nice way of putting this. There's a good chance

that this guy's boss doesn't really care. Or the radio won't work. Or he's had a really bad, goddamn blood thirsty day. You understand?"

He held her gaze for a long moment, trying to discern from her eyes alone what emotion she was feeling. He sensed first confusion, and then something he assumed was fear. But just as quickly he sensed a shadow of resignation. Almost consent. He turned away.

"What you're saying is they're gonna kill us anyway," she said, her voice flat and distant.

Sonny looked at the Arab. He had always counted on his ability to read faces and body language. Now in the span of a radio conversation... whim, good luck or bad luck... whatever... and their fate would be decided. And this juvenile, murdering prick's face would tell it all.

He looked at the three *janjaweed* still surrounding them. The one closest to Sonny held his Kalashnikov loosely in his hands. He could play the hero, go for the rifle. A slim to none chance. The best he could hope for was that it might end quicker.

A long moment passed as the Arab attempted to raise someone on the radio. Sonny recalled how unreliable a PRC-25 could be, especially if it hadn't been maintained. A burst of static and a scratchy voice came through. The Arab shouted into the radio, something about *Medecins Sans Frontieres*, a few other words he recognized. The word for woman. Then *Firinzi*. Another moment passed before the Arab, obviously angry, tossed the radio to one of his companions and strode back towards them, his swagger noticeably diminished.

He stopped and leaned down, his face inches from Sonny's, close enough that Sonny could smell the sour tang of his breath. With his one hand he shoved Sonny's head back, with the other he pulled a small ceremonial sword from beneath his robe and pressed it to Sonny's throat. He held it there a moment, then reared back and struck Sonny on the cheek with the handle. The force of the blow knocked Sonny onto his heels.

13

"Good fortune, infidel," he said as he placed his boot against Sonny's chest and kicked him onto his back. As Harper tried to scramble away, the Arab grabbed her by her hair and pulled her face tight against his thigh, muffling her pleas. He held her there for a long moment.

"*Inshallah*," he muttered finally, shoving her back onto the ground beside Sonny.

Their captors turned in unison toward their mounts and rode off in a wild shuffle of lumbering camels and dust. Neither of them moved for what seemed a minute, both of them stunned by their good fortune. Sonny started to struggle to his knees, then fell back, unsure he could even stand. His stomach rolled, and he felt the bile rise in his throat. He lay there a moment longer, then spit and rose to his knees.

"You all right?" he asked.

She made an effort to nod as she wiped the bloody snot from her face with the back of her hand. He started to reach over to remove a clump of dirt from her hair when he noticed his hand trembling. As he touched her hair, she grunted and pulled away.

"Come on," he said, pulling her to her feet. He felt unsteady, shaky with adrenalin. "We need to get out of here before they change their minds."

She leaned against him for a moment, and then bent down and picked up what remained of her shirt and draped it over her shoulders.

"You're bleeding," she said. "A lot. Here," she said, pointing at her own face.

She tore off a strip of her shirt and handed it to him.

Sonny touched his cheek, gingerly probing the laceration with his finger. It felt deep enough for stitches.

"You're the one they would've killed," she said as she struggled to tie up one of her bra straps that had been torn. "You know that, don't you?" She gave up on the strap and looked at him. "They would've let me live. It's what they would have done."

14

Something in her eyes was different now. Revulsion mixed with what he sensed as defiance. She turned and walked over to the scattered contents of her duffle and picked up a T-shirt. With her back to him, she undid what remained of her bra, and slipped on the shirt.

"Here. Don't forget this," he said leaning down to retrieve her camera from the brush where he had thrown it. He tossed it to her and she caught it in both hands, stared at it a second, before slinging the camera around her neck.

She hesitated a moment, then as if an afterthought, glanced over to the smoldering brush where Khatir had sought refuge.

"Your friend. Don't you think we should bury him?"

"Not much point," Sonny said, picking up his backpack. "He wasn't my friend. He was just someone that..." He paused for a moment before dropping his pack. "Okay. We bury him. But we need to hurry."

2

Harper Harris winced as she slid the camera bag off her shoulder and slumped back onto the sandy slope that marked the boundary of the sprawling refugee camp. She still ached where her assailants had held her down, the skin on her shoulders raw and abraded. Earlier that morning, she had studied herself in a jagged shard of mirror in the crude canvas shower stall, inspecting the vague, hand-shaped bruises on her biceps. The cut on her upper lip and the abrasions on her face had started to scab. Her appearance reminded her of a mug shot taken of her years before by the Atlanta police after she had been arrested while covering a Ku Klux Klan march for her college newspaper. An acquaintance on the force had given it to her, a souvenir she now kept taped on the wall in her New York loft. The bruised face of a previous incarnation.

She raised the camera to her face for a moment before lowering it again and scanning the scene before her. A seething, dust-choked tide of humanity ebbed and flowed as the long, uneven lines of refugees filed by the scattered feeding stations. The sun hovered just above the opposite hillside, and in the rapidly cooling air, the dust seemed to meld with the bluish wood smoke drifting up from the hundreds of cooking fires on the valley floor. Oddly enough, the unworldly, almost poisonous hue transformed the stark landscape into something vaguely idyllic. A National Geographic moment, she thought. It was only when she looked closer, and smelled the acrid odor of the massed humanity, that the grandeur gave way to reality, and a queasy claustrophobia again took over.

The first day in the camp she had simply gone through the motions, still in shock over what happened the day before. She had shadowed the harried aid workers and medical personnel in their rounds, snapping pictures, coaxing conversations out of the few willing to give her the time, all the while avoiding the solitude of her mind. She preferred the despair of the camp to reflecting on her own misfortunes and estrangements. This realization always made her feel wretched.

Strangely enough, no one had asked questions about her wounds or why she was even there, her circumstance of little concern when measured against the surrounding disaster. As for her fellow American, he had simply disappeared within minutes of their arrival at the aid compound. She had sensed his hostility, assuming he held her responsible for what had happened to his companion. After they had buried him, he had picked up her duffle bag and started off to the camp, always keeping several strides ahead of her. Her attempts at further conversation had elicited only the most rudimentary replies.

Now as the sun lowered, she took advantage of the light, framing shot after shot until she had almost used up an entire memory stick. Peering through her viewfinder, she focused the lens on several of the aid workers hauling blue plastic buckets of porridge to waiting refugees.

A clamor arose from a clump of people gathered around one of the dozens of canvas blister bags that provided water. A small boy clutching a wooden bucket tried to flee from two women attempting to tear the bucket from his grasp. It was only then she saw him. He waded through the mob and stepped between the boy and the women, shielding him until he could disappear into the crowd. Harper quickly raised her camera to see him more clearly, but he was gone, swallowed by the refugees as they surged around the watering station.

Her queries about him had revealed next to nothing other

than a first name. Sonny. No more. Sonny. *Le Americain.* In a place like this, any help was welcome, no questions asked. One of the doctors told her that Sonny had shown up about three or four months ago, hitching a ride in on a supply truck. He had quickly settled into the dreary, numbing routine of feeding the refugees, helping out in the dispensary, and burying the dead. When he wasn't working, he kept to himself, secluding himself in one of the supply tents along the far edge of the compound.

The same doctor had shown her to a cot in a cramped, make-shift vestibule just off the main dispensary. The guest bedroom, he quipped. That first night, among the constant coughing and keening of the sick and dying, she replayed over and over in her mind the .incident on the road in the hope the endless repetition might weaken its hold. Instead, with each reenactment, she grew more anxious. She also obsessed about the enigmatic Sonny and where she had seen him before. Finally, unable to sleep, she surrendered to a sleeping pill washed down with a shot of tequila from a bottle she had hidden in the bottom of her bag.

It came to her on the second night, bubbling up into her consciousness from some long forgotten file of minutiae. She sat up and searched frantically for her flashlight, and then reached for the notebook she always kept beneath her pillow. It was a habit from her childhood, re-enforced by her obsessive-compulsive mother, and her own desire to illuminate every stray thought.

She scribbled the name Dade, underlined it, paused and wrote beneath it the word   Spain. No it wasn't Dade, but something like that, she thought scratching it out. Daly? Day? That was it. Day. His first name was maybe Arnold. No. Something more unusual. She suddenly remembered. Arliss. Arliss Day.

He was supposed to be in prison somewhere in Spain. Forgotten. His fifteen minutes of notoriety used up. Could she be mistaken? If it was really him, what was he doing here in the Sudan?

The story had been a brief sensation in newspapers both in the States and Europe, creating an international incident of sorts. Arliss Day. A former official of the U.S. State Department convicted of manslaughter in a Madrid court for the death of an elderly German tourist. Witnesses had testified Day had been pursuing another car in what appeared to be a high speed chase when he struck the German as he crossed the street. The other car was never identified and Day held to his silence, pleading no contest to the charges.

The State Department had adamantly disavowed him or knowledge of the incident, yet in the heated climate of anti-American sentiment, the European newspapers had had a field day. There were rumors that Day had at one time been involved with the CIA in Central America, and the ensuing accusations of political intrigue only fed the tabloid frenzy.

Some months later, she had read a short piece in the New York Times about his sentencing and then he was forgotten; buried in the obscurity of a fifteen-year sentence in a Spanish prison. It was implausible that an early release would not have rated at least a small headline somewhere. Where had she been four months ago when he had arrived at the camp? Georgia? Mired in despair. Hiding out at her mother's farm. She could've easily missed the story. And now, strange as it might seem here he was in the middle of the Sudan.

She sat on the hillside for a moment longer watching the sun edge the horizon before putting her camera away and finding her way down into the swarming mass of refugees. As she approached the throng, they parted and fell silent, making way for the tall, strange woman with red hair. A few of the children reached out to touch her, their hands grazing her pant leg. The women, their faces gaunt and numbed by misery, stared back at her as if she were some alien being. She tried to acknowledge each of them, holding their gaze if even for a second, the gesture as much one of respect as payment for the use of their likeness.

For too long she had traded on images like theirs, sold their misery in the guise of a news story to the highest bidder. She forced herself to assume the guise of indifference, numb to the pain beyond her lens. Perhaps it wasn't indifference as much as resignation. But today, she felt raw - aware, like a minute change in her aperture setting. Enough so that some little voice in her head counseled caution.

She decided earlier that afternoon that she would leave in the morning, hitch a ride with the bi-weekly supply run. Lifting her gaze to the olive drab island of tents that marked the compound, she thought of him. Was it mere curiosity or some perverse need for completion? Either way she knew she wouldn't leave without first seeing him.

She found his tent at the edge of the camp, a crude canvas lean to, three of its walls formed by a stockade of stacked crates. The open portico overlooked the latrines, whose yawning pits were laid out in an almost impossibly precise grid that stretched to the dim horizon. Some of them, surrounded by thin piles of brush, almost resembled miniature dwellings, no doubt crude attempts at privacy. When the wind shifted to the south, the hellish stench consumed the camp, almost incapacitating all but the hardiest of the volunteers. She wondered what contrivance of circumstance had resulted in this particular site for his living quarters. Perhaps it was banishment. She failed to even consider it might be choice.

She stepped around the corner of the tent and paused a moment to allow her eyes to adjust to the dimness. She didn't see him at first, his profile momentarily hidden in the shadow until revealed by the flare of his cigarette as he inhaled. Gradually, he emerged like a photograph in a developing solution. He sat on what appeared to be an aluminum chaise lounge. If he noticed her presence, he gave no indication, but lifted his cigarette and sucked at it noisily.

"Love your view. Rent controlled, I hope."

He turned to glance at her, and then shifted his gaze back to the approaching dusk.

"I thought I'd run across you in the camp," she said in response to his silence. When he still didn't answer, she wondered if she had made a mistake in coming.

"My last cigarette," he said after a moment. "I made a bet

with myself you'd show up before I ran out. Good timing. At least now I feel like I'm breaking even."

"I'm leaving in the morning. I just wanted to thank you. And apologize."

He looked at her now, his expression masked by the shadow. "Apologize?"

"Your friend. You waited for me. If you hadn't..."

"No. They saw the smoke. It's why they came back. If anyone's to blame, it's me. Was my stupid idea to burn them."

She detected a drawl she hadn't noticed before, and recalled reading that he had grown up in Texas.

"You're Arliss Day, aren't you?"

He took another pull of the cigarette before flicking it at a stray dog that had started to root at the bottom of the sagging plastic construction fencing that separated the tent from the latrines. Another long moment passed before he said anything.

"You've come a long way for a short story no one cares about."

"If it makes you feel any better, I didn't come here looking for you."

"That's a relief'. Let me guess. You're doing a travelogue for Conde Nast."

"Budget Traveler, actually."

He made a sound halfway between a bark and a laugh and shook his head.

"I'm doing a project with World Refugee Alliance. Photographing the camps, writing a piece about the aid workers," she said, tripping over a box as she moved closer.

"Hold it," he said, leaning over and sliding the box aside. "Don't want you screwing up the feng shui."

She watched as he retrieved a lantern from beside his chair. He gave it a few perfunctory pumps before lowering it on to a packing crate laden with books and what appeared to be the rem-

21

nants of his supper. Other than a cot, a couple of folding canvas chairs, and a mud tracked carpet remnant, the tent appeared bare.

She studied him as he lit the wick with his lighter and adjusted the flame. He wore a grimy, sweat stained T-shirt and baggy floral print shorts. The harsh white light exaggerated the creases in his face, making him look older then she had earlier guessed. His close- cropped, salt and pepper hair only added to the impression. As he turned his deeply tanned face, she could see the jagged track of the sutures on his left cheekbone. His only soft features were his lips, which were full, almost fleshy. She tried to conjure up in her mind the photograph of his arrest she had seen in the newspapers. At the time, she thought him roguishly handsome. Even in handcuffs and disheveled clothes, his face had revealed an irresistible mixture of vulnerability and romantic tragedy.

"Sit," he said, nodding at one of the frayed canvas chairs.

She hesitated for a moment, still unsure of her intention, before dropping into the chair. "I brought you something," she said, reaching into her camera bag. She pulled out the bottle of Sauza Commerativo and placed it on the crate between them.

Day considered it a moment before reaching for it. He unscrewed the top and sniffed.

"Jesus. This was in your duffle? How in hell did they miss that?"

She smiled and pulled a small plastic shot glass from her bag. "Had it wrapped in my dirty underwear. I guessed it would be the last place they'd want to rummage through. Sorry, but I had to surrender all my limes at the border. Something about a quarantine, or stopping a plague. I guess irony knows no bounds."

He moved closer, leaning across the table to reach for the jigger. He avoided looking at her, his deep-set eyes hidden in the flickering lamplight. She watched as he filled the glass with the tequila before passing it to her.

"Ladies first."

She took a tentative sip and then finished it in one swallow. She handed the glass back to him and he rewarded her with what passed for a smile. He carelessly refilled it, spilling a small amount on the table. "Sorry," he mumbled as he leaned over to sip the overflow before tilting it back in one quick motion.

He filled it again, this time with exaggerated care, and handed it back to her. She noticed then that he was missing most of his right index finger.

"The guy you should thank is that gallant, young *janjaweed* stud. Or Allah. Or Jesus. Or Howdy fucking Doody. Any one of them might've kept you from getting gang raped and your throat slit, but it sure as hell wasn't me."

They watched each other as she downed the jigger and handed it back to him.

"Now that I've plied you with liquor, are you going to tell me what you're doing here?" she asked.

"Fund raising."

"Okay, so it's none of my business. So we stick to small talk. Maybe you can just tell what's there to do around here on the weekends?"

That earned another smile. She now noticed the creases around his mouth, and could almost imagine that once upon a time he smiled a lot.

"You said you were leaving in the morning," he said. "Where to?"

"Back to Lokichokio, then Nairobi, and maybe Khartoum. See how the other half lives. Have to be in New York in a couple of weeks. How about you?"

He tossed back the tequila before answering. "You're not going to let go of this, are you?"

"You can understand my curiosity, can't you? Last anyone heard you were in a Spanish prison. I would've expected they'd thrown away the key. And now you're here."

He didn't reply, his attention fixated on a pair of moths circling the lamp. After a moment, he poured another shot and offered it to her but she shook her head. He shrugged and downed the tequila in one swallow.

"You familiar with the term *samma*? It's Buddhist," he said without waiting for an answer. "Means right. Like it seemed the right thing to do at the time. Coming here, that is." He laughed. "The Buddha had a fucking sense of humor. I'll give him that."

He sat back in the lounge chair and shook his head. "Right thought. Right action, and all that. There was this book on Buddhism that got passed around the prison. Only thing in English besides some raggedy ass copies of Playboy. Buddha and Hugh Hefner. Now that'll sure as hell provide you with an interesting philosophical viewpoint."

A sudden breeze carried the miasmic stench of the latrines and the muted sound of voices from somewhere in the camp. A second later, they heard a woman's plaintive wail. They both glanced at each other in the brittle silence that followed.

"How do you stand it?" she asked after a long moment had passed.

Some inchoate emotion crossed his face. He leaned down and retrieved a small jar of Vick's Vapo Rub from a pile of paperbacks at his feet. "This helps. A little in each nostril and you don't notice the smell so much."

"That's not what I meant."

He rolled the jar between his fingers for a moment before replying. "First week I was here I asked one of the doctors that very same thing. You know what he said? You get used to it. Can you believe it? You get used to it. Well, you never get used to it, but you do learn to accept it. Not the same," he said, turning to look out into the darkness. "So how do you stand it? Recording the world's misery?"

"People want to know. They need to know about what's happening here," she said, put off balance as much by the tone of his voice as the self-righteous sound of her own.

"You really think they want to know? Three minutes on the evening news and it's forgotten by the first sitcom. What you're doing is a definite step up on the food chain though. Serving up guilt to soft-handed Presbyterians."

"I don't know what's worse," she said. "Your cynicism or your piety."

"Ah, finally a worthy opponent." He swiped at the moths, and then leaned back again and looked at her. "Hard to pick fights with most of the people around here. I used to think they were too noble. Then I figured out that they're just too damn tired." He smiled at her. "Don't disappoint me, Harper Harris. Yeah, I know who you are. I've read your stories. Seen your photos. You did that long, dreadfully beautiful shot of that beach after the tsunami. With the bodies sticking out of the sand. Got you on the cover of Newsweek. Good story by the way. Bet that drained a few wallets. Charitable folks do love misery."

She felt herself flush with anger. When he looked back, she turned away, unsure of herself. "I should go," she said, pushing back her chair.

"No, you shouldn't," he said, grasping her wrist. "You came here to talk about it. And spare me the sad, weak kneed apologies about what happened to my friend. This is about making what happened out there real. Am I right?"

He pulled a pack of cigarettes from his pocket, poked his finger in it, then crumpled it into a ball and tossed it into the darkness.

"You figured you have to share it with someone. Someone who knows what it feels like. Because no one back in the world's really going to understand. No one you're that comfortable with. Talking about it is too…" He glanced up at the ceiling as if searching for the right word. "Intimate. It's like fucking pillow talk."

He looked at her and grinned. "Excuse the drama. I'm having a bad day. That and I happen to have a case of the ass for journalists." He picked up the bottle of tequila and contemplated it a moment before pushing it across the table. "Best you put this up. I'm getting ugly."

25

"No. Keep it," she said, trying to hide her irritation.

He shrugged and set the bottle on the floor beside him. They stared at each other.

"The other day. Out there," he said, leaning forward. "That wasn't the first time, was it?"

She held his gaze, struggling to remain impassive, all the while wondering what she had said or done, what she had revealed, what he knew. She tried to push the memory from her mind, but the panic she thought she had buried rose up and made her tremble. The smell of the cold, dank mud in her nostrils, the feel of the soldier's coarse wool against her thighs. And the face of the young Serbian militiaman who rolled her over. A boy's face. Too young for this, she recalled thinking just before he punched her. She looked away.

"You did good."

"I did good?"

"You showed guts. That's all I meant," he said, his voice almost lost in the quiet. "You handled yourself better than most. The rest of us. We try." He paused, the silence building for a long moment. "I came here because I had nowhere else to go."

"What?"

"You wanted to know. Why I'm here." He shifted his gaze, his eyes seemingly fixed on some spot just over her shoulder. "They let me go," he said after a moment. "Gratis. Details don't really matter, but the short and so far unpublished story is that I saved a guard's life." He shrugged. "The guard happened to be the warden's nephew. This warden figured I had served enough time. So the paperwork goes missing. As far as he was concerned I had paid my debt. Can't help but wonder though whether that old man I ran over would feel the same way." He shook his head as if perplexed. "Anyway, I'm off their books. But as far as the State Department and the press are concerned, I'm still busting rocks in Extremadura." The lamp started to sputter, and he paused to pump it a few times before going on.

"Two weeks later, I'm wandering around Charles de Gaulle,

staring up at the departure board, hoping to see...I don't know what. Either the next flight to Miami or life's goddamn purpose. And this woman comes up to me. One of those stealth nuns. You know the kind. No habit, civilian garb. But she's wearing these butt ugly, sensible shoes. Work boots for chrissakes. It's how I knew she was a nun. Women in Paris don't wear ugly shoes. Not even the really beautiful ones." Something like amusement passed behind his eyes. "So she hands me this brochure about Darfur. Doesn't say a thing, just walks off. Was like some kind of sign. From God. The universe, or the Buddha himself. Who the hell knows? But it was a sign. So here I am. That satisfy your journalistic curiosity?"

"Arliss."

"Sonny. My friends call me Sonny."

"Sonny Day." She shook her head and smiled, then looked out into the darkness. She was not someone who revealed herself easily. After one failed marriage, two near misses, and countless lovers, intimacy still seemed a commodity to dole out in increments

Sonny was right about her need to share what had happened with someone who understood. Harper sensed the same need in him. It was like a one night stand. Take it off. Bare ass, bone to bone. I'll show you mine if you show me yours. The tequila was talking and she knew she should go.

They sat there in silence each consumed by their thoughts, each in their own way acknowledging what they shared. Finally, giving in to instinct and discomfort, she pushed back her chair and made an effort to stand.

"I better go," she said. "Thanks again."

"For?"

"I'm not sure yet. I imagine it'll come to me."

He nodded and smiled. "I like that. Very Zen."

"Tell me something," she said, picking up her bag. "What are you going to do?"

"I don't know. I think I'm just waiting for the next nun," he said with a faint smile.

For the first time she detected a melancholia. When he looked up at her, she also saw a look of bewilderment that made her pause.

"Is there somebody back home I can call for you? Tell them you're all right."

He turned his head, his eyes fixed on something as he thought about what she had just asked. "No. I don't think so," he said after a moment.

She reached into her bag and pulled out a card and a pencil. She jotted her number, on the back and handed it to him. "My cell number back in the States. Ever make it to New York, call me."

He took it from her without looking at it. "Yeah, I'll do that."As she turned to leave, he said, "Harper."

"Yeah?"

"Nothing. Have a safe trip."

She nodded and slipped into the darkness.

3

PART TWO
Santa Fe, New Mexico
Three Months Later

"They were low-life's. Border trash," was how Ray Cortese's father had explained it to him. "And they sure as hell got what they deserved."

His father had uttered this disclosure one night in a moment of vodka induced candor as he drove Ray home from a football game. This rationalization had always struck Ray as false and somewhat self-serving. What the old timers at the Agency referred to as constructing a false identity. A legend was what they called it. It was a legend all right - the night his father killed two men with his bare hands in a bar fight in Del Rio, Texas.

The first time Ray heard the story he was thirteen, a good decade after the event. A schoolmate had recounted it word for word from his own father's account. His friend's father, the local judge, had a reputation for being close-mouthed and a paragon of truth, so thus the story must have been true. By then Ray's father had long since ceased being someone he looked up to, even if he was famous.

Ray leaned over the dashboard and craned his neck to stare up at the leaden sky. A sixty-percent chance of snow and a rat's

29

ass chance it would make it above freezing, he thought pushing back against the seat to straighten his leg. Any time he sat for too long, his bad leg ached and stung as if a dog were chewing it. He grimaced as he swung his right leg onto the seat beside him. He was a large man and every movement he made seemed to take up more space than was needed. It was why he liked to drive old Crown Victorias. It seemed no one made cars with bench seats anymore.

He glanced across the parking lot at the knot of young men huddled beneath a bare poplar; the skeletal tree the only hint of vegetation awarded the bleak landscape of the low slung city housing project. Every once in a while the group parted just enough for Ray to catch a glimpse of someone sprawled on a weight bench.

He watched the guys gathered around the weight bench a moment longer and then checked his watch. Thirty minutes had gone by since he had last looked. No sense putting it off, he thought, removing his glasses and slipping them into his shirt pocket. He dog-eared a page of the tattered Garcia Marquez novel he had been reading and tossed it on the seat beside him. He started to open the door and then hesitated as he remembered the small, pearl-handled Beretta semi-automatic tucked beneath the passenger seat. A pimp's gun was what his father would have called it. Only good for scaring women and wearing out your pocket. Forget it, he thought. Not nearly enough of an advantage anyway.

Opening the door, he swung out his good leg, then planted his feet and pulled himself up with the aid of the door strap. Retrieving his cane, he paused for a moment to let the pain in his right knee subside before slamming the door. Then he started his uneven walk across the parking lot, all the while unbraiding in his mind what exactly he was doing here.

The group of young men huddled around the weight bench failed to even notice him, with the exception of a scraggly teen in chains and summer weight hip hop gear who offered him a brief sneer. The man walking by them could hardly have been intimidating; a balding, slightly overweight white guy limping along with a cane. If the kid had been asked later to describe Ray, he might have remarked on the silver goatee and the eyes. The eyes, deep set and gray, were the one feature Ray had inherited from his father. The kid would have remembered the eyes.

The only photograph Ray had kept of his parents was a yellowed Kodachrome that revealed a handsome, larger than life, swarthy young man with eyes as shallow as cheap paint and a smile that promised too much. His mother, much like the photograph, seemed washed out by comparison, her cat like face and reddish hair hinting at her Irish lineage. Something in her expression, a wariness perhaps, lent itself to speculation as to the exact nature of their connection.

Every once in a while, Ray would study his father's face in the detached manner one might consider that of a vaguely familiar stranger, searching fruitlessly for some connection from a safe distance. Something in that emptiness rendered him indifferent to consequence and regret. Fertile soil for a life of duplicity a woman friend had once remarked with more insight than Ray had sought at the time.

Ray paused at the entrance to the long, open portico that separated the two wings of the tenement, squinting in the dim light at the numbers above the doors. Half of them were missing one or more of the digits. It was only then he noticed a young Hispanic wearing warm-ups and a leather bomber jacket sprawled on a tattered sofa beside a doorway halfway down the hall. As Ray approached him, the guy bounced to his feet, blocking the doorway.

"I'm looking for Freddie Ascensión," Ray said, offering up a smile.

The young tough rolled his shoulders and looked past Ray. His left eye was milky, making it difficult to tell if he was looking at Ray or not. Two small teardrop tattoos adorned his cheek just below his good eye. Ray could see the sculpted outline of the man's pectorals through the muscle shirt he wore beneath his jacket. By the sag in his jacket, Ray guessed his piece was stuffed in his right pocket.

"Freddie Ascensión. He lives here, right?

"He call you?"

"No."

"Nobody live here wit' that name."

Ray stared at the man's good eye and shifted his weight off his bad leg.

"I need to see him, *Comprendes*? I'm not leaving until I see him, okay?"

The doorman started to reach for the lapel of Ray's coat, but Ray slammed his right forearm into the man's throat, using his weight to push him against the wall. As his opponent tried to retrieve his gun from his pocket, Ray dropped his cane and grabbed the man's hand. Before he could pull it free, Ray head butted him twice. He heard the man's nasal cartilage pop, but instead of giving up, the asshole slammed his knee into Ray's bad leg. As Ray's leg started to buckle, he hung on to the man's gun hand, at the same time ramming his elbow as hard as he could into his opponent's stomach. As the other guy doubled over, Ray managed to jerk the gun from his grasp. Sagging against the wall for support, Ray placed the barrel of the .45 against the man's forehead.

"Okay, that's it, fuck-head. Enough. *Basta*! Shit, that hurt," he muttered, grasping his knee.

The young man had slumped to the ground on all fours, fighting for breath and gagging on the blood streaming from his nose. Ray bent down on his good leg to retrieve his cane.

"Now let's go see Freddie," Ray said, nudging him with his foot.

But instead of giving up, the man swung wildly at Ray's crotch. This time Ray dropped him by cracking him behind the ear with the butt of the automatic.

That was smart, he thought slumping against the wall to catch his breath. Not exactly the way to make friends with Freddie Ascensión. He slipped the gun into his pocket and started to knock on the door. Before he could react, however, the door flew open, and he found himself staring down the barrel of a sawed off shotgun. The face on the other end appeared to be an almost exact copy of the guy on the ground, only with two good eyes and decidedly more edge.

"*Tranquilízate!* Stay cool," Ray said, flashing his open hands. "I just need to talk to Freddie."

Ray looked past him into the dim foyer. Someone stood leaning casually against the wall at the end of the hallway. Ray glanced back at the man wielding the shotgun who had lowered his eyes to take in the motionless figure at Ray's feet.

"Your *amigo*. He must've tripped."

"*Esaí*," the figure in the hallway said quietly. "*Déjalo entrar.*"

Esaí motioned with his hand for Ray to step inside, and as Ray stepped across the threshold, he grabbed Ray by the collar and spun him against the wall. He jerked the cane from Ray's grasp and tossed it aside. Jamming the shotgun into Ray's spine, he patted him down, removing the .45 from his pocket and just as deftly the switchblade from his boot.

"*Pase*," he said, nodding his head to the back of the apartment. Esaí followed Ray down the corridor. They passed several rooms that to Ray's surprise, had been tastefully decorated, painted in bright pastels and furnished with heavy, Colonial style wood furniture. The room at the end of the hall was small and bleak in comparison. A tiny kitchen occupied one side, on the other a simple metal table and chairs. The walls had been painted a revolting shade of purple. Puce is what Macy had called it. Not something as common as eggplant but puce. A color she had once suggested they paint the restaurant's foyer. He glanced over at the slight man in a red sweatshirt and jeans leaning against the counter pouring a cup of coffee.

"Café, *amigo*?" the man asked, turning his back to rummage through the dish rack for another cup.

"Sure. I'll take it black. You're Ascensión, right?"

Esaí placed the .45 and Ray's knife and cane on the counter. The other man turned and nodded at Esaí. *"Corre a ese pendejo de mi puerta."* He waited for Esaí to start down the hall before looking at Ray. "Is no good. Body lyin' outside your door. The neighbors talk."

Ascensión looked older than what Ray expected. Early forties, maybe with a shaved head, a nose that had been broken a few times, high, Indian cheekbones, and narrow eyes. A web of tattoos covered one side of his neck. The look of almost benign amusement reflected on his deeply pitted face belied the harshness of his features. Only his mouth, thin lipped and wide, revealed an appropriate tension.

"¿Habla Espãnol, se? Senior Cortese?"

"¿Sabes quién soy?" Ray asked,

"We should speak English," Ascensión said, tilting his chin at the hallway. "Yes, I know who you are. You own that restaurant off the plaza. By the river. *Es* nice place. *Es muy caro."* He handed Ray a cup of coffee and motioned for him to sit. "You have bad leg. I have bad back. You sit, I stand." He slurped his coffee as he studied Ray. "You are here because of Enrique, no?" Ascensión grinned. "He says you scare him. Now maybe I know the reason he say this, and now you owe me a watchdog," he said, nodding at the front door.

"Yeah, well, I might've overreacted some."

Ascensión nodded. "Enrique's mother," he said after a moment. *"Eeee.* She is a beautiful woman. *Muy hermoso.* Enrique told me his mother works for you. At the restaurant. So, you ever fuck her? Mebbe why you bring her up here. To *el Norte?* For this thing?"

Ray took a sip of the coffee before replying. "You know I had just about rid myself of all my bloody thoughts."

Ascensión smiled. *"Muy bien.* Now I know how far to go with you. *Muy importante.* No? Knowing this. So forget what I say about his mother. Is test. So, what is your business with

34

me?"

"Enrique. I want you to leave him alone. Same goes for my other employees. You've already ruined my best cook."

Ascensión cocked his head. "I don understan'."

"Your boys were feeding my cook's habit. So he doesn't work anymore. Doesn't feed his kids. Pay his bills. He's nothing. 'Cause of that shit. *Queso*. Isn't that what you call it?"

Freddie appeared to consider this a moment before replying. "They say these people work for you, are legal, yes? People you get the green cards. Should be plenty, no? *La tarjete verde*. Way I see. This is America. Land of the Free. They got... how you say? The right to fuck up. Yes? And get fucked up. Your America."

Ray took a sip of his coffee. "All right, suppose we look at a different way. You're a businessman, right?"

Ascensión shrugged. "Maybe one day I am *un empresario independiente*. Like you. I have dream. In my dream, I don do this thing," he said, opening his arms. "Not forever. *¿Comprendes?* But I think you understand this, Ramón. Okay I call you Ramón?"

Ray nodded. "What I don't want are any more enemies. I'd guess the same is true for you. You've got enough already. Between the cops and the competition. *¿Verdad?*"

Ascensión drained his cup and set it on the counter behind him. "You wish to make some kine of... how do you say? *¿Como se dice? ¿Acuerdo?* Agreement, yes? Maybe I do this. Then what? We do business together?"

"No business. But I hear things. I hear things about you."

Ascensión didn't reply, but instead bent down to pick up an enormous black cat that had appeared between his legs.

"I hear rumors. People talk too much. Know too much. A dangerous thing, no?"

Ascensión dropped the cat onto the counter and made his way over to the door leading to the hall. "And what do you hear?" he said, closing the door.

"I hear you want out. Out of Mara Salvatrucha. But they're a real bunch of hard asses, aren't they? *El miembro para todo su vida.* They're not going to let you just walk away, are they?"

"*¿Quien es? ¿La* DEA?"

"No, I'm just someone who needs a favor. You do me this one thing, and maybe I can help you someday. You just have to know there are some favors you don't ask. Some lines I won't cross. We have this understanding?"

Ascensión tilted his head in appraisal. "Enrique, he tole me you spend lots of time in Central America. *En la dulce cintura.* I come here from Honduras. But something tell me you know that, Ramón. And I ask myself, if this is true, how he know that? Mebbe Enrique's right. You are scary. *Muy peligroso. ¿Más café?*" he asked, refilling his own cup.

Ray shook his head.

"San Pedro Sula? You know it?" Freddie asked.

"I've been there a couple three times. Once I..." Ray's cell phone rang. Out of habit, he pulled it from his pocket and squinted at the number. Macy. Someone else had also called and left a number. An area code he didn't recognize. He turned it off and slipped it back into his pocket. "I had a job there once. Some asshole banana farmer needed a bodyguard. I got a lot more choosy after that."

Ascensión smiled and nodded when Ray didn't offer more. Ray wondered what the odds were that Freddie had spent time in the prison outside Tegucigalpa. Ray had been there once on an unsuccessful effort to spring an informant. A singularly unpleasant place as he recalled, a dangerous and overcrowded hell hole. He wondered what someone like Ascensión had done to survive that.

"So is it true? That you want out?"

Ascensión picked up the cat that had been rubbing at his elbow. "I have *familia. Ninos. La vida diferente.* Yes, I want to leave this life. To go home. Mebbe have a little *finca* like my father. For that, I need money."

"Where's your family?"

He dropped the cat and smiled. "Somewhere away from here, *amigo*."

"In the States though?"

"*Quintana Roo, su restaurante es...* how you say? *Zona prohibido...*off limits?" he asked, quickly changing the subject. "Okay. I tell my people. Is not going to make some of your people happy, you know? And if I tell my people I don' want Enrique around, then mebbe they get wrong idea. He mebbe get his *cojones* kicked." He shrugged. "So I take you for your word. You owe me this favor. Mebbe someday, I come to your bar. I been there once, you know. Nice bar. So I come in. Have a mojito, hokay?"

Ray slurped the last of the coffee. "Probably not the best idea," he said after a moment.

Ascensión laughed. "*Cabrón.* You are... how you say? A hard ass? Hokay, we make a deal. Mebbe one day, we drink together. *Compañeros empresarios, si?*"

Ray pushed his chair from the table. "Maybe. I have to go. Can I have my cane back?"

"Tell me," Ascensión said, handing him his cane. "Where you hear these rumors 'bout me?"

Ray cocked his head to the hallway. "You trust him? You trust anyone?"

Ascensión smiled and opened the door. "*Mi hermano.* You cannot trust your brother, then who you trust? *Esaí! La puerta!*"

Ray turned and started down the hallway.

"*Amigo. Su filero.*" He tossed Ray his knife. "I like the man who carries a knife. *Muy valiente.*"

Ray nodded and headed for the door where Esaí stood waiting. His fallen colleague was nowhere to be seen. Ray paused at the doorway to one of the side rooms, his attention drawn to a faded bull fight poster tacked to the wall. He knew the town in Spain, had passed through it once on leave from his barracks in Frankfurt. He smiled at the flicker of a memory of the young woman who had accompanied him. His commanding officer's wife, a woman he never should've let go of. He turned and looked at Esaí. He bore little resemblance to Ascensión. Maybe he merely meant a brother in arms. Ray looked at the poster again.

"You ever had a time in your life you'd give anything to get back?"

Esaí stared at him mutely. Ray repeated the question in Spanish, but it still didn't elicit a response.

"Didn't think so," he said, slipping past the man and stepping out into dim cold light of the approaching dusk. It had started to snow and a thick layer of powder already coated the uneven sidewalk. He paused before stepping out from below the portico and pulled a blister pack of Nicorette gum from his pocket. The homies had finished their workout, the only occupant of the yard an ancient looking German Shepherd who snapped ambivalently at the drifting flakes. Ray popped his chewing gum, then took out his cell and hit redial.

"Hey, babe. What's up?"

"Where in bloody hell have you been? Sadie just called. You were supposed to pick her up at four. It's half past five already."

"Oh, hell. I'm sorry. I got tied up with something. She's still at school?"

"Of course not. She's at the dance studio. Where do you expect her to be?"

"She's waited before. It's not like she's alone. You at the restaurant?"

"Yes, and it's all balled up with this snow and all. One of the cooks called in. Jaime's late. I need some help."

"Let me get Sadie settled with supper and her homework and

I'll be there. I'll call Corina to come watch her. Okay?"

He took the silence on the other end as assent mixed with a good dose of disgust.

"Macy? Did you hear me? I'll be there in less than an hour."

"Right. By the way, a friend of yours called."

"Who?"

"Dunno. Said he was an old army buddy."

"He didn't give a name?"

"Not that I recall. I tried to chat him up but he was a bit murky."

He thought about the out of state number on his cell. "Say where he was calling from?"

"No, like I said, he wasn't too talkative. I gave him your cell number though. Did he call?"

"No. He sound American?"

"Of course he was American. He was with you in the bloody army, wasn't he?"

A door somewhere behind him slammed and he turned and watched as an old woman swaddled in what appeared to be half dozen layers of clothes shuffled along the portico before disappearing around the corner. Was it Sonny that had called? Could he already be Stateside? He thought about the email. It had been short and to the point.

Footloose. Need an author and a banker. London if possible. Reply this address ASAP.

The willful boy

The willful boy. Sonny was nothing if not willful.

Ray had called in some favors and spent a whole day on the phone before emailing Sonny back with a name and phone number of a guy in Kensington who could forge him a new passport and possibly supply him with some fake credit cards. That had been what   four days ago? Sonny wasn't wasting any time.

There hadn't been anything recent on the Internet or the newspapers about Arliss Day. No deal, no pardon, no reported prison escape in Spain. Nothing. He glanced up again at the drifting snow.

"Ray? Are you still there? Listen to me, Ray. You better not be up to your old games again. I told you, you get involved again, Sadie and I are gone. You understand that, don't you? Ray?"

"Yeah," he said, glancing down and noticing his bloodstained jacket cuff. "Just chill, okay? It's just an old buddy. Sit tight and I'll be there in an hour."

He started to put his cell phone away then thought twice. He fumbled in his pocket for his glasses and squinted at the number in the fading light. It was seven something-- 718. If his memory served him right that was a New York area code. He dialed the number. It rang a half dozen times before someone answered with an abrupt hello.

"Who's this?"

"Who you want?" The accent sounded foreign. Asian maybe.

"Where am I calling?"

"What you mean? Don't know where you are calling? This airport. Newark Airport. Who you want?"

Ray snapped the phone shut and slipped it into his pocket as he limped to the car. The willful boy had landed. And just when he thought things were getting boring.

4

NEWARK INTERNATIONAL AIRPORT

Sonny sipped his coffee as he watched the parade of people passing through the concourse. Years ago, when he had been flying frequently between D.C. and Latin America, he had cultivated the habit of passing time by picking out a passerby and fabricating a dossier from nothing more than his or her appearance. A guy he had met once in the airport bar in Miami had told him it was a great way to hone one's observational skills.

He watched a pair of fleshly middle aged men in ill-fitting suits for a moment. Eastern European, he surmised from the cut, and their cheap shoes. Not tourists, but most likely business types from the way they yammered away on their cell phones.

Earlier, he had been intrigued by a woman in a stylish silk burkha that had just come out of the bookstore across from where he sat. She had paused long enough to stuff several copies of Vanity Fair in her carry on. In the process, she dropped her purse, spilling across the floor an amazing array of cosmetics along with a carton of Winstons. When she glanced up, she met his gaze with a look of obvious amusement. From the shade of her eyebrows, she looked blonde. She quickly shoveled her belongings back into her purse, offered him one more smile and disappeared into the crowd.

Newark Airport certainly was a far cry from the airport in

Nairobi, he thought, glancing around for his next subject. And a lot friendlier, too. Everyone from the flight attendants to the immigration agent had been almost too pleasant. After what he had been through the past two years, he found the civility jarring. The immigration agent, a beet faced cracker transplant, had been overly solicitous, passing him through with only a cursory glance at his passport and a "Good to have you back, Mr. Bass."

At customs, they had performed a cursory search of his lone piece of baggage, a battered leather valise. They failed to find the duplicate of his original passport that had been sewn into the bottom. Its dog eared predecessor no doubt still resided in some forgotten file drawer at the Ministry of Justice in Madrid. Fortunately, they had not bothered to check the pockets of his raincoat or they would have easily found the five thousand in crisp, folded one hundred dollar bills. He counted on the cash lasting him a while before he would have to use the bogus credit cards issued in the name of one Samuel T. Bass of Kansas City, Missouri.

He glanced at his watch and realized he had spent an hour gazing at the faces of passersby, half- hoping, half- dreading he might recognize someone. To his amazement, he actually had recognized someone - a young woman who had once worked at State. They had shared a long conversation about Mexican economic policies at a reception hosted by the Argentinean consulate. He no longer remembered her name and doubted that she would even recognize him. Maybe it was all for the best. Arliss Day didn't exist anymore, at least not the Arliss Day that had left from this same airport almost two years ago.

Earlier that day, he had studied himself in the restroom mirror and for the first time felt taken aback by his physical transformation. He doubted his own mother, God rest her soul, would recognize him. The desert and prison had taken its toll, but it was more than that. Something reflected there reminded him of a word he had come across in the tattered Buddhist tract he kept beneath his mattress in the prison. Duhka. He learned it had various meanings. Dissatisfaction. Confusion. Pain. A state of imbalance. Craving for existence. Craving for non-existence. After a while, the equivocal semantics began to annoy him.

He glanced over at the bank of pay phones. The phone whose number he had left on Ray's cell had rung twice. Once was a wrong number, the other time, a passerby had grabbed it before Sonny could get there. The man had quickly hung up after saying a few words. He thought about calling again. But if Ray didn't answer, he didn't want to sit around waiting for him to call back. There were plenty of flights to Albuquerque, so he could make in the next day or two. He would try again in the morning.

It had been impossible to get comfortable on the flight from London. A mother with a young child had occupied the seats next to him; the child crying for most of the trip, the mother dutifully apologetic. London itself had been a series of interminable waits in dim bars. The two hour nap in the backroom of Ray's forger contact had merely aggravated his fatigue. Then there had been the one fitful night in the fleabag hotel in Nairobi; the mind numbing eight hours waiting in the hanger at Lokichokio. But that had been when? Six days ago? Eight? He wasn't quite sure anymore.

His gaze settled on a news magazine someone had abandoned on the seat beside him, the cover of which depicted an Afghani family grieving over the corpse of what appeared to be a child amongst the bombed out rubble of their home. He stared at it for a moment before reaching into his pocket and retrieving a small tattered notebook. Thumbing through the pages, he finally found the number he had jotted in the margin. He thought for a long moment before making his way to the pay phones.

As he dialed the number, he found himself questioning his motives. Was it merely loneliness or just boredom? He hesitated to think it could be desperation, but the sad truth was that other than Ray, there was no one else with whom he retained any connection. He had long since lost contact with his ex-wife. Most of his kin had passed on and he had long since burned the bridges to his ex-lovers. There were perhaps a handful of former friends, none of which he could trust to keep quiet. So why the Harris woman? She was a tenuous connection at best. Was he just reaching out to a kindred spirit or just reverting to his old predaceous ways? So much for duhka, he thought.

He let it ring five times. Just as he was about to hang up she picked up, her voice thick with sleep.

"Yeah?"

"Harper?"

He thought he heard the soft clink of teeth on glass and her swallow.

"Who's this?"

"Sonny Day."

"Who?"

"Arliss Day. If this is a bad time…"

"No. Wait." The phone dropped and he heard a shuffling sound and some music in the background and then silence. "I must've fallen asleep. What time is it? God. Where are you?"

"Newark. The airport."

"I'll be. I can't believe it. What's it been? Three months? You've been in Darfur all this time?"

"Guilty."

"I was wondering when you would show up. I mean I knew you would. Eventually. What took you so long to get out of there?"

"Couldn't bring myself to break the lease."

She laughed, a mannish snort that ended in a cough. "So. Passing through or what?" When he didn't reply, she waited a few seconds more. "We need to talk,.Sonny?"

"Listen, I just thought I would call and say hello."

"Are you hungry? I slept through supper. I could meet you somewhere. Where are you staying?"

"Out here I suppose. I'm flying out in the morning."

"I know a great place to eat, if you don't mind coming into Brooklyn."

He hesitated, suddenly ambivalent. "Sure, I guess I could. One condition. We don't talk about Darfur."

"Deal. You like Asian? Chow's on Fifth Avenue," she said, not waiting for a reply. "Don't recall the address, but it's at Fifth and Garfield. Cabbie should be able to find it. Probably take you a good hour. Maybe more."

"An hour," he said just as she hung up.

5

The cabbie was a beefy young African who for the first ten minutes carried on an ardent soliloquy on his cell phone in a dialect that at times sounded pleasingly melodious; at other times like someone calling sheep. Sonny couldn't be sure, but he guessed it was something West African, Yoruba, maybe. Even though the cold rain had turned to sleet, the cabbie drove with the usual Third World abandon, his one hand clasping his phone to his ear, the other somewhere in the vicinity of his lap. An accident stalled them just before the Holland Tunnel and the cabbie snapped his cell phone shut and glanced at Sonny in the rearview mirror.

"Coming home, sir?"

"You could say. Where are you from?"

"I come from Lagos."

Sonny nodded and looked out the window at a police squad car edging its way through the stalled traffic. "Long way from home. Tell me something, what do you like about the States?"

The cabbie thought for a moment, glanced at him in the mirror and offered a toothy grin. "I like de money. And de women."

"And what don't you like?"

"De women," he replied, laughing. "And you nevah get good bananas. Not like back home." He held Sonny's eyes in the mirror. "I miss Nigerian girls, too." He sighed. "And too cold here."

They rode the rest of the way in silence, their progress slowed by the icy streets. Sonny didn't care for the cold either. One of the many things he never got accustomed to living in D.C. At one point he had realized that most of his adult life he had resided in climes below the thirtieth parallel. Other than the last tour at State and the three years in Lima he had languished in the warm bosom of the tropics. So what did he like about the States? He wasn't sure about the women. The cabbie was right about one thing, though, it was hard to find good bananas.

By the time the cabbie rolled up outside of Chow's, the sleet had turned to wet, quarter sized snowflakes. After tipping twice as much as he should have, Sonny turned up his collar and lingered on the sidewalk, overcome by a reticence he still couldn't place. He wondered if it might be the simple discomfort that Harper knew who he was; what he had done. Anonymity had become his second skin.

Peering in the window, he spied her sitting alone. Her hair was shorter, redder than he remembered. She was dressed in a short sleeve blue silk blouse that seemed a bit unsuitable, considering the weather. She held a martini glass in one hand, her posture relaxed, visibly free of the tension of that night in his tent. He watched her for another moment before making his way inside.

She spotted him immediately and raised her hand to get his attention. As he approached, she stood and leaned forward as if she were going to hug him but instead offered her hand, palm down.

"Welcome home, sailor," she said her Southern accent more obvious than before. Her smile opened up her face, and he felt his reticence fading. "If I would've known what the weather was going to be like, I wouldn't have dragged you out."

"Don't worry about it. Good to get out of the airport for a while," he replied as he shed his raincoat and gazed around the restaurant. The dimly lit dining room was furnished in teak and leather and populated with well dressed professional types. Diana Krall crooned in the background. He wondered what the denizens of the refugee camp would make of such a place. The dissonance set him back for a moment.

"You look different," he offered, slipping into the booth.

"I should hope so. Sorry I can't say the same for you," she said, her eyes taking in his wrinkled shirt and unshaven face. "And something tells me that's the sum total of your luggage," she said, nodding at his valise.

"The movers are taking care of the rest," he replied, studying her in the soft light. Her neck was more slender then he recalled, her facial features more rounded. Her makeup made her look so dissimilar from her appearance at the camp. Younger? Older? Oddly enough, he wasn't sure. With women of a certain age and complexion, it was difficult to tell.

They settled into an awkward silence as her gaze shifted back and forth between him and the dining room behind them. She finally settled on something and motioned with her hand. A waitress materialized at Sonny's shoulder.

"We're ready, Nana. But first I'll have another one of these. My friend…"

"Whatever she's having is okay."

Harper's smile segued into something more sober, her eyes revealing some hidden tension. "This is strange, seeing you here. But I knew you'd call."

"You're awfully sure of yourself."

"Intuition. So when did you leave?"

"A week ago, maybe. Give or take."

"And?" she said when he didn't offer more. "You're just passing through?"

"Yeah, you could say so. That's the thing with those frequent flyer miles. Use 'em or lose 'em."

"My. You're just as glib and evasive as ever."

"Tell me something. Have you told anybody, I mean about

48

running into me?"

She seemed to hesitate. "No. Why do you ask?"

"Because it's probably best if everyone thinks I'm still back there. You know, in Spain."

"Why would I tell someone? If you think…"

The waitress interrupted, setting their martinis on the table with a theatrical flourish. "Ready to order, Harper?" the waitress asked. Harper was obviously a regular.

"I'll have the ahi."

"I'll have the same."

"And we'll share a green papaya salad. Thanks, Nana," she said, handing her the menus.

"Look, I just meant that I'm not ready for certain people to know. It's complicated. I'm not even here under my own name."

"Doesn't surprise me. After all, secrecy and deception are you people's bread and butter."

"You people? What's that supposed to mean?"

"I mean I did some checking. That's what we journalists do."

"Meaning?"

"Meaning I know a lot about you. Let's see, your father grew up in East Texas. Beaumont, as I recall, the last of a long line of unreformed Southern Baptists. He spent his youth on a shrimp trawler before joining the Marines where he met your Mom, an Italian American from Massachusetts. I imagine that was a marriage made in heaven."

He contemplated his parents' marriage while Harper took a long sip of her martini. She was right. The joining of a Yankee Papist and a fundamentalist redneck was as unnatural as the mating of a goat with an elephant. Needless to say, his childhood was one of ever shifting allegiances, the perfect upbringing to prepare him for a life of moral opportunism.

"Your Dad died of cancer when you were just seven. Mother never remarried. Taught school up until she passed in '87. You were an honors student and star jock in high school. You earned a Master's in Latin American Studies from the University of Texas at the tender age of twenty-three and followed that with two years in the Army. Doing what I could never find out. First red flag," she said, cocking one finger in the air. She took another sip of gin.

"Let's see. 1978, you show up in Nicaragua working for the Agency for International Development. AID's always been a good cover."

"Yeah, well, believe it or not I was helping people start up coffee plantations. And you don't know what you're talking about."

"You drop out of sight for a couple of years. Second red flag. What do they call that again in the trade, developing a legend? Next you show up in Peru working for the State Department again. Cultural attaché or some such crap." She sought his eye. He didn't flinch, so she continued. "You married a local woman. She doesn't follow you when you turn up in D.C. five years later. Then Honduras, Mexico City, Costa Rica and a long stint in Guatemala as political attaché that time. You picked up a couple of Indian dialects along the way—and another wife. Back to D.C. Divorced after five years. Moved up to assistant to the undersecretary for Latin American Affairs. Then two years ago, you suddenly up and resign."

He held her gaze and took a drink. It was a better than average martini. Dry with a hint of some spice he couldn't place.

"You're leaving out a lot of the good parts," he said.

"I'm not done. In D. C. you played racquetball five days a week with your boss. You had three lovers that I could find out about. I've got names," she said with a sly smile. "You're afraid of flying. Found that sort of odd. And you had this huge record collection of Cuban music from the fifties. Leave anything out?"

"Okay. So why?"

"Why what?"

"Why'd you go to the trouble?"

"I'm inquisitive. Figured there might be a story in there somewhere, one you're going to have to tell me eventually."

He smiled. "Ah! Now I remember what I liked about you. You're direct. That's good."

"You think? So tell me, how did you lose half your finger?"

"Home improvement project. Got distracted."

"Jesus. All right. For once be honest. Why did you call me?"

"Truth? Had time to kill and came across your number." He shrugged. "Here I am."

She cupped her glass in both hands and looked at him as though he was at a distance she would have to cross. He noticed her hands for the first time. They were large for a woman, the fingers long and elegant.

"I suspect what you really mean," she said after a moment, "is you need a friend and all you're left with is me. Okay, what-ever," she said when he didn't reply. "Almost forgot, I brought you something." She picked up a manila envelope from the seat beside her and handed it to him.

He took it from her, opened it and slid the contents into his one hand. It was a black and white photo of him, his hand out-stretched toward the lens. Just over his shoulder Khatir stood scowling.

"I thought you might want it."

"I thought Darfur was off the table," he said, sliding the pho-to back across the table.

"Nothing's off the table."

"What's that supposed to mean?"

"It means maybe we can work something out."

He picked up his glass and looked at her. "There's nothing to work out. You've got no story. Don't you read the papers? It's already been told. I killed an innocent man in Madrid. It was an accident. A tragedy. End of story. Now drop it."

She stared at him without expression for a long moment before draining her glass.

"That must have been horrible. I can't imagine how you must feel."

"No. You can't."

Neither of them said anything for a long moment.

"Who else knows you're back?" she asked. When he didn't say anything, she went on. "You're going to see someone, aren't you? Will she mind me coming along?"

"God, you never let up, do you?"

"She can think of me as a researcher."

"One, I'm not going to see a woman, and two, why would you think I would want you to come along? I get it that you think there's a story here somewhere. But enough, okay?"

"Ah, dinner," she said, tilting her chin and smiling. As the waitress served them, Harper leaned back and smiled, a look of satisfaction on her face.

"What if I told you that I have your record collection? Would that change your mind?"

"You have my records? How?"

She stuffed a large forkful of papaya salad in her mouth and chewed for a moment before answering. "God, this is good. Here, you have to eat some of this. Your ex-landlady, bless her soul, put all your stuff in storage," she said while dissecting her tuna. "I told her I was your ex-wife and you wanted me to hold them for safekeeping. Her gullibility and two hundred dollars and now I've got them. Don't' worry, they're in a safe place. So, you want to tell me what you were doing in Madrid?"

He shook his head in amusement. She was putting on her seductive look in the hope feminine wiles would carry the day. In the old days it might have been worth her effort, he thought, holding her gaze.

"I don't give up easy. I can wait."

Sonny took a bite of the ahi and sat back in his seat. He

couldn't decide about her. He was out of the practice of reading women. Why was she pushing this? It couldn't be just the story. He smiled as he thought of his records. He could get the records from her. He wasn't worried about that. Getting her to keep her mouth shut was another matter.

"What?"

"You really have my records?"

"Yeah, I do."

"What's my landlady's name?"

She paused as she was about to place a forkful of ahi in her mouth and stared at him, her face expressionless. "Mrs. Colfax. She said she has a whole box of photos, too. I didn't bother with them. Privacy and all, you know."

"That old bitch."

"Hey, be nice. She hung on to your records for you." She picked up her empty glass and twirled it between her fingers.

"So where did you find out all the background about me?"

"I have a friend. Ex-boyfriend actually. He's a cop with Major Crimes here in New York. Anyway, he's on loan to Homeland Security. So he has some access. Obviously not to everything. But he heard some scuttlebutt about why you went to Spain. Rumor had it you were in Madrid looking for someone, someone you had some grudge against from years back and just a whiff of something about Nicaragua. What did you do down there again? Seventy-eight, seventy-nine. That was back during their civil war, wasn't it?"

His estimation of her had just gone up. He held her gaze, thinking that she had done her homework. Which begged the question; did she know more than she was letting on to?

"You're good at making assumptions."

"Give me some credit. I started off doing investigative reporting. Ten years of it for the Atlanta Journal. I learned how to connect the dots."

53

Sonny started in on the papaya salad to buy some time. He made a show of looking at his watch.

She glanced around the dining room. "Must be hard. Being back. All this?"

"It's a bit strange. With your line of work, I imagine you could give me a lot of advice on reentry."

"To be honest, most of the time I lock myself in my apartment and, you're going to think I'm crazy, but I clean. Scrub my floors, the oven. Takes me two days until I'm satisfied everything is clean. Then I go see my shrink and unload about…" She shook her head, as if she were shedding herself of some unpleasant thought. She raised her martini glass and started to drink from it before realizing it was empty.

"Tell me something, Sonny. Do I have to be afraid of you? I mean, I usually have a feel for people, but you're hard to read. You've got this aura of…I don't know. Menace maybe?"

"Menace? I'm too tired for menace."

"I've just never shared dinner with an ex-con. Guess technically you're not even that because you're still supposed to be in jail. Oh my god. Even worse. I'm having dinner with an escaped con." She sat back and fanned herself. "Is it hot in here? I think I drank too much."

She nearly looked embarrassed, an emotion he guessed she wasn't that familiar with.

"And I guess I ought to be getting back. Hate to get swept up in any manhunt."

She turned and looked away, her jaw tightening. Some obvious change in her had occurred; her light demeanor replaced by tension. A swirl of something passed behind her eyes. Part truth, part lie. Neither of them spoke for a moment or made any effort to get up from the table.

"Where are you staying?" she asked, finally. When he didn't answer, she went on. "You know with this storm, the traffic is going to be dreadful. Maybe take two hours." She shook her head. "I hope I don't end up regretting this. My apartment's right around the corner. Has a fold out. It'll buy you at least another hour or two of sleep."

He thought for a moment. "I wouldn't say no. But I suspect it's some kind of ploy to get full disclosure."

"You're a fast learner. Shall we?" she said, motioning for the waitress.

Her apartment was a typical New York walkup. Three narrow rooms, a kitchen the size of a large walk-in closet. One wall in the cramped living room was given up to dozens of unframed photographs tacked randomly to the wall. He recognized a few from Darfur. A solitary window opened up to a view of another apartment building, the brightly lit windows of her neighbors obscenely close.

Sonny watched in silence as she pulled out the sofa bed and pulled back the sheets. "Give me a few minutes and the bathroom is yours. I'll bring you a pillow," she said, disappearing into the bathroom. He peered into her bedroom. An elaborate stereo system covered one wall, the surrounding shelves holding several hundred CDs. No records, though. He leaned his ear to the bathroom door. She was brushing her teeth.

Walking back to the small den, he paused to look at her desk. A scattering of illegible hand written notes littered the surface. An unframed, curled black and white photo was tacked to the wall above the computer monitor. A police mug shot of a young woman in an Afro, her face bruised and swollen almost beyond recognition.

Suddenly overcome with fatigue, he walked over and sat on the edge of the sofa bed and stared at his mud stained boots. He needed some new clothes. And a shave. He flopped back onto the bed and closed his eyes.

6

Harper lay awake in the gray dawn, ruminating about the previous evening and her possible motivations for having invited Sonny Day into her life. She couldn't figure him out, but then figuring out men had never been her strong suit. For most of her adult life, she had stumbled through the usual progressions of boyfriends, lovers, and a few affairs that could have been easily mistaken for marriage. How had some writer put it so aptly? McMurtry maybe. Pastures of plenty, pastures of less than plenty, and pastures you should get the hell out of.

To her credit she had married only once, to a jazz musician called Beadie. To his credit, Beadie had been a generous and affectionate partner, so much so that he felt he had to share these qualities with every woman he met. Still, for five years they had maintained a complex attachment born of loneliness and a complicated carnality. It had ended badly, worse than they both deserved. After several months of therapy, Harper took up with a woman she met in the condominium's laundry room, a nurse with the hands of a sculptor and the libido of a sixteen year old boy. What proved more disheartening to Harper was that she didn't seem to get women either. Male or female, they all challenged her poorly honed instincts. The assignment in Serbia came soon afterwards. And soon after that came the realization that she might be the wrong person for her own life.

She raised her head from the pillow, alerted by a noise in the

56

other room. He was talking to someone, his muted voice just audible through the thin bedroom walls. Dropping her head back, she stared past the near empty glass of wine at her alarm clock. A little after seven.

She sat up and studied herself in the dresser mirror. No point in preening, she decided, running her fingers through her hair. Thirsty, she downed the last of the wine before making her way to her bedroom door. As she slipped into her robe, she leaned close to the door, hoping to overhear what he was saying. She distinctly heard the word Dallas, one p.m., and a moment later, what sounded like "get into Santa Fe". Carefully turning the knob, she cracked the door and peered into the living room.

He was standing in front of the window with his back to her, a cell phone held to his ear. She could smell coffee and something else. The primal stink of an unwashed male? Nothing that disagreeable, she decided opening the door all the way, but all the same foreign, as no one other than a pizza delivery boy had crossed her threshold in at least a year.

He turned at the creak of the door and glanced at her as he continued his conversation. As she made her way to the kitchen, she heard him snap the phone shut and toss it on her desk.

"Thanks for making coffee," she said, pouring herself a cup. "If you're hungry, I could make us some breakfast." When he didn't answer, she turned and looked at him. She could see that he had picked up a sheaf of papers from her desk. He leafed through them, occasionally pausing to study one before tossing them onto to the desk.

"Mind me asking where you got these?"

She didn't answer, but instead buried her face in the open refrigerator.

"You think you know things, but you don't. This is garbage. I told you there's no story here. Are you going to say something or just stare in that empty, sad ass refrigerator?"

"I told you. I was curious," she said, her gaze fixed on a lone carton of cottage cheese. I'm a journalist. Journalists see the world as just a bunch of stories. Satisfied?" She turned and looked at him.

"It's bullshit, spin and hearsay," he said after a moment. His voice barely concealed underlying anger. "Those guys at Langley couldn't tell the truth if their lives depended on it." He looked at the page in his hand and then crumbled it up and threw it at the wall. "I do have to hand it to 'em. They do a good job of covering their asses."

She leaned against the kitchen counter and sipped her coffee, waiting for him to say more. After a moment, he met her gaze.

"The stuff about Nicaragua. You separated it out from the rest. How come?"

"I don't know. Personal interest partly. I was there once. After the war, Newsweek hired me to do a piece on the contras, back when I didn't have any ideals to speak of or much of a bank account. Anyway, it was one of your so-called Langley shitheads who got me the introduction and arranged my being....what do they call it these days? Embedded? Sounds innocuous enough, doesn't it? I don't know who was scarier, the contras or the creep who smuggled me across the border."

"Across the lake?"

"The lake?"

"Came in from Costa Rica, right? A skiff across Lago de Nicaragua. Moonless night and all that."

"Not exactly. A bumpy flight from some dark airstrip in Honduras to an even darker airstrip somewhere outside of a place called Jinotega, if I recall."

She watched him as he turned and stared out at the neighbor's window.

"Don't do that, looking in their window. You'll make them nervous. They're Chinese and I doubt they're legal."

He ignored her request.

"Please."

He turned back, but he appeared distracted.

"So why after all this time..." She paused and started over. "You went looking for somebody in Madrid, and I gather not with the friendliest of intentions. My ex-boyfriend says you apparently made some people real nervous."

"I bet I did." He looked down at his coffee. "Any of this left?"

"No, but I can make some more." She busied herself refilling the carafe, all the while gauging how far to push. "That file says something about you getting flown out because you had gotten beaten by a street mob or something," she said, her back turned to him. "It also says you weren't working for Central Intelligence. At least not then." She stopped to look at him. "But you did later. Right?"

"Drop it, Harper. No good can come of this."

"Of what?"

"Look. I have to go," he said after a moment's hesitation. "I have a flight out of La Guardia in three hours. I could use a shower, but if you don't mind, I'd like to use your Internet first. Part of reentry, you know, catch up on the news, check out the employment ads."

They stared at each other for a moment. "Have it your way," she said, retreating to the bathroom.

Later, when she turned off the shower, she heard him talking again, the conversation unintelligible. A few minutes later, she heard the door to her apartment close. She took her time putting on her makeup before going out. Other than the unmade bed and the coffee cup on the counter there was no sign he had ever been there. No thank you note. No nice to share dinner.

"Asshole."

She sat at her desk and stared at the computer. She clicked the mouse. There was nothing on the screen that would help. She thought for a moment, then picked up her cell phone and hit the redial.

"That sure was sloppy," she said, staring at the number, a 505 area code. She pulled out her telephone book and leafed through the front. 505. New Mexico. Northern New Mexico to be exact. Santa Fe? She thought for a moment and hit the redial again. Might as well see how careless you really are, she thought listening to the ringing tone that was followed by a taped message.

"Quintana Roo is currently closed. We serve a selection of dishes from the Yucatán and the interior of Mexico for your enjoyment. We also offer a full bar. The restaurant and bar are open from lunch to midnight every day but Monday. Please be aware that reservations are not accepted." The woman's voice on the recorder had a British accent.

She put down the phone and stared at the wall above her desk for a long moment before dialing another number. The person on the other end picked up almost immediately.

"Hey. It's me," she said. "He's here. You know. Arliss Day. No, not in my apartment. I mean here in New York." She listened for a moment. "I don't know. He didn't say. I mean he just got in last night. Well, so much for your goddamn watch lists. I told you, I don't know!" She listened again for a moment and sighed. "Look, we had a deal. The background in exchange for a heads up if he ever got in touch. So that's what I'm doing, okay? Sure, I'll let you know if he gets back in touch but don't hold your breath."

She snapped the phone shut and thought for a moment before opening the desk's file drawer. Rifling through the contents, she quickly found what she was looking for. Even if he had looked, he wouldn't have thought to look under 'Fashion shots''. She placed the file in front of her, unopened. Should she have given it to Sonny? Traded it? Traded it for what? She still didn't know why she was doing this. Was she merely desperate for a project, or was this more personal; more about him?

As she lay in bed the night before she had briefly contemplated her attraction to him. Perhaps this was nothing more than a nascent carnal craving. She had resisted that notion from the beginning. Or had she? Change of life, a friend had suggested, noting her general restiveness. Maybe that was it, just simple melancholy at the prospect of diminishing prospects. When she was thirty, she regarded any obstacle as a challenge. At forty, an illness, a night spent sleeping on the ground a mere nuisance. Now, at fifty-one, came the realization that her missteps keep repeating themselves. So much for ten years of therapy.

She opened the file she held on her lap and began leafing through the photos and Xeroxed articles. Nicaragua was old news. But obviously not for Sonny, she thought as she pulled a photo out of the sheaf. She stared at the image looking back at her. If not for what was in the accompanying file, she might convince herself the picture was that of someone's jovial grandfather. Balding, a pear shaped face, the brushy white moustache that barely obscured the fleshy lips. The man was smiling, but his eyes surely weren't.

I wouldn't have been doing him any favors giving him this, she thought. No good could come of it. Isn't that what he had said? She knew Sonny wouldn't drop this. So why not help him? She thought for a moment before picking up her cell phone and hitting the redial. For a moment it crossed her mind that she might be better off calling her therapist.

"Hey, tell your friends I want to make a new deal."

7

SANTA FE, NEW MEXICO

Ray adjusted the rear view mirror so he could watch a pair of young women remove their luggage from a van. They were underdressed for the weather in gauzy silk pants and long sleeved jerseys. Tourists heading back to warmer climes. He watched them for a moment longer before leaning closer to study the bruise on his forehead. He had told Macy he had hit his head on the car door. It would've been an easy enough lie. But then, telling lies had long been his strong suit. The problem was Macy usually saw through most of them.

He looked at himself in the mirror. Let's try this.

"Remember that guy, Sonny, I introduced you to once? He's coming through town. Thought we'd catch up. Talk about old times."

Hell, I can't even convince myself, he thought, straightening the mirror. He had never told Macy much about Sonny. Not their shared history or anything about Sonny being in prison in Spain. Sonny and Macy had actually met each other once, a perfunctory and accidental, quick introduction when Sonny came by their apartment. Sonny, he told her, was a foreign officer with the State Department. He had known him from the embassy in Mexico. He knew better than to think she believed him, but still she hadn't asked to know more.

He slurped the last of his coffee, dropped the Styrofoam cup on the floorboard beneath his feet, and cracked open the car door. For a moment, the cold air made him shudder, his breath suddenly visible in the late afternoon sunlight. Last night's storm had dropped the average daytime temperature to the mid- twenties along with another foot of snow. In the ten minutes since arriving at the airport, the storm's tail had broken, revealing the ragged silhouette of the Ortiz Mountains, and just beyond, the snow covered hump of Sandia Peak. In the frigid afternoon air, the mountain loomed much closer than fifty miles away.

He pushed open the door and pulled himself to his feet before zipping up his parka. Due to flight delays across most of the Southwest, there was little activity at the Santa Fe Airport. In fact, his car was only one of a half- dozen in the parking lot across from the small, unimposing adobe style terminal. The lack of a decent airport was actually one of the things he liked most about Santa Fe, the effort needed to either get here or leave. Another stake holding down his tent was how he liked to think of it.

Barring some unforeseen delay in Dallas, his flight was due at any moment. Sonny had been curt on the phone, whether from fatigue or stress, Ray couldn't tell. He assumed a bit of both. All he had said was "I'm coming in from Dallas at four." Sonny had never been one given to long conversation. Or revealing his intentions. It's what had bothered Ray when he first met Sonny.

He thought back to that first occasion. It was in the bar of the Intercontinental Hotel in Managua. August 22, 1978. Ray remembered the exact date because it was the same day a band of Sandinistas occupied the National Palace, their objective an exchange of hostages for some of their imprisoned comrades. The bar's patrons, the usual mix of journalists, idle expatriates and their bored, upper class Nicaraguan mistresses, were huddled around the bar's radio listening to a breathless female reporter's coverage of the ensuing panic.

Ray had just fallen short in his effort to seduce the wife of the Nicaraguan Agriculture Minister, her attention consumed by the drama occurring just a mile across town. Dejected, Ray retreated to his usual table, a booth with an unobstructed access to the rear exit, only to find it occupied by a young couple. At first, neither of the two acknowledged Ray's presence, their attention focused on what appeared to be a sheaf of drawings bound in a heavy leather portfolio. A row of empty Cerveza Victoria bottles lined the near side of the table.

After a few seconds, the woman looked up at him. Her skin, extraordinarily pale for a resident of the tropics, seemed almost too tight for her face, making her black eyes appear drawn, almost Oriental. Her skin color along with her chestnut hair, confirmed what Ray already knew. Definitely a Criollos, her ancestry old line, pure blooded Spanish. Her full lips however were a hundred percent Nica, an attribute embellished by the slash of red lipstick.

"You want something?" her partner asked.

Ray suddenly recognized Sonny as someone from AID, the Agency for International Development. He vaguely recalled being introduced to him at an embassy briefing. He was probably about Ray's age, although his crew cut and boyish face made him appear much younger.

"We've met before, haven't we?" Ray asked."The embassy, right?"

The guy nodded. "Arliss Day. AID."

Ray glanced at the young woman.

"Aminta Garza Segovia. I don't believe we have met," she said, offering her hand, her English almost without accent.

They all looked at each other for a moment in awkward silence before Ray smiled and walked off. Ray had heard the stories about Aminta. She was a fairly well known artist and the daughter of a wealthy family from Granada. He had also heard the rumors that she had Sandinista sympathies. Apparently, her father's connections were the only thing keeping her clear of Somoza's secret police.

Ray glanced up, stirred from his thoughts by the commuter

jet passing overhead. He wondered again about Sonny's reason for coming to Santa Fe. There hadn't been any further developments since the incident in Madrid. Sonny had gone to prison for who knew how long, off the radar. So Ray had dropped it. What was the point? His life had taken another direction. He was a husband, a father, a respectable businessman. Or so he liked to tell himself.

Ten minutes later, the first thin line of arriving passengers began to emerge from the doorway. Skiers mostly, their shoulders draped with boots, their skis held at port arms. A few of them blinked at the intense sunlight reflecting from the snow packed parking lot. After a moment, a lone figure dressed in a raincoat separated from the second clot of arrivals, paused to scan his surroundings, and then nodded in Ray's direction.

Ray watched Sonny pick his way through the slush. If it wasn't for the unmistakable stride, he doubted he would have recognized the approaching figure as his old friend. They stood apart for a moment, each silently appraising the other.

"Arliss."

"Raymond."

"You look like hell."

"Christ, one more person tells me that and I'm going to start believing it."

Ray clasped Sonny behind the neck and pulled him into his arms. "Man, and you stink," he said, shoving Sonny back and grinning.

"That I believe to be true."

"That's all you're carrying?" Ray asked, nodding at the valise.

"They didn't leave me with much." Sonny paused and patted the hood of the old Crown Victoria. "Been hitting the police auctions? I would've figured you for something Teutonic and silver."

"Yeah, well, the seats fit my fat ass."

"Where's the cane?"

"In the back. I have good days and bad days. I'm scheduled for a knee replacement next month, so it's good you showed up now."

"You look sorry to see me," Sonny said, sliding into the front seat.

"Should I be?"

When Sonny didn't reply, Ray turned the ignition and backed out. "It's good to see you, man," he said, gripping Sonny's shoulder. "Glad to have you back." Sonny grunted and gazed out the window at the passing landscape of the occasional warehouse and scrubby Junipers and Cholla.

"You got a new passport, right? Cards?"

Sonny nodded. "The guy in Kensington does good work. You can tell him I said so. Far as I know, everybody thinks Arliss Day's still in a Spanish jail."

"Tell me you didn't bust out."

"Nope. Early release. Good behavior, so to speak."

"So tell me. How was it?"

"What do you mean, how was it? White beans and stringy pork six nights a week, a glass of rotgut Tinto on Saturday and a cell so small I had to leave it just to change my mind."

Ray laughed."Cell so small... That's a good one. Have to remember that one. Meet any senoritas?" Ray asked, still hoping to lighten the mood.

"You're an asshole."

"*Eeee*, those Latinas. Remember those two we hooked up with that time in Mexico City? *Dos tipos de cuidado*. That's what they called us. Two dangerous characters. Man, those were some times. I know what you're thinking. I didn't screw up your marriage. Dorinda was never your type anyway. "

"How about you? You still hooked up with the Aussie gal, the one used to be a nun or something?"

"Macy? She used to be a nurse, not a nun. And she's not Australian, she's a Brit. Come to think of it, she might as well have been a nun. She was a tough nut to crack."

"And the kid?"

"She's almost twelve. My little Mayan princess. The best thing I got going. And for that I'll always owe you, man." He laid his hand on Sonny's shoulder.

"So you guys are good," Sonny said, cranking down the window. "You must still like it here."

"Yeah, it suits me. I can keep my profile low; stay out of trouble. Mostly," he said, thinking about yesterday's encounter with Ascensión. "Restaurant's doing great. I take care of the bar, Macy runs the kitchen. Can't complain."

Ray did like Santa Fe. He liked the town's eclectic mix of Native Americans, artists, Hispanic immigrants, politicos, fourth generation locals, and the wealthy refugees from Texas and California. And there were more than enough wackos to qualify as some exotic New Age game preserve. The tourists he could do without. Still the place had just enough edge without the undercurrent of dark tension of other Sun Belt cities. Or so he liked to think.

They drove in silence now, along Airport Road, past the golf course, and down a long straight stretch lined with Mexican groceries and pancerias, pawn shops and low rent apartment buildings. Little Chihuahua, the locals called it in reference to the high population of immigrants from the Mexican state to the south of New Mexico.

The setting sun had turned the snow covered mountains that overlooked the town a rosy pink. The Sangre de Cristos is what the early settlers had named them. The blood of Christ and that of a lot of murdered Indians. He glanced over at Sonny.

"You gonna tell me what happened?"

Sonny shot him a look but didn't answer. His eyes betrayed a heaviness Ray hadn't seen in a long time.

"You know what happened," he said after a moment. "I killed someone, an old man out for a walk. One minute he's enjoying the afternoon and the next....I never even saw him but still my fault. He's dead. No way around it."

Sonny looked away and in the ensuing silence, Ray sensed Sonny had cut himself adrift, slipping away in the receding waters of the past. Finally, when at last he looked back, he seemed to have let go of whatever it was that had held him.

"Mind me asking how you found Granera?"

Sonny didn't reply at first. "Caught a lucky break," he said, finally. "I had put out the word some time back. A guy I know at DEA said Granera's name came up. Some Columbian wanting to cut a deal tossed his name out along with everyone else he was willing to rat out. Said Granera was living in Spain under his own name, if you can believe it. It was easy from there." Sonny shook his head. "Living in the open without a care in the world, until I showed up downstairs. I almost had him."

"And if you would've caught him? Then what?"

"I don't know. Anyway, he's in the wind. Like me. What can I say?" Sonny turned his head and sniffed his sleeve. "I have to get out of these clothes. Any place on the way I can buy some?"

"Yeah, there's a mall just up ahead. So now what?"

"You're asking me if I'm done with it?"

"Thirty years is a long time to...."

"This is where you tell me to get a life. Right? I had one," Sonny said, looking over at him. "Didn't like it all that much."

"I don't know where he is, Sonny. Haven't looked. Don't care. You know, we all have to move on. Leave things behind. You get that, don't you?"

"So Ray Cortese, the scourge of the Americas, is finally housebroken. Good for you, *amigo*," Sonny said, tapping Ray affectionately on the shoulder. "But I have to ask, you still know anyone at Langley that'll talk to you?"

"Come on." Ray shook his head in frustration. "Listen, all

the old guys are tight assed career flunkies. No way anyone's gonna risk their goddamn pensions, and anyone willing to talk is out of the loop anyway. I do have a good buddy at ICE, but that's about it."

"Immigration won't be much help. He'll have new papers. Probably high dogging it in Miami as we speak. How about Chico? He still around?"

"Last I heard he was a Rent a Dick in Dallas."

"What about Kazmerak?"

"Christ. He's just about the dumbest bastard to ever sit between two shoes. You're still dead set on this, aren't you?"

"Did I say that?"

"You're asking me about goddamn Langley."

"Just curious is all."

The silence built as they waited in the traffic at the busy Cerrillos Road intersection.

"You still have that painting?" Sonny asked..

It took Ray a long moment to answer. "Yeah, I still have it."

Sonny nodded but didn't say anything.

He should've never told Sonny about it. And I'd be a damned fool if I tell you about the other one, he thought. As they waited for the traffic light to turn, he let his gaze wander up to the mountains to the north of the city. In the quickly fading light, their summit had turned from crimson to an icy blue, the foothills lost in dark shadow except for a necklace of lights from the high end real estate clinging to the slopes.

"What you say we get you cleaned up, change of clothes, get a Bistek Encebollado and few cervezas in you. Tomorrow's a new day." Tomorrow he would tell Sonny about the other painting and let the dice roll.

8

Ray had dropped Sonny at his house so he could freshen up, staying only long enough to show Sonny the guest room before heading back to the restaurant. After a long shower, Sonny changed into his new clothes and made himself a cup of coffee. The house was a rambling, low slung adobe with rough hewn pine ceilings and what looked like the original wood floors beneath expensive looking Oriental rugs. The thick plastered walls bespoke the house's age. The spare, mostly modern furniture didn't seem to quite fit, but still the house felt comfortable.

As Sonny sipped the coffee, he wandered around the house, examining the photos and art work on the walls, the music collection, the casual litter of a family, much like an anthropologist might study an excavation site for clues to the lives of its former residents. He lingered in what he assumed was the master bedroom, held by the scent of lotion or perfume.

He checked the other rooms and only afterwards acknowledged to himself that all the while he had been looking for the painting. It wasn't anywhere, at least anywhere obvious. In the hallway, he took a moment to study a collage of photographs of a young girl he could only assume was Ray's adopted daughter, Sadie. She had the slightly round face and high cheekbones of a Mayan. The only photograph he had ever seen of her was a passport photo taken right after Macy and Sonny had taken her from the orphanage eleven years ago.

When he finally left the house, it had started to snow again, enough so that the light from the street lights cast an orange glow onto the lowering sky. Even though it was still early, there was little traffic on the narrow side streets. The only sound other than Sonny's boots crunching on the icy sidewalk was the muffled barking of a dog. He tilted his head back and sniffed the air. The smell of pinón smoke and damp pine suddenly reminded him of nights spent on holiday in the Guatemalan highlands. The nostalgia fanned a faint glimmer of optimism. Amazing what a set of clean clothes will do for you, he thought, turning up the collar of his new ski jacket. Maybe Ray was right. A good meal, a good night's sleep, and tomorrow he'd wake up with an improved outlook on life. He could always hope.

His new found hopefulness was still not enough to quell his sense of disorientation. Less than two weeks ago he had been in Darfur, sitting in his makeshift lean to, struggling with his decision to leave the camp, all the while enduring the despair of his surroundings. And now here he was, strolling through a world many times removed, an affluent neighborhood of narrow private streets, three hundred year old acequias, and people sitting down to dinner discussing the stock market and little Tommy's attention deficit disorder. The dissonance between those two worlds could hardly be greater.

He paused on a bridge and glanced over the railing. Ray had referred to it as the river, but it looked more like a small stream at best. He waited for a moment as a young couple picked their way arm in arm past him on the icy sidewalk. He suddenly thought of Harper and how wrong it had been to leave that morning the way he had. From that first day in the desert, he had sensed in her a connection of sorts, albeit one that might be grounded in nothing more than a shared dysfunction. Perhaps her curiosity about his past was only mutual recognition of that bond. Still, her prying had opened a wound. Once this was over, he would call her and apologize. Who knew, maybe he would try looking her up again. He couldn't deny his attraction to her. Was that the reason he had neglected to cover his tracks? And what if she did manage to find him? He didn't have an answer.

71

He picked his way through the ankle deep snow along Old Santa Fe Trail as he tried to recall Ray's directions. After a few minutes, he spotted the carved wooden sign hanging above the sidewalk. The words Quintana Roo were faintly visible in the reflected light of the doorway. He paused at the entranceway to kick some snow off his boots before opening the heavy wooden door and stepping inside.

He was immediately assaulted by the sound of Ruben Blades and the pungent aroma of grilled meat and seafood. A huge stone fireplace divided the bar from the dining area which sat for the most part empty except for what appeared to be the over flow from the bar. The pink, diamond-finished walls, the high, barrel-arched ceilings and soft lighting transported him back to another place and time, the memory fleeting and elusive. The bar patrons, while raucous, appeared to be an older and more conservative crowd than what he would have expected. Professional types, politicians possibly, recalling the state capitol was a mere two blocks away. A few looked like they might be tourists. The only exception was a compact Hispanic looking man with a shaved head dressed in a turtle neck and a heavy leather biker's jacket hunched over a beer at the far end of the bar. The guy met Sonny's gaze and held it for a moment before turning away.

Sonny scanned the room for Ray before pushing his way through the crowd to the bar. Blades was singing something about another day, another love. The bartender, a wizened old black man in a white guayabera flicked his eyebrows in query.

"Ray around?"

The bartender shrugged. "He round. Mebbe in office. I don see him for a while."

Sonny could've sworn the guy's accent sounded Cuban.

"¿Usted es Cubano, si?"

The old guy nodded. *"Si. Soy de Las Tunas.* You know de place?"

"No, only the song. The one about the cane workers." He glanced up at the liquor bottles behind the bar. *"Flor de Caña anejo con limón. No hielo, por favor,"* he said, sliding a ten across the polished mahogany. *"¿Donde esta la oficina?"*

"Arriba," the bartender said, tilting his head at the stairs at the end of the bar.

Sonny glanced down the bar and saw the Hispanic guy at the end staring at him, his acne pitted face impassive. On second view, the man looked more Indian than mestizo. Sonny nodded a tenth of an inch and looked around the rest of the bar. Ray had done all right for himself. Sonny wouldn't ask where the money came from. In all the years they had known each other, Ray had never been known to be able to hold onto a dime.

He took off his parka as he listened with one ear for a moment to two guys next to him talking about some real estate deal that had gone sour. The bartender handed him an oversized tumbler of the dark Nicaraguan rum with two slices of lime impaled on the rim. Sonny took a sip of the rum, allowing the warm smokiness to sit in his mouth before swallowing it, and made his way through the crowd to the stairs.

A door stood half open at the top. He paused and knocked, and when no one answered, pushed the door open and stepped inside. The room, lit only by a pair of small desk lamps, seemed to occupy the entire second floor. One side was taken up by a massage table, an exercise bike and a rack of barbells, the other side had a pair of leather sofas and a small bar. A heavy wooden desk occupied the center. Through a French door set off to one side he could see the snow had begun to come down more heavily.

He took a bite of the lime along with a sip of the rum and looked around. A large split image video monitor hanging from the ceiling above the sofa displayed two views of the bar with such clarity and detail that he spent a good minute staring at it. He slid his gaze to the wall behind the desk. It took a moment in the dim light for him to realize what he was looking at. With his free hand, he bent the arm of one of the desk lamps to illuminate the wall.

The painting took up a good part of the wall. Its sheer size had always seemed to draw the viewer in. Part of its hold, he thought as he stepped back in order to better study it. The muted colors she had chosen were an aberration, the style more pensive and sedate than her usual kinetic realism. The young woman reclining on the rumpled bed was nude except for the sheet draped across her thigh. She held her chin in one hand; the other clutched a beer bottle. Her eyes held the viewer, the gaze wistful and vaguely questioning. Behind the bed, an open window framed the conical silhouette of a volcano and a palm frond. It took the casual observer a moment to notice the barely revealed figure in the rattan chair next to the window. A trousered leg and bare foot propped on the window sill. The out flung arm, the gold wrist watch, and the crooked hand clutching a glass. The crown of a man's head was just visible over the top of the chair back.

He glanced at the lower right corner. The words La Pausa were scrawled in red along with the initials AGS and a date. 1978. La Pausa. She had always referred to those afternoons as the pause, an interruption of the world outside; a brief escape from the subterfuge and brutality that had overtaken her country. He lifted his gaze back to the young woman's face, his eyes holding her for a long moment before he exhaled.

"What do you make of their relationship? I mean aside from their being lovers?"

Sonny turned and looked at the woman leaning against the door frame.

"They're obviously not married," she added. "Accomplices, perhaps."

He had forgotten how much Macy reminded him of a certain actress. Meryl Streep, maybe. Something about her face. More petite though and a good decade older than Ray. She wore a simple white cook's smock and jeans. Her dishwater blonde hair was pulled back into a tight chignon and she had a pair of glasses perched on her forehead.

"You're Sonny, aren't you? I believe we may have met once," she said, without leaving the doorway.

"Macy, right?" He nodded, turned, and looked back at the painting. "Accomplices, huh? Yeah, I can see that."

"Have you seen it before? The painting? Ray has this odd attachment to it. Doesn't look like him, does it? The guy in the chair? Bloody, better not be," she said, drawing up beside him. "I like it though. Much more than the other one. The other one is a bit...I don't know...What's the word I'm thinking of? Baroque, maybe? Not my taste at the least."

Sonny looked at her. "There's another one? Same artist?"

"Yeah, Ray keep's it in the liquor cellar. Thank god." She flicked her glasses down onto her nose and smiled.

Sonny always found it odd how easily a woman could rearrange her face with a simple prop. Her pale eyes looked bigger now, more intense. He didn't answer her, but instead looked back at the painting.

"Did you meet Sadie?"

Sonny turned and looked at her, at first too preoccupied to be sure what she had asked. "Sadie? No, she wasn't home when I left. Ray showed me a picture though. She's beautiful."

"No credit to us," she said, glancing up at the monitor. "Ray's back."

Sonny looked up at the screen. Ray was leaning over the bar and talking to the Hispanic guy he had seen earlier. Their conversation appeared one sided with Ray doing most of the talking. The other man's expression remained just as impassive as before until Ray said something that made the Hispanic grimace and turn his head. After a moment, he nodded and walked off.

"I'll let him know you're here and send up some food," Macy said, interrupting his thoughts.

"Yeah, that'd be great."

She started for the door, then hesitated. "Tell me something. Were you ever posted in Guatemala? We may have met there before. I used to run across a lot of diplomatic people. Maybe back in '97?"

He stared at her a moment before answering."Yeah, I was down there around then. Don't recall meeting you though."

"I gather you and Ray go a long way back."

"You could say that."

She regarded him silently for a long moment. "Do me a favor. Don't ask too much of him." She shot him a cold, hard glance. "He's not the same man you knew," she said, turning and walking out of the room.

None of us are, he thought as he stared after her. He walked over to the French door and looked out at the night. The snow had eased up and he could make out the steeple of the Loretto Chapel, and beyond that, the pair of blocky steeples of the cathedral. The whole setting seemed almost surreal in the reflected glow of the street light. It made him wonder even more at the dissimilarity of this and the world he had fled a little more than a week ago. Oddly enough, it only heightened his ambivalence about what he was doing here. During those months in Darfur, he had tried to make sense of his life. He had even seemed to convince himself that he had put Nicaragua behind him. Of course, he had convinced himself of that once before.

He finished off the rum. It left a warm taste of a time less complicated. He walked over to the desk and twisted the lamp back to where it shone on the desktop, and then walked over to the sofa and sat back on the cool leather. He had no sooner settled when Ray limped in followed by a young Hispanic woman bearing a tray of food.

"Ready for some grub? I promised you bistek ecebollado, so steak it is."

The smell of the grilled meat and onions filled the room. Sonny hadn't realized until then how hungry he was or when the last time he had had a meal like this. The young woman slid the tray onto the coffee table and left without speaking.

"That's the last time I go up those goddamn stairs tonight," Ray said, pulling out a couple of Negro Modelas from the small refrigerator beneath the bar. He set them on the coffee table and turned on a floor lamp.

Sonny nodded up at the monitor screen."Who's the *cholo* you were talking to at the bar? Thought you didn't circulate with that type anymore."

"Just somebody I trade information with. You know me. Old habits. Have to know what's going on in my territory. Information's always been worth more than gold."

Sonny cut a piece of steak, dragged it through the small bowl of salsa and forked it into his mouth. He relished the taste of the smoky ancho peppers and lime. He chewed as he watched Ray settle into his chair. He looked distracted.

"Not the kind of bar I expected."

"You were expecting what, a biker bar? Lot of people in this town like to spend money. Makes them feel better. I look at it as legalized money laundering."

Sonny took a swallow of beer and nodded over to the painting. "Why'd you keep it?"

Ray sat there, motionless, ignoring his question. "The thing about information," he said, finally, turning to look at the window. "is that more often than not you find out things you don't really wanna know." He looked over at the painting. "Was a nice house Aminta had there. View of the lake and all. I happened to stop by there the last time I was down there. It's gone. Burned out. Nothing left but an old concrete slab and that banana orchard. You know I'd sit there in the dark in those banana trees, getting chewed up by mosquitoes and I'd wonder if you knew I was there."

"Why'd you stop? Watching us, I mean."

Ray met his gaze. "You know why. Shit, there's no point..." He got up from the sofa, walked over to the desk, and picked up his glasses.

"I've been thinking," Sonny said, "about what you said. About letting it go. You're right. Was a long time ago and nothing good will ever come of it."

Ray didn't look up but instead went through the motions of looking at some papers.

"I'd just like to know when you were going to tell me about the other painting."

Ray dropped the papers on the desk and took a long swallow of his beer. "Macy, right?" He leaned on the desk, hands spread, as if he were holding it down. He looked up at the painting. "Okay, so you know about it. You wanna see it? Let's go," he said turning to look at Sonny.

"It can wait. Food's too good," he said, taking a mouthful of the grilled onions.

"I didn't tell you before because I only bought it six months ago. The woman who owns the gallery where I got this one," Ray said, pointing with his thumb over his shoulder, "she calls me up and tells me she's got another one by this same artist. When I pushed her as to where she got it, she said she bought it at an art show in Houston, said she didn't want to sell it but she needed the cash."

"And you didn't ask any questions, right?"

"Didn't see the point."

Sonny chased a bite of steak with the beer. "And you bought it anyway. Why?"

Sonny sensed the hesitation in his reply. "A fucking impulse. What can I say?" Ray said, his attention suddenly drawn to the doorway where Macy had appeared.

She looked at Sonny. "Somebody's asking for you. I told her I'd ask Ray if he had seen you."

They both glanced up at the video monitor.

"The lady in the baseball cap and the fur parka, just down from the end."

"Hold on," Ray said, reaching for the remote. One half of the screen suddenly displayed a view from a vantage point behind the bar.

"I'll be," Sonny said. "She's smarter than I thought," he muttered, getting to his feet to look more closely.

Harper's face was partially obscured by the baseball cap. She was talking to an older man who was rubbing his hair like he still had some. The presence of an attractive woman amidst the paucity of other females hadn't gone unnoticed. The Cuban bartender leaned over to take her order, and for a brief moment her eyes seemed to look into the camera lens.

"Who is she?" Ray asked.

"Trouble," Sonny said, smiling and shaking his head.

9

Harper took a sip of her martini and gazed in the bar's mirror at the knot of male patrons huddled behind her. Several of the men tried to make eye contact. Lounge lizards were the same the world over.

"Would you like a table?"

She turned and saw it was the same woman the bartender had summoned when she first asked about Sonny. The British accent sounded more obvious now, the same voice that was on the answering machine when Harper happened to call the restaurant from New York. She appeared to be amused by something.

"Or I can serve you upstairs with the boys if you'd rather. Sonny said I should send you up," she said in response to Harper's obvious surprise.

"He's here?" Harper asked, amazed at how easy it had been.

"Don't disappoint me. I'm hoping you might prove to be the diversion the situation requires. I'm Macy by the way," she said, taking Harper by the elbow and leading her back through the crowd. "Snapper or steak," she shouted over the din. "Appetizers? What would you like to eat?"

"No thanks. Maybe later."

"Suit yourself. They're up there," Macy said, pointing up the stairs before disappearing through the door that led to the kitchen.

Harper made her way up and paused at the top of the stairs before stepping through the doorway into the dimly lit room. Sonny sat on a sofa with his back partially to the door, leaning over a plate of food. The guy sitting across from him lifted his eyes to take her in but said nothing. He looked fiftyish, slightly balding, with an olive complexion and hooded eyes. He wore what appeared to be black pajamas. It made him look like some aging, doughy ninja. Harper's intuition made her immediately mistrust him.

He watched her without reaction before glancing over at Sonny, who sensing her presence looked up. Sonny smiled through a mouthful of food.

"You're good, I'll grant you that. How'd you find me?"

"Trade secret."

"Harper Harris, meet my friend."

"Your friend? Oh, I get it. Names only on a need to know basis. You guys," she said, smiling and shaking her head. "You must at least have a cool code name?" she said, turning to Sonny's companion. "Black mamba or something equally venal?"

He didn't reply but stared at her blankly. Harper took off her cap and ran her fingers through her hair. She started to slip out of her parka when he finally spoke.

"Sonny says you're poking around where you shouldn't be. That's not a smart thing to do."

Harper looked at Sonny and then back at the other guy. "Listen, I've been told that once already today and I'll tell you what I told the other asshole. It's my business to ask questions and no one tells me I can't. Live with it."

No one said anything for a long moment. The silence grew until Sonny started to laugh.

"Call me Ray," the man on the couch said, smiling broadly and extending his hand. "Have a seat," he said sliding over on the sofa. "Sonny was right. Said I'd appreciate your attitude.

Would you like another martini?"

"Sure," she said, taking his hand and dropping down on the sofa beside Ray."Bombay. Up with lots of olives. And I apologize for the bitchiness. Too many airports in one day."

Ray nodded, pushed up from the sofa and picked up his cane.

"Oh, never mind," Harper said, noticing the cane.

"Don't worry about it. The stairs are my physical therapy. Sonny. Another rum?"

"Sure."

"I guess there's not much point in asking why you're here," Sonny said after Ray left.

"I'm not going to lie. I came to see you."

They looked at each other for a moment longer before Sonny finally spoke. "No story. No questions. Is that right?"

"I didn't say I wouldn't ask questions. I just said there's no story. I told you, I'm inquisitive by nature."

"I can live with that. I'm sorry about leaving the way I did. Wasn't feeling quite civilized at the time."

"You look better," she said, moving onto the sofa beside him. "I hardly recognize you. You even smell halfway human." She settled back and glanced up at the monitor. Ray was behind the bar mixing drinks. "This Ray's place?"

"Yeah," he said, turning sideways to look at her."You're not going to tell me how you found me?"

"Easy, I hit the redial after you left." When he didn't react, she shook her head in realization. "You did it on purpose, didn't you? To see if I... Now I'm the one that feels foolish. Jesus, you're a shit."

"If it makes you feel any better, I really didn't think you'd look."

"So then why'd you do it?"

He smiled and looked up at the ceiling. He likes games, she

thought. Did that come as any surprise? It's what these guys did. Rather than unsettle her, it only stoked her interest. She finished her martini and looked around the room, only now noticing the painting on the opposite wall. She had missed it at first in the dim light. She stood up and walked over behind the desk to look at it more closely.

"Interesting piece. Surprised he doesn't have it hanging downstairs." She leaned closer and squinted to look at the title. "Mexican artist?" She turned and looked at Sonny but he didn't reply, his face suddenly devoid of the animation of a moment earlier.

"I used to paint. Back in college," she said, hoping to reengage him. "Never was that good at it. Not like this," she said, looking back at it. "The atmosphere…"

Ray came in, followed by a young Hispanic woman carrying a tray of drinks. He looked at each of them as if smelling out the mood. "So do we have détente?" he asked, handing Sonny a tumbler of brown liquor. "And a martini for the lady." He handed the glass to Harper. "*Gracias*, Anna," he said, nodding to the young woman.

"I was just admiring this painting. You know the artist by any chance?"

She saw the two of them exchange looks before Ray shook his head.

"No, I don't. I bought it at an auction."

"C'mon Ray, tell Harper about the artist," Sonny said, downing half of the tumbler of rum. "What's it going to hurt? Harper's…inquisitive. So am I. It's why she's here. Why I'm here."

She looked at Ray, whose whole countenance seemed suddenly cautionary.

"Tell her why you have it hanging up here where you can look at it every goddamn day. Tell her. Then maybe we'll all saunter downstairs and look at the other one." Sonny finished his rum and banged the glass down on the table.

"Okay," Ray replied after a long moment had passed. "Yeah, we knew the artist. Her name was Aminta. And Sonny and her were an item once upon a time." He glanced back at Sonny who stared at the table. "She's dead and Sonny can't let it go. It's why his life is so fucked up. Does that about sum it up, *amigo*? Shit," he muttered, turning his back on both of them.

In the ensuing silence, Harper could hear the murmur of Latin rhythm and a raucous cheer from downstairs followed by laughter. Sonny looked up at Ray.

"I want to see it. Then we're done. You. Me. All of it."

Ray sighed. "If that's what you want."

"That's what I want," Sonny said as he stood and headed for the door.

Ray hesitated a moment before pushing off from the desk and starting after him. Harper grabbed his arm.

"What's this about?"

Ray turned and looked at her. "Listen, I don't know why you're here or what you and Sonny have going on. I don't care. But if you're as smart as you think you are, you'll walk away."

"Walk away? You obviously don't know me."

"Maybe not, but I know your type. I've seen what you people do. You fuck things up is what you do. You think turning over some rock is gonna expose something we all want to see. That it'll make things better. Well it won't. Not this time. So why don't you just get the hell out of here?"

Ray glanced at the door and then back at her. "I don't get you. You don't know anything about him. About any of this. He said he already told you there's no story here. So what is it?"

"Like Sonny said. I'm inquisitive. And stubborn."

"All right. Stay if you want, but I'll tell you the same thing he did. No story."

"Okay." She set her drink down and followed him out the door.

10

Ray winced as he picked his way down the stairs, pausing halfway down to glance back at Harper. From the little bit of her background that Sonny had revealed, he knew better than to expect she would stay behind. He had run across plenty like her over the years in places like Nicaragua. Guatemala. Mexico. Places that were the news du jour, the disasters and the dirty little wars. For the most part people like her were nothing more than high minded vultures, serving up bad history as news. Neatly packaging misfortune for a short news cycle, and then off again to somewhere else, like a botfly seeking out shit. He had played ball with them, used them, had even liked a few of them. The women were the worst in that they always played out as the wild card. Then again, maybe he was misjudging her. She had obviously been around.

He paused again at the bottom to survey the crowded bar area and the nearly deserted dining room. Sonny was nowhere in sight. He turned and looked back toward the kitchen. The door to the liquor cellar was open and Macy stood beside it, wiping her hands on her apron. She waited as he made his way over.

"He wanted to know where the cellar was. What? I shouldn't have told him? Ray?"

Ray brushed past her and started down the stairway, sensing both the women following behind him. He knew he should stop them but also knew any attempt would be met by stubborn opposition. He paused at the bottom of the stairs, the pain in his knee making him feel faint. He gripped the handrail and pivoted on his good leg to glance down the narrow aisle way that led to the rear of the cellar. In the dim light of the naked overhead bulb, Ray could see Sonny standing motionless, his attention focused on something in front of him. Ray reached up on the wall beside him and flipped a light switch. The effect on Sonny was almost instantaneous. He seemed to slump, then caught himself, hesitating a moment before stepping forward and out of Ray's line of sight. Harper tried to slip past Ray, but he stopped her with his arm.

"Wait a minute. Leave him be."

In the ensuing silence, Ray thought he heard Sonny mutter something. He waited another moment before making his way through the stacked cases of liquor and foodstuffs. He no sooner had reached the end of the aisle before Sonny stepped back into view. To Ray's surprise, the look on Sonny's face was one of confusion.

"There's something you're not telling me," Sonny said, his voice flat and barely audible in the tomb-like silence.

Ray shot his eyes up at the painting suspended on the far wall and then back at Sonny.

"What do you mean?"

"I mean you've been lying to me all along. And I just want to know why," Sonny said, pushing Ray back against a stack of empty cartons, knocking them over. Ray struggled to keep his footing as Sonny grabbed him by the shirt.

"That's not her painting. Can't be. She never finished it. She couldn't have. I saw it. The day before. It wasn't like that. It's either a goddamn fake or you're lying."

"I don't know what you're talking about."

Sonny swung at him, the blow only grazing Ray's cheek, but still enough to send him stumbling back against the wall. Sonny stepped back and pointed to the painting.

"If that's her painting, then she can't be dead. You told me she was dead." He lifted his fist as if to hit Ray again but instead turned away. "God damn you Ray! Don't you see? You fuck up people's lives...hell, people die because of your...games."

Ray looked at the painting, a tiny vein of panic opening inside of him. He should've known all along something wasn't right about it. It wasn't anything like Aminta's other works. It was different. How many times had he looked at it and felt some strange dissonance that he couldn't quite put his finger on. He had never considered the possibility that it was a forgery. That or Sonny had to be mistaken about her never finishing it. There was no other explanation. Ray had seen her. Christ, Aminta was dead. He couldn't even begin to consider any other possibility.

Sonny stared at the painting for a moment, and then turned and pushed past Ray and went up the stairs.

"Sonny," Harper said.

"Let him go," Ray said, grabbing Harper's arm.

Harper glared at him. "He shouldn't be alone. You're his friend, why don't you..."

"I told you. Leave him alone. There's no point." Ray dropped down onto a large wooden box behind him. The pain is his leg made it difficult to think.

"Macy, hon. Do me a favor and get me some Advil. And a cigarette. Don't give me that look. One lousy cigarette."

Macy stood there, arms crossed, regarding him silently for a moment before walking away. He leaned forward, rubbing his knees, his gaze fixed on the floor. When he finally looked up, he saw Harper standing in front of the painting.

It was much smaller than the painting in his office. A portrait of sorts if one could really label it as such. The title was crudely scrawled in large cursive script along the bottom. *Un Retrato de Las Penas,* followed only by the initials AGS and no date. The viewer could hardly fail to sense the mood of the painter. A melancholia overlaid by something that the woman who sold it to Ray labeled, "a perverted tranquility". Ray had thought it more like some simple, numb acceptance.

The subject, a young woman dressed in a diaphanous red gown reminiscent of the Elizabethan period complete with a cowl like, jewel encrusted collar, leaned forward from the curled cusp of a pale yellow calla lily. Her left hand clutched her breast, her right held what on close inspection appeared to be an amputated heart. A thin dribble of blood coursed down her fingers onto the creamy floral orifice encircling her waist.

Her hair had been shorn close to her skull. That along with her pale skin gave her an ethereal, gaunt appearance. Her eyes were lowered and focused off to the side, her mouth slightly open in a vague smile. A shroud of smaller calla lilies surrounded her, their stems spewing from a mound of various multicolored tropical fruits. A montage of jacaranda and traveler's palms completed the background, and beyond the trees the faint silhouette of a conical volcano, a thin tendril of smoke sketched against the pinky orange hemorrhaging dusk. If the viewer's eyes lingered long enough, small figures emerged from the muted shadows. Naked children, an old man carrying a bunch of bananas, a young soldier holding a skull in his outstretched hand, and in the bottom corner an infant swaddled in what appeared to be banana leaves.

It was almost too much to absorb. And too disquieting he had decided to exhibit in the bar or dining room. Macy had immediately vetoed its presence in their home, so here it resided, amongst the sacks of dried beans and the dusty crates of tequila and Spanish olives.

"Sort of stops you, doesn't it?" he said, his voice cutting the stillness.

Harper turned and looked at Ray. "It's quite..." She searched for the words. "I don't know. It's difficult to put into words. Beautiful. Disturbing. All at the same time. Reminds me of this medieval tapestry I saw once in this cathedral in Prague. It's another one of hers, I take it? This Aminta woman. She was pretty talented," she said, returning her gaze to the painting."What does the title mean?"

"A Portrait of the Sorrows."

"Yeah, I can see that."

Macy returned, carrying a glass of water, a Ziploc bag of ice cubes and a single cigarette. She handed him the cigarette and dropped some pills into his open palm. Ray dry swallowed them, ignoring the glass of water Macy offered him. She dropped the bag of ice in his lap and joined Harper in front of the painting.

"I hate it. And I especially hate when you bastards hide things," Macy said. "Bloody men," she said, turning and fixing her gaze on Ray.

Harper nodded at the painting."I want to know about her and Sonny."

Ray sat there motionless for a long moment, staring at the two women, before screwing the cigarette between his lips. In some part of his mind he was already surveying his memory, calculating what it would cost to relive that time. It wasn't only Sonny or Harper that needed answers. He suddenly had his own doubts.

He leaned into the lighter and sucked greedily, his eyes closed. When he opened them, he stared at the smoke leaking from between his fingers, lost in the story that he had already screened on the back of his mind.

"That one upstairs. I never should've told him about it. I should've known he wouldn't let it go. He'd start asking questions. Start looking for Granera again."

"Who's Granera?" Macy asked.

"General Reynaldo Granera-Holman. He was in charge of Somoza's prisons. Not a very nice person from what I gather," Harper said.

Ray looked at her with astonishment."Sonny tell you about him?"

"No. I figured it out on my own."

Ray regarded her a moment."Why do I get the feeling you know more about this then you're letting on?"

89

Harper shrugged. "There's always more, right?"

"Okay. You want to know what happened?" He pushed himself to his feet. "Let's go upstairs. It's a long story and my ass can't take this box much longer."

After they were settled back in Ray's office, Macy left them alone to arrange for some food to be brought up. Harper remained silent as if lost in thought. Occasionally, she would glance up at the painting as if trying to reconcile it with the one she had just seen in the cellar. Ray held to his own silence, replaying and rehearsing the narrative he was about to reveal, editing out the irrelevant sidebars, editorializing in parts that he hoped might put him in a better light.

"So is she really dead?" Harper asked.

Ray met her gaze but didn't reply.

"Do you even know?"

"Let's not get ahead of ourselves," he said after a long moment had passed. "How much do you know about what happened down there?"

"The war? Enough. I was down there once. During the Contra War."

"Then you probably know what kind of shit our side was involved in. Guys like me."

"And Sonny?"

He picked up the bag of ice and dabbed it onto his cheek. "No, Sonny was straight back then. He was AID, not Agency. His whoring came much later. What?"

"I don't know. I just thought …The newspapers said he was probably CIA."

"No, he was never one of us. At least not officially. Let's say we used him for some things. He was too much the clear eyed idealist to take up with the Agency."

Macy came in carrying a large tray of food and a bottle of red wine. The smell of the food immediately filled the room. "Salbutes and tacos," she said, setting the tray on the coffee table. The artfully arranged apertivos reminded Harper of a photo shoot she once did for Gourmet Magazine. Macy lowered herself to the floor opposite Ray, cradling the bottle of wine between her legs. Reaching into her blouse pocket, she pulled out a cigarette and held it out to Ray.

Ray took it from her and slid it behind his ear.

"Well," Harper said.

Ray took a deep breath. "Like I said. It's a long story."

"Come on, Ray. Long stories are what I do for a living."

"You'd had to been there."

"Put me there, then."

He thought about it for a moment. "I could've warned him off," he said finally. "Warned both of them. But I didn't. You see, I didn't trust him. Truth be told, I had orders not to. And I sure as hell couldn't trust her."

He took the wine bottle from Macy and poured himself a glass. "Christmas Eve, 1978,. Sonny and I were having a drink at the Intercontinental Hotel in Managua. It was crazy there that night. People celebrating like no tomorrow. Beginning of the end, and they all knew it," he said. "And who shows up but Granera. With goddamn Aminta on his arm. I should've figured it out right then." He downed the wine in one swallow."Yeah, it was the beginning of the end."

11

"Come on, Sonny. *¿Que dice?* Tell me what's got you so goddamned blue. It's Christmas Eve for chrissakes. *Saturnino, otro ron y cola!*" Ray gestured with his empty glass to signal the bartender who lingered discretely at the end of the bar. When Sonny didn't reply, he spun around on the barstool to observe the smoky barroom.

In honor of the holiday, someone had decorated a few of the potted plants with strands of blinking multi-colored lights. Draped above the doorway was a sagging banner proclaiming "*Feliz Navidad'* in cheesy, handcut letters. A piano had been moved into the small alcove by the door, and the piano player, an elderly black man, pounded away on the keys in an attempt to be heard over the cacophony of laughter and conversation. Apparently, he knew only a handful of tunes, an off key rendition of White Christmas he had already played three times in a half hour, a few Broadway show tunes and a tediously languid version of the Bee Gees' "Staying Alive."

A raucous group of Americans populated the far end of the room, journalists mostly along with a smattering of diplomatic types Ray recognized from the embassy. One table on the edge of the contingent seemed taken up by a clot of guys in crew cuts, their casual tropical shirts contrasting with the more formal wear of their fellow countrymen. Military advisors, he assumed.

A group of Nicas occupied the other end of the room. A few, Ray guessed, were out-of- uniform soldiers. Several of the others were business men and their wives or mistresses mingling with some upwardly aspiring government ministers that Ray recognized from his dealings in the capital. Some of them he knew because they were on the Agency's payroll.

"Might wanna check this out," Ray said, nudging Sonny.

A chorus of drunken greetings announced the arrival of an entourage of a half dozen or so men, several of them garbed in natty military attire replete with gold braid and the usual vulgar excess of campaign ribbons and medals. They surrounded a tall, slender raven-haired man of about forty dressed in an impeccably tailored gray silk suit and a red club tie. His wide open face and dark eyes possessed an attractiveness enhanced by full, almost feminine lips. The lips had earned him the nickname El Labio. Of course, only his enemies dared to call him that.

As he turned to kiss the hand of an elderly female admirer, Aminta suddenly appeared at El Labio's side. She wore a red evening gown and an unseasonable white ermine stole across her bare shoulders.

"What the hell?" Ray muttered, turning to look at Sonny who was studying the crowd in the reflection of the bar's mirror. He saw Sonny and Aminta briefly exchange glances before she turned away to talk to a couple at a table.

"You mind telling me what's going on? I thought you were meeting up with her later. She is your girl, isn't she? I mean…"

"This isn't high school, Ray," Sonny said, his eyes never leaving the mirror.

"I just wouldn't have figured Granera for her type, that's all."

Sonny shot him a look in the mirror but didn't say anything.

"I'm going to ask you again, and you better be straight. What's she doing with him?"

"It's none of your business, Ray"

"That's where you're wrong, buddy. Everything that bastard

does is my business. He's like a cornered dog. He can still bite. Aminta should keep her distance. I warned her…"

"I told you not to talk politics with her."

"Why? Because she's playing both sides? I don't trust her, Sonny. You wanna know what the intel reports are saying about her these days?"

"Don't tell me any of that stuff either."

"Don't worry. Word around the shop is you have too many of the wrong friends."

"The wrong friends? You mean those guerilla spies I slip messages to in the restroom at the Parador?"

"It's your business what you do in the john. I hear a lot of mariquitas hang out there. You know queering around is a sure fire career killer at State."

"God, Ray. You're an asshole. I told you I keep my mouth shut. I do my job. That's it."

"You're apolitical, right? Like Aminta."

"Keep her out of this."

"That's the problem. She's in it up to her tits. And if you're not careful, you're gonna get caught up in it."

The bartender placed their rums in front of them and started to turn away.

"*Saturnino. Por favor. Decirme. ¿Quién será victorioso?* Huh? Who's gonna win? *¿Las Somocistas o las Sandinistas?*"

The bartender shrunk back and looked around to see if anyone had heard Ray's question before scurrying back to the other end of the bar.

"You're a bigger asshole than I thought."

"Just checking the political barometer. I guess it's still safe for pricks like Granera to drink here. Tell me something, *amigo*. What happens with you two after *la revolución*? Big wedding? Kids and a place in the suburbs along the lake?"

Sonny threw back his rum, emptying half of the glass."Comes down to it, I resign, stay on."

"You think the Sandinistas are gonna welcome a *Yanqui* into the fold that easy? Especially one that worked for the *Diablo de la Norte?* Think again. I meant what I said about Aminta. You need to step back for a while."

"Did I ask you for your advice?"

"All I'm saying is her family connections won't protect her forever. There'll come a time..."

"Shut up, Ray."

"Hear me out. They know about her. They have to. They're not stupid."

Sonny emptied his glass, reached into his shirt pocket and tossed a wad of bills on the bar. Then without saying another word, he stalked out of the bar.

Ray watched him go, allowing his gaze to briefly take in Granera and his friends. If they had observed Sonny's exit, no one had given any sign. No one except Aminta. She watched him leave and then gathered her stole and made her way to the bar.

"Interesting company you keep," he said as she slid into Sonny's empty seat.

"I am sure your friends at the embassy will find it interesting."

"I have to tell you, that's one of your countryman I'll be happy to see go."

"You think he will go?"

"Come on, Aminta. You know things are about to get ugly. I give it six, maybe eight months before Somoza and his bunch bail."

"Bail?"

"Leave. *Escapar.*"

"*¿De verdad?* One can only hope. But as I have said before, our country is not truly ours. Not as long as your leaders have their puppet Somoza."

"Oh, spare me. It's over. Okay? Your side won. *Salud*, he said, emptying his glass. He gestured to the bartender to bring him another. "I was at this bar down off the plaza the other night. This one guy had too much to drink. Jumps up and yells *Viva la revolución! Viva Sandino!* Crazy thing was. Nobody even batted an eye. Hell, three months ago, no one would've dared mouth off like that. Writing's on the wall. Our *Presidente* Carter's cutting Somoza loose. Torrijos and his Panamanian other pals are turning up their noses like he's bad tuna. The Costa Ricans are starting to supply your boys in the south. Like I said, six months tops."

Aminta met his gaze in the mirror and smiled. Ray could see why Sonny was so enchanted with her. She had the kind of smile that made you forget where you needed to be in five minutes. He leaned closer for no other reason than to smell her. She smelled like the tuberose one of the embassy secretaries always wore in her hair.

"My side, you say? You think you know things, Ramón. About me. About my political convictions. You know you could be wrong. Perhaps I am much more... *desviado*. Maybe more than even you."

"Is that why you're here with Granera?"

She shrugged. "I have known him since I was a child. He is a friend of my family. It is Christmas. I am here merely as a courtesy. The holiday is supposed to be a time of peace, no?"

"Even though he's a murdering asshole?"

"Por supuesto. Él es un cerdo," she muttered, reaching for the rum the bartender had just slid in front of Ray. She took a long swallow and handed it to Ray. "Yes, he is a pig and your people pay him."

"So I hear. Look, all I really care about is that Sonny doesn't get hurt in all this. You forget he's got a career to worry about."

"I think you don't know your friend. Sonny thinks nothing

of his career. He is *un idealista.*"

"*Exactamente.* An idealist. It's why I worry about him. He thinks this is some political game. He underestimates people. People like him," Ray said. He nodded at Granera who was making a toast, the platitude lost in a new revival of the Bee Gees.

Aminta fell silent, her mood suddenly dark, as if some cloud of worry had passed over. Ray had little doubt her mercurial nature was another of her many enticements. He felt a brief pang of jealousy. If Sonny wasn't his friend. He'd what? Pursue her himself? He pondered how that would complicate his life and shuddered. He didn't need things more complicated.

"Tell me something, Aminta. Do you really love Sonny? Or is he just useful?"

Her face darkened, her eyes flaring in anger. "*Bastardo*! You know nothing." She looked way. When she turned back, her face had softened.

"Love is not so easy. Not in these times. Not when one never knows. When one can't know tomorrow. It is … *¿Como se dice? Ajeno?* Something makes no difference."

"Irrelevant?"

"Is the right word, yes? It doesn't matter. I mean it does. *Justo…*" She looked away."There is more to life than love. Things more important. Sonny knows this. He knows. *El precio para amor.* "

"All I'm saying is the price better not be more than he can afford."

She lifted her eyes to glance at Granera in the mirror. "You are no different than him."

"Maybe, sweetheart. Yet go figure, here you are drinking with the both of us. Makes me ask myself what you're really up to?"

"I told you. It is Christmas. A time to forgive your enemies. Make peace."

"I don't believe you, Aminta. They know about you. I hear

things. It's dangerous, what you're doing."

She pulled a small mirror from her purse and checked her makeup. She wiped her lips with a napkin and looked at him. "And what am I doing? If you know so much, then why don't you tell your friends. Stop me. Have me arrested. Otherwise, leave us alone."

"Us?"

She gave him a quick peck on the cheek. *"Feliz Navidiad, Ramón,"* she said and walked away.

Ray watched her rejoin Granera as the piano player started up again with White Christmas for perhaps the fifth time. A few of the Americans began singing along, the lyrics lost in the drunken banter. A group of Nicaraguans at an adjoining table listened to them with a sort of sullen wistfulness. Ray guessed that more than a few of them were wondering what next Christmas would be like. He contemplated ordering another drink, but instead paid his bill and walked out, his mind heavy with the realization that his own prognostications were no less dark.

12

Harper leaned back against the sofa and watched Ray fall into silence. The music from downstairs as well as the din of conversation had stopped some time ago, leaving the upstairs room in a cocoon of silence reinforced by the silent snow falling outside the windows. The only sound was the occasional clatter of a pan from the kitchen. Several minutes seemed to pass before anyone spoke.

"You think he's all right? He left his coat," Macy said, nodding at the barstool. She glanced at her watch. "Maybe we should call the house. See if he's there. Sadie should still be up."

Ray continued to stare down at his hands, her proposal left for dead by some unspoken, shared inertia. Another long moment passed before Ray raised his eyes and looked at Harper. He was fixed on some interior landscape only he could see.

"She was desperate. That's why she did it," he said, finally. "Truth be told, it wasn't all that bad a plan. But there's always something you can't account for. The goddamn wild card." He picked up the beer bottle and when he realized it was empty, set it back down.

"You have to understand what Nicaragua was like near the end. The back room deals, the plotting and maneuvering that was going on. It made everything that much more dangerous. Never knowing who to trust. Everybody desperate as hell. And

Somoza's bunch wanting to get out before it was too late.'

And then there were our people at the embassy still thinking they could pull it out at the last minute. On the other side the hard line Sandinistas were all salivating at the prospect they were gonna win. And then there were the *terceristas*...the middle-of-the-roaders who wanted Somoza out but not a socialist bunch of crazies taking over. They were praying for some miracle. And everybody in between just trying to keep their heads down.

"That night at the bar, Aminta already knew what she was going to do. Turned out Sonny did, too. I should've seen it coming. Maybe I did and just didn't want to. I don't know."

Harper reached for her glass of water and the distraction seemed to bring him back to some thread, for he took a deep breath and sat back.

"It was probably the amnesty that started it," he said, clearing his throat. "Somoza declared this amnesty a few weeks before Christmas. Let go a couple a hundred prisoners, Sandinistas most of them. It was supposed to be a gesture of good will. A way of sucking up to Uncle Sam mostly. He was still counting on us to grant him asylum. Would be the answer to his problem." He fell silent for a moment before going on.

"Thing was Aminta had friends in prison and none of them made the cut. That's the only reason I can think of why they did it. I had this informant that said a lot of 'em were already dead and that's why the amnesty wasn't bigger. Like I said, there were lots of rumors. Everybody figured Somoza was hanging on to the rest of the prisoners. His bargaining chips. There was even talk..." He looked up at the ceiling and shook his head.

"I'm sure neither of you ever heard of the Casa de Vampiros. It was what they called this... this hospital that Somoza owned. A giant blood bank was what it really was. The Agency figured Somoza's share of the take at twelve million dollars a year. Selling blood overseas. Donors were the poor, the péons. Selling their blood for food. But there were also stories that Granera took blood from his prisoners. And after the amnesty, the stories started up again. Granera was padding his escape fund by selling blood. Squeezing every goddamn drop out of 'em. All this was why I figured Aminta did what she did. To save her friends. Before it was too late."

God, Ray. Get on with it, Harper thought, fidgeting in her seat. It was tedious. All the "why she did it" crap. Did what? The journalist in her begged for the opportunity to ask just a few succinct questions. But her instincts told her Ray needed to reveal it layer by layer. Cut by cut. So she held back. Macy also suddenly seemed anxious, whether from tedium or dread, Harper couldn't tell. She had moved away from Ray as if avoiding the contagion of what was to come.

"I found out." He started over. "I had this informant that worked for Somoza's secret police. He told me most of what happened. The rest I got later from one of Aminta's... co-conspirators," he said with bitterness. "It turns out Granera had been trying to seduce Aminta for years. Apparently ever since she was a teenager. Did he know about her being a Sandinista sympathizer? He had to. At least at the end. Maybe that was part of his obsession, why he came onto her so hard towards the end. So this bright idea came to Aminta and some of her friends. They were gonna lure Granera into her bed. Kidnap him. Then hold him for ransom. Trade him for all the other prisoners. Crazy, huh? Well they almost got away with it. Must've seemed to her the only way to save her friends. It's the only reason I figure Sonny agreed to help them.

"Her family had this house outside of Granada. She was going to get Granera there, up in her bedroom, and then her buddies who were hiding in the closet would nab him and take him by boat to Ometepe, this island on the lake where they had friends who would hide them until they made a deal. Sonny was going to arrange for this boat. Wait for them. At least that was the plan.

"But somebody must've talked. Not long before they pulled us out of the country, I heard a rumor that it was some Sandinista that sold them out. Somebody playing both sides. Bottom line, Granera got wind of the whole thing." Ray dropped his head into his hands. "If I would've asked the right people, I could've found out ahead of time. Maybe stopped it."

He looked down at Macy, and she reached up for his hand. Perspiration glistened on his forehead, and Harper could see that he was struggling to control his emotions. She sensed that he didn't show his feelings easily, and this admission of vulnerability was obviously costing him.

"They jumped Granera, just like they planned. But they never even made it out of the house. Granera's men had the place surrounded. Aminta and the rest of them barely got out the door before they get ambushed. The shootout lasted all of about half a minute. Two of her friends get killed, the rest they arrested. None of them were hard core guerillas or anything. Just wannabes and college students, mostly. They folded and that was that. They should've just shot the bastard and went out guns blazing. Would've been better in the end." He shook his head. "And Sonny. He waited by that boat. Just long enough for someone to talk.

"I found out the next day when one of my informants called me. Said Granera had Aminta and an American. And if I ever wanted to see either of them alive again I'd better start calling in some favors. No way I was gonna call the embassy. Not until I knew what they knew."

He slumped back again, his despair at having to relive those emotions evident in his face. In the silence that followed, Macy moved up onto the sofa beside Ray and put her arm around his shoulders. They sat this way for a while before Ray went on.

"It got all fucked up after that. Jesus. And he thinks she's still alive. She isn't. She can't be."

"You're sure?" Harper asked.

"Hell yeah, I'm sure." He shook his head. "She can't be because I was there when she died. We both were. And I was the one that killed her."

13

Ray quickly glanced at Macy, sensing what her reaction would be to what he had just revealed. His apprehension was justified as he saw her stiffen, her face suddenly drained of color. She brought her hands to her mouth and then slowly stood and turned her back to him. He started to reach for her but then let his arm drop onto the seat beside him.

"What do you mean you killed her?" Harper asked.

"I didn't have a choice."

Macy turned and looked at him. "Ray. What…what did you do?"

"I told you. I didn't have a choice."

"Ray…"

"Goddammit! You have to understand what happened."

"Well then I guess you better tell me what bloody happened. No," she said when he again reached for her. He could tell she was about to cry.

No one spoke for a long moment as Ray seemed again to be collecting his thoughts. "Give me another cigarette," he said finally.

When Macy made no move give him one, Harper got up and reached for the pack in Macy's pocket. Macy knocked her hand away and shot her a cold hard glance before tossing the pack on the coffee table.

Ray picked up the pack. "I told you, I had this informant. He told me where Granera was holding them." He took his time lighting one of the cigarettes before slumping back on the sofa. "I wasn't sure what to do. I couldn't just go to my guys and tell them Sonny was involved a plot to kidnap one of Somoza's generals. But I had to do something. Otherwise Sonny..." He stared up at the ceiling. "I was scared. Not just because I knew I was on my own. But because if I fucked it up, Sonny's was gonna die. Aminta...I already knew there was nothing I could do about her."

He took a drag of the cigarette and thought back to that morning and remembered the smell of the garbage pit; the taste of bile rising in his throat. The taste of fear. He'd never forget it. Or what he did.

He slid down in his seat as he gazed out though the windshield at the nondescript cinder block warehouse. The building was secluded, strategically located at the end of an unpaved dead end street that ran through what was the municipal dumping ground. Smoking mounds of trash extended in either direction as far as the eye could see. Rag pickers, old women and children mostly, rooted around at the edges in fevered competition with a herd of slat sided pigs. The cloyingly sweet smell of the refuse was mixed with what he knew was most likely the stench of decaying flesh. Obviously someone had given careful consideration in locating a jail adjacent to a dumping ground.

He knew that these unofficial jails were reserved for detainees that might require discretion for reasons of politics, or more often than not, blood lines. Nicaragua was a small country, and over the years families had intermarried so often that allegiances became complicated. Families were often split by politics to the point where brothers or cousins fought on opposite sides of the struggle. It was common for prisoners to be either released or executed solely because of family ties.

His informant had told him that Aminta and her friends had been brought there the night before, the American arriving just before dawn. Enough time for suitable pressure to be applied to even the bravest of them to reveal anything and everything, to betray friends, lovers, their souls.

He had been sitting in the car for almost an hour, paralyzed partially by his own fear and partially due to a lack of any idea of what he would do. He sketched in his mind one possible plan after another, discarding them as all but useless against the odds he faced. If he got in, no mean feat in itself, what could he do? He had no idea of the situation he might find. A dead embassy employee? Or one barely alive. Then what? He was on his own with no back up, and no political leverage.

A solitary guard dressed in jungle fatigues lounged in the thin shade of a stunted papaya tree at the heavy steel gate that led into what appeared to be small open yard. From the look of how he slumped in his chair, Ray guessed he might be napping and might easily be overcome. Still not much of a plan, he thought as he bent his neck to capture the last of his cigarette with his lips. He took a deep pull and flicked it out the window. Get in first, and then play it by ear was all he could do. He picked up a crumpled envelope off the seat, then took his embassy ID card from his wallet and placed it inside along with a sheaf of twenty dollar bills. He listened for a moment to the sawing drone of the cicadas, then as an afterthought scribbled something on the outside of the envelope, and stepped out of his car.

He paused for a moment to rethink what he was doing, and then reached beneath the front seat for the .45 he kept there. He stuck the automatic in the back of his waist band, covered it with his shirt and started down the street. The only other inhabitant of the dusty street was a speckled mongrel dog inexplicably sleeping in the middle of the road. The dog barely took notice of his passage, opening one lazy eye but otherwise not moving so much as an ear. The guard had not stirred either, and when Ray prodded him awake with his foot, the guard leapt to his feet, startled by Ray's sudden appearance. The guard thrust the barrel of his M-16 in Ray's face.

"Cuidado, mi amigo." Ray held his hands up and away from his body and forced a smile. *"Dentro. El dinero es tuyo. Dar la dotación al general, por favor."* Ray nodded at the envelope he held in his right hand.

The guard eyed him for a long moment before jerking the envelope from Ray's outstretched hand. He glanced inside and quickly removed the money and stuffed it into his tunic pocket.

"Espera aqui," he said and slipped through the gate, locking it behind him.

Ray glanced back up the street to his car. A couple of feral kids had already found it. He waved them over, handed them each an overly generous five dollar bill and told them there would be more if his car was still there when he got out. He desperately wanted another cigarette and briefly contemplated searching through the guard's kit bag left abandoned on the chair. But before he could act, the guard yanked open the gate and jerked his head for Ray to follow him.

As the guard busied himself with locking the gate, Ray scanned the small courtyard. He couldn't see another exit. The concrete walls were topped with the ubiquitous broken beer bottles and exposed rebar. There would be no way out unless it was on their terms.

"Pase adelante," the guard muttered. He prodded Ray with the stock of the M-16, pointing him to a heavy wooden door manned by a stocky young man dressed in slacks and a guayabera that appeared to not have been washed in ages. A large hand gun protruded from the pocket of his slacks. The young man frisked him and quickly found Ray's automatic. He clicked his tongue and then motioned for Ray to follow him. They passed through the door and then down a narrow hallway. Ray glanced into a large open room to his right. Three, possibly four bodies lay in a bloody heap. The wall behind them was streaked with blood. Ray averted his eyes in the hope no one had noticed. He had no desire to be a witness.

106

From somewhere ahead of him he heard someone yelling, the outburst overlapped by a long scream. He slowed his pace in an attempt to locate the source, but the guard tugged at his arm, leading him to the entrance of an adjoining room. The guard motioned for Ray to wait outside. A moment later, he emerged and motioned for Ray to enter.

"Come in, my friend," Granera said from behind the door.

Ray stepped through the doorway, closing it behind him before turning to face the man sitting behind a large mahogany desk. Granera wore a pale yellow polo shirt and white linen slacks, his impeccably casual attire marred only by the large rings of sweat below his armpits. He rested one of his Gucci-clad feet on the desk. He held Ray's .45 lay loosely in one hand.

Ray nodded but said nothing, aware now of the sweat trickling down his own armpits. The air in the small office was stiflingly hot, the anemic efforts of the small window mounted air conditioner no match for the tropical humidity and midday heat. A small rubber tree plant bearing two wilted leaves sat in the corner of the office. A pair of cheap portraits hung on the wall behind the desk. One was of Somoza, the other a faded pastel of some hot-eyed liberator from Nicaragua's checkered past. Otherwise, the room was devoid of furnishings.

"We have met once before, no? At your embassy, perhaps. I believe it was a dinner for one of your senators. Thurmond, I think it was."

His English was almost without accent, thanks to four years at Florida State and a tour at the infamous School of the Americas, the US Army's training school for the military elite of their Central and South American allies. Critics of U.S. policy held it up as more proof of the government's collusion in human rights abuses throughout the Third World. Ray had heard accounts of the various interrogation techniques taught at the school, and from what he had seen here in Nicaragua, the stories were more than likely true.

Granera took a swig from the beer bottle he clutched in his left hand, his face empty of expression. "So, let us not waste each other's time," he said. "You are here for your friend, no? Your note said you wish to make a deal." He smiled when Ray made no attempt to answer. "If your wish is to negotiate, why do you bring this?" he said, sliding the automatic across the desk.

"I'd like to see my friend," Ray managed to say. "I'd like to take him back to the embassy. With all due respect, I hope he's all right and we can avoid any kind of incident."

"Incident? Your friend was helping the enemies of my country. Your country's enemies. I suspect his motives were perhaps more influenced by *puta* then politics. We are men after all. We all sometime stumble at the sight of a woman with her legs open, no?"

"You can't afford to let anything happen to him. You know that. Not after your guys just killed that journalist. Wouldn't be good publicity. Especially not now. What you need now are friends."

Granera's smiled. "Perhaps. But what if your friend disappears and his wallet is found on a dead criminal. Something easily explained. Or would you rather explain your friend's indiscretions to your superiors? I think not."

"What do you want? Money? Information? What?"

Granera studied him, his face impassive. After a moment, he began sifting through some papers lying on the desk in front of him. "You know yourself that your government already pays me. Quite generously in fact. You could say, you and I are fellow employees, yes? It is not so simple anymore. There are many things to consider. But perhaps we can reach an agreement. You want your friend, yes?"

"And your promise that my embassy doesn't find out about this."

Granera considered this before nodding in apparent acceptance. "In exchange, I wish to know if and when your country's policy towards me changes. Which way the wind will blow, yes?"

"I can do that," Ray said, reaching down to pick up his ID

from the desk. He started to reach for the automatic but Granera covered it with his hand.

"I also require a list of your informants."

"That can't happen and you know it."

"Then…" Granera shrugged.

"How about if I told you my people know where your money is, know the account numbers of the bank in the Caymans. They can take it back anytime they want. I bet you didn't know that."

Granera looked at him with all the equanimity he could muster. "That is useful information, my friend. But you have shown me your cards too early perhaps. Now what else do you have to bargain with?"

Ray started to reply when a sudden shout from the hallway, followed by the sound of something being dragged, momentarily distracted him. When it was again silent, he looked down at Granera whose attention again seemed diverted by the papers on his desk.

"What about the girl?"

"Aminta? She is of no use to you. Forget her. I will deal with her in my own way, at my own time."

"There might be some money. Something else I…"

"No," he replied quickly although his voice betrayed uncertainty. "She is a Nicaraguan and no business of yours."

"Are you sure?"

"If you wish to leave with your friend, I suggest you not ask for more than I am willing to give." He smiled. "I will need your assurances that you and your friend will remain silent."

"About what? This place? Aminta?"

"And other things."

"So, you'll let my friend go?"

"As I said, you have left yourself with little to bargain with. You come in here with empty hands. And alone. Remember the unfortunate accident I mentioned? How tragic if two Americans would meet such an end."

Ray felt a twinge of panic. It would be easy enough for Granera to arrange for them both to disappear. It happened every day. Who would know the truth? There was always the chance his informant would come forward later. Too late for them.

"There's nothing else you want? Money, passports. What?"

Granera smiled. "Perhaps, there is something. Something that will ensure your silence and your future cooperation." He ran his finger across his lips. "All that is required is that you deal with her. With Aminta. Perhaps if you were responsible for her… disappearance, let us say."

"No."

"A more than a fair exchange for the life of your friend. And yours."

Ray suddenly regretted not telling the embassy. To hell with Sonny's career, even if they decided to prosecute him. It would have been better than this. He had been a fool.

"Perhaps if you see her. It might help you to make up her your mind. Come."

Granera rose to his feet. He picked up Ray's .45 and slipped it into his waistband. As he brushed past Ray, the scent of his sweat and cloyingly sweet aftershave lingered in the dank air. Ray hesitated a moment and followed him out the door and down a narrow hallway leading to the rear of the building. The further they walked into the recesses the more suffocating the still, heavy air. The smell of piss and shit and blood was overwhelming.

The only light was provided by three widely spaced low watt bulbs recessed into the planked ceiling and a small rhomboid of daylight cast from a barred window set high in the cinderblock wall at the end of the passageway. It was sufficient to make out the line of heavy wooden doors that he assumed were cells. It also allowed him to see the streaks of congealed blood that stained the dusty floor. Granera paused in front of one of the doors, flipped open a small shutter and gestured with his hand.

Ray hesitated, then stepped forward and peered through the small barred opening. It took a moment for his eyes to adjust to the dim light but what he saw made him flinch. A young woman hung suspended by her wrists from a rope attached to the ceiling. She had been stripped naked and her feet bound together with wire. Her bloody, matted hair and battered face prevented Ray from being able to tell if it was Aminta.

"You son of a bitch."

Granera laughed. "Careful, my friend," he said, raising his hand as Ray stepped toward him. "You want your friend, no?" He smiled in obvious pleasure at Ray's helplessness. "Come."

They walked further down the passageway to a small alcove recessed into the wall. A pair of guards dressed in jungle fatigues slouched against the walls on either side of another wooden door. Granera motioned to one of them to open the door.

"Come out, Señor Day. It seems your friend has rescued you."

After a moment, Sonny appeared at the door. Other than a swollen, split lip and a puffy, bruised eye, he appeared uninjured. Granera grabbed him by the shirt and shoved him towards Ray.

"So what will it be?"

"Where's Aminta?" Sonny said. "I'm not leaving without her."

"Come on, Sonny," Ray said, grabbing his arm. "Let's go."

"I told you I'm not leaving without her."

"Sonny…"

"Very well," Granera said. He nodded at one of the guards who took Sonny by the arm and pulled him down the hallway to Aminta's cell. Ray tried to stop them but the other guard blocked his way. Granera and the guard grabbed both of Sonny's arms and shoved his face against the small window in the cell's door. It took a second or two for him to react.

"No! Aminta! Goddammit!"

Ray recoiled at the sound of his friend's wounded scream. Sonny tried to break loose from the guard, but Granera punched him in the stomach, dropping him to his knees. Granera kicked him in the side, one, two, three times. Before Ray could react two more guards appeared from behind him and restrained him from coming to Sonny's aid.

"So it is your choice," Granera said, pulling the .45 from his pants and offering it to Ray.

Ray shook his head.

"We shall see. *Detener lo!*"

The guard shoved Sonny to the ground and knelt on his back, pinning him to the ground. The guard handed Granera a pair of what appeared to be pruning shears. Granera stuffed the automatic in his belt.

"Granera! Wait! Don't," Ray yelled.

"It's simple what I ask, no?" he said, jerking his head at Aminta's cell.

When Ray hesitated, Granera twisted Sonny's arm behind him and in one swift movement, grabbed his hand, and clipped off one of his fingers. Sonny screamed and writhed in pain. Ray pulled his eyes away.

Granera leaned down and lifted Sonny's head by his hair. "Take my word for it, *cabron*. She is not worth it. Not anymore." Granera pulled the automatic from his belt and pointed it at Sonny's head. "So Señor Cortese, which one will it be? *¿Tu amigo o la puta?*"

Ray exhaled and leaned forward, his face in his hands. He couldn't find it in himself to go on. No one spoke for a long moment, the silence filling the room.

"You shot her?" Macy finally asked, her voice quavering.

Ray raised his head, his eyes unwilling to meet hers

"What could I do?" he said quietly. "He was my friend."

Macy made a sound like some small animal in pain. For what seemed like minutes, no one said anything, each of them unwilling to acknowledge the horror of what they had heard. After a while, Macy rose from the floor and draped herself over Ray's shoulders. She started to sob, burying her face in Ray's neck. They held each other tightly like this until Ray finally pulled away.

"He doesn't know, does he?" Harper asked.

Ray shrugged. "They beat him senseless. I don't think he was even conscious when it happened. Don't you understand? I didn't have any choice. He was my friend. And she was already as good as dead. I never told him. I couldn't."

Ray swiped his hand across his nose and rubbed the tears from his eyes. "You try to forget, you know? What it's like to kill someone. But you don't forget. I just buried it. After a while you almost convince yourself that none of it ever really happened. That none of it did." He paused before going on.

"It didn't stop there. About six months later, the day before the Sandinistas rolled into Managua, I came across one of the guards. The one who had held Sonny down." Ray glanced up at the ceiling for a moment before going on. "I killed him. But not before I got him to tell me where the others were. The other guards. I was gonna kill every last one of them." He took another deep breath and stared at the floor. "Thank God, he was the only one I ever found."

"What happened to Sonny?" Harper asked.

"Soon as I got him out of there, I patched him up and flew him out. Told the embassy we had been attacked by a mob of Sandinista supporters. I took him back to Texas and left him. I flagged his passport so he couldn't come back. "

"And Aminta?"

Ray looked up at Harper, barely able to suppress his anger. "What do you mean? She's dead. I shot her, for chrissakes!"

"You're sure? That she's dead?"

"Stop it!" Macy said.

"No," he said, holding up his hand. "I know what you're thinking. That she could've lived." He disappeared back into that moment briefly and looked up at each of them in turn."I took the gun. And I shot her. I know I did. All I know is nobody ever heard anything, nobody talked about her. Not her family. Nobody. It's like she never existed. They had a name for that. *Desaparecidos*. The disappeared. Most likely they threw her body in the garbage dump along with the others."

"What about Granera?" Harper asked.

"I never saw him again. I tried to find him but he disappeared. I heard later he got out with a bunch of the National Guard. Took a boat out of San Juan del Sur. Rumor had it he was in El Salvador. I put some feelers out but I never heard anything. And that was that. Until Sonny found him in Madrid."

"You're not going to tell him, are you?" Macy asked.

He shook his head. "What'll that change? You saw him. How he reacted to that painting. He's not over her. Something that happened thirty years ago. I tell him I was the one killed Aminta…"

"Something tells me he's not the same man," Harper said. "He can't blame you."

"You have to understand something. I'm his only friend. He doesn't have anyone else. Wives, colleagues. None of 'em stuck. Ever since then, he hasn't let himself get that close to anyone. His last friend tells him something like that…"

Ray sat back, lost in thought. "What I'm really afraid of," he finally said, "is that he'd go after Granera again. Only good thing is that bastard's gonna be a lot harder to find now. If I knew where he was, I'd kill him myself. End the whole fucking thing."

"Don't even think about it. I told you…"

"Yeah, yeah. I know," he said, cutting off Macy. Ray held her gaze then looked away. "But I sure as hell might pay somebody to do it."

"What if I told you I know someone that might know how to find him?" Harper said.

Macy got to her feet and walked over to Harper, her face inches from hers.

"You do, and I promise I'll make your life so miserable you'll bloody well wish you were dead. I want you and Sonny gone," Macy said, shoving Harper. "You hear me?"

"Macy. Leave her alone. Hey," he said as Macy grabbed Harper's arm. He struggled to his feet and pulled Macy away. "This is on me. It's something I should've done a long time ago."

Macy turned and looked at him. "What? You're not going after this Granera guy. That's all there is to it. If you do, I…"

He pulled her into his arms and held her even as she struggled to be free of him. He looked at Harper. "Get out of here. Now. And if you see Sonny, tell him… Just get out of here."

Harper stood there a moment before grabbing her coat. "I'm not telling him anything," she said."That's what friends are far," she said and turned to the door.

14

The cabbie took a sip of his coffee and squinted at Sonny in the rear view mirror. The old guy's eyes reminded Sonny of some cartoon marsupial. quarter size, bulging and bloodshot. Like some color animated lemur that had been up all night chain smoking.

"My old lady. The one I tol' you about before. She used to like to drive around with me all night. If I didn' have no fare. She'd sit in the back, same side as you so's we could see each other in the mirror." The cabbie rolled down the window, dragged some phlegm from his throat and spit. "Better than sittin' at home, she'd say. Truth be tol', she just didn' trust me. Never gave her reason not to either." He turned to look over his shoulder. "What's your reason? Why you like drivin' round all night? For what you said you'd pay me, you coulda been sleepin' in the La Fonda."

Sonny took a swallow of his coffee and looked out the window. A few wisps of cloud scudded across the impossibly blue sky.

"You said two fifty for the night, right?" Sonny pulled out his wallet and thumbed through some bills. "Here, keep the change," he said, opening the door.

"It's about a woman, idn't it?" the cabbie said. "The old lady tells you not to come back until you figured it out. Something

116

like that, right?"

Sonny smiled and shook his head. "Yeah, something like that," he said, stepping out into the cold morning air.

The cabbie had talked almost incessantly through the night, not the least bothered by Sonny's unwillingness to reciprocate. His rambling monologue had seemed to cover most of the cabbie's life, the key chapters highlighted by vignettes of memorable fares and the routine maintenance involved with a string of bad marriages. Fortunately, Sonny had been able to tune him out. It was a skill he had learned in prison where the cacophony of daily life required some form of retreat in order to survive with a semblance of sanity.

Sonny stood there a moment watching the taxi back out of the narrow side street before turning to look back at the house. Ray's Crown Vic and a beat up, vintage Land Rover sat parked in the driveway. Maybe they would all be asleep, he thought rubbing his eyes. The endless permutations that he had gone through his mind over the last eight hours had left him raw and irritable. The thought that he might have to explain himself made him suddenly regret sending the cab away.

He slogged across the snow to the front door as he fumbled in his pocket for the key Ray had given him. As he started to slip the key into the lock, the door suddenly opened. Macy stood in the entranceway in a pair of sweats, a cup of coffee in one hand, a set of car keys in the other. She gave him a look that telegraphed her unease. Finally, she nodded with her head for him to come in.

"Wish I could say I'm happy to see you. But I'm not. For what it's worth, Ray was worried. He thought someone would find your bloody corpse frozen along the road somewhere. Come on, Sadie," she shouted over her shoulder, her eyes never leaving Sonny's. "We're going to be late."

Something in her gaze told him she knew everything. There was pity reflected in her eyes, mixed with trepidation, maybe even revulsion. He leaned against the wall and began pulling off his boots. Just then, a young girl dressed in ballet tights entered the hallway. Her long coal black hair framed a face marked by high cheekbones and dark almond shaped eyes. She gave Sonny a cursory glance before picking up her gym bag and glancing at Macy.

"Sadie, say hello to your father's friend Sonny."

"Hi," she said shyly, her gaze taking in the fact that he wasn't wearing a coat.

"Nice to finally meet you, Sadie. I've heard a lot about you," he said, offering his hand.

She took his hand and smiled. "My Dad said the last time you saw me I was just a baby."

Macy looked at Sonny, her eyes registering some unspoken question. "We better go," she said. "There's coffee and scones in the kitchen. Ray's out back. In the hot tub. You're welcome to join him. There's a robe and a towel hanging by the door. Just no rough stuff, please," she said, dropping her smile.

"Thanks." He glanced past her.

"If you're wondering about your lady friend, I told her to bugger off. Told her, I for one, would be happy if I never saw her again."

"Let's go, Mom or I'll be late," Sadie said, hoisting her gym bag.

He watched them leave before making his way to the kitchen. A plate of scones sat on a plate on the counter next to a carafe of coffee. He picked up one of the scones and walked over to the window. A small courtyard enclosed by high adobe walls backed up to the rear of the house. A thin cloud of steam lingered in one corner. It took a few seconds before he spied Ray's balding head protruding from the snow covered edge of a sunken sauna. He held the scone in his mouth as he peeled off his clothes. After pouring a cup of coffee, he grabbed a robe and a towel and walked out onto the patio.

Ray turned at the sound of the door opening. He watched without comment as Sonny tossed the robe and the towel on to a nearby chair.

"I'd appreciate if you wouldn't eat in the tub," Ray said.

Sonny ignored him and slid into the tub, the scone still in his mouth.

Neither of them said anything for a minute.

"You okay?" Ray asked.

"Is it always this goddamn cold here?"

"You take off in the middle of the night without a coat. What do you expect? Where'd you go?"

Sonny swallowed before answering. "Took in the town." He stared at Ray for a moment."How's your face?"

"What? This?" he said pointing at the bruise on his cheek. "Anyone ever tell you that you hit like a girl?"

"How much did you tell them?"

Ray looked away for a moment before answering. "I told them enough. Okay? You didn't exactly leave me a lot of choice. Leaving like you did."

Sonny swallowed the last bite of scone and licked his fingers. "Curious to know which version you told."

"Don't give me that shit, Sonny. You were there."

"Yeah, I was there. Lying on the goddamn ground, sucking on my hand, and dodging kicks. That's about all I remember. You remember everything though. Least, that's what you always told me. And I know what you're going to say next. That I should be appreciative you hauled my ass out of there in one piece."

Ray just looked at him. "Why'd you come here?" he asked finally.

"Tell me something, Ray. You ever talk to anyone else about what happened down there? Reason I'm curious is that I've only heard the whole story that one time. Right before you hauled me out of Managua. I can't help but wonder if there're some details you left out."

Ray didn't say anything, his eyes fixed on Sonny's.

"You didn't tell a friend, maybe. Macy? After too many drinks one night."

Ray held to his silence.

"Come on. You must've told somebody. Keeping secrets was never your style."

Ray grunted and looked away. "Okay. It came up once. In therapy."

"Therapy? You? Mr. Touchy Feely."

"What can I say? It's Santa Fe for chrissakes. Everybody here's in therapy. Anyway, it came up in the context of what I've been doing with my life these last thirty years. You know what this shrink called it? Incoherent living. Shit, that almost makes it sound worth doing over again."

"Incoherent living, huh? Yeah, I like that. Has a lot more cachet' than what they always told me I have. I get Post Traumatic Stress. You get incoherent living. Doesn't seem quite fair."

Ray lifted his chin. "Let's just call it an ass full of bad memories. And it's high time it stopped. No point to it." He leaned back and looked up at the sky. "She's dead, you know. I looked. I asked around. Wasn't a trace to be found and that's the god honest truth."

Sonny gazed up at the azure sky visible through the bare limbs of a huge cottonwood. "I think you're lying," he said, meeting Ray's gaze. "You were never that good at it. My guess is lying is what got you in that mess down in Mexico."

Ray shook his head in a way that left the meaning unclear.

"Look, I just want to know about the painting. Who might've finished it for her."

"What about Granera?" Ray asked.

"What about him? I could care less. That's over."

"So you keep telling me. I still would like to know what you were planning on doing when you caught up with him."

"I had plenty of time to think about it." Sonny smiled. "And the odd thing is, I still don't know. Guess that means I'm not rehabilitated."

"How much do you know about your friend Harper?"

"Why?"

Ray shook his head. "Just that I can't figure out why she's here. She's either hot for you or after a story."

"She's an acquaintance, that's it. What?"

"Nothing."

"I take it Macy doesn't care for her."

Ray shook his head. "It's just Macy doesn't like anyone coming in and disturbing the status quo. Stirring up things from my past. We've got something good here. With Sadie. The restaurant. She doesn't want something bitching it up."

"You don't have to get involved. I just want to know about the painting."

"And what if you find out things you don't want to know?"

"What do you mean?"

"Say you find something that leads to Granera."

"What did I just say? To hell with Granera."

"You're in a scratchy goddamn mood."

"You try not sleeping for a week. I told you, I just want to know about the painting. That's all."

Ray took a swallow of his coffee and set the cup in the snow beside the tub. "Okay. We can go see the woman I bought them from. Her name's Trapani. Her house is right up the road. She told me she needed the money is why she finally decided to sell the other one. I didn't believe her so I checked her out. Moved here from Vegas. Her old man was some big shot in the casino business. He's dead. She was a show girl when she married him. She's got to be in her late sixties, early seventies, but she's had some remodeling done so she doesn't look it. And she's got money. So I don't buy the bit about her being hard up for cash.

Which leads me to wonder why she didn't offer to sell me the other painting the first go around."

"So let's go see her."

"Say when."

Sonny slipped lower into the tub. Basking in the hot water made him realize that maybe things were moving too fast. Not even two weeks ago he was in Africa with nothing more on his agenda then leaving the camp. And now he was sitting around drinking coffee in the lap of relative luxury and contemplating God knows what? He had felt an odd sense of grace the day he left Darfur, a tentative bliss. Was it because he was about to leave Arliss Day behind? Discard that one life like a snake shedding its skin? He had a second chance and now it seemed like he was about to blow it. You need some perspective, his ex-wife always used to tell him. Maybe she was right.

"Which hotel is she staying at?"

"Who? Harper? The Inn at Loretto is what she said. If Macy hasn't run her out of town."

Sonny stood up and reached for the towel on the bench behind him.

"Where're you going?"

"To get some perspective."

You need a ride? To this perspective?"

"No. I can find it on my own," Sonny said, sliding the towel across his buttocks.

"She knows something."

"Yeah, well, I kinda figured that."

"She knows things about Nicaragua. She knows about Granera. Look, all I'm saying, is watch your back."

"I always thought that was your job," Sonny said, turning toward the house.

15

Harper shifted in her chair so she could gaze out at the empty patio. The shapeless form of a pool chair was just visible under the blanket of fresh snow. She leaned over, her nose almost against the window, and looked out at the blue patch of sky.

"I'll bet you know exactly where I am," she said, cradling the cell phone on her shoulder. She reached for another piece of toast. "You guys with all this high tech spook stuff. Someone's tailing me, right? Humor me and tell me how many cups of coffee I've had."

She turned back to look across the bar, half-expecting see some non-descript, middle-aged woman who had no business sitting in a bar at eight o'clock in the morning. Instead, she saw Sonny walking through the lobby towards her.

"So what do you mean Langley's not interested anymore? I told you. He's here. And he's supposed to be in prison in Spain. I'm surprised your guys don't know that." She listened for a few seconds as she watched Sonny scan the room. He hesitated a moment before making his way through the empty dining room.

"He's ancient history? That's really what they said? I don't believe you. Sounds to me like they're trying to keep you in the dark. Listen, all I want is some help finding someone. This is someone the Agency should have no trouble finding. Ah, come on." She smiled at Sonny as he approached her table. "Look,

I'll get back to you. Asshole," she muttered as she snapped the phone shut. She looked up at Sonny. "Not you. You ever sleep?"

He dropped into the other chair and reached for a piece of her toast, his eyes never leaving hers.

"You want something to eat? You're welcome to this," she said shoving her plate across the table. "I can't handle green chile. Want some coffee?"

He nodded as he took a bite of the toast.

She looked around for the waitress. "You'll never guess who I was just talking to," she said, her back turned. She got the waitress's attention and then looked back at him so she could see his reaction. "Your friends at Langley."

He stopped chewing for a second before turning to look out at the pool. When he looked back, he was smiling.

"You don't play fair, do you?" he said.

"You mean you guys do?"

He reached for her glass of water and took a swallow before picking up her fork and starting on the *migas*. "So they know about me? Did you tell them or are they better at this than they used to be?"

She held his gaze. "Seems they don't care. You're old news."

He didn't reply, his mouth full of eggs and chile.

"Okay. I told them. All I said was that you were back but I didn't know where you had gone. Satisfied?"

He turned away and chewed deliberately, one mouthful after the other until the plate was empty. She took the opportunity to study him, casting for something, a mannerism, some facial gesture, anything that would allow her a better grasp of how she should deal with him. She thought about what she learned the night before, measuring it against the person sitting across from her. Her gaze settled on his hand, the missing finger. The thought of how he lost it made her flinch.

When she lifted her eyes, she realized he knew what she had

124

been looking at. He smiled.

"Mind me asking why you told them?" he said, reaching for the rind of her half eaten slice of orange.

"I made..." She paused as the waitress filled their cups. She cleared her throat. "I made a deal. Background in exchange for a heads up when you contacted me. That's all."

He took a swallow of coffee and started on the sprig of grapes on the edge of her plate.

"Listen. You have a right to be angry. It was unethical. Desperate is what it was. I'm sorry. Say something."

"I was just thinking," he said. "About how long it would take them to find your body. Snow might melt in a few days, week at the most. I'd be in Costa Rica by then. Or somewhere."

"Sure. That's if I'm dumb enough to leave here with you. Which I don't plan on doing. Not yet. Maybe after we talk some more."

He smiled with obvious amusement.

"Do they know what name I'm using?"

"I don't even know what name you're using. Look, all I told them was that you were here, and now you're not. That's all."

"Samuel T. Bass. That's who I am," he said in response to her look of confusion. "See if you can parlay that into something."

"They'd have to goddamn torture me before I'd tell..." She stopped herself as she saw the brief riff of pain in his eyes. "I'm sorry. That was insensitive."

He looked out at the pool for a moment before turning back. "I take it Ray told you pretty much everything. So now you have your story. Is that why you're coming clean? Easing your conscience?"

"There's no story. Not anymore. I just wanted to know."

He reached across for her napkin, swiped at his face, and leaned across the table. "Then you'll be leaving?"

She cocked her head. "Depends. Is there more?"

125

"Is there more? You don't quit, do you?" When she didn't reply, he fell back into the chair and shook his head. "I'm beginning to think you care about this more than I do."

"I didn't get that impression last night. That painting…"

"Yeah, the painting. She didn't paint it, you know. I know that for a fact. One, she never finished it. Two, it's different from the sketch I saw her do."

"Maybe she did two versions."

"No. The reason I know is she would talk about her paintings. She'd compose them in her mind before she'd ever start. She didn't do two versions. She just didn't."

"But it's her work, isn't it? Her style. That's what's bothering you."

He didn't reply.

"You don't think she's dead, right?"

He still didn't say anything. She watched him, sensed that he was reliving something. She waited for it to play out.

"I can see her painting it," he said finally. "Just the way it is. Even though it's a little darker than the work she was doing back then." He shrugged. "I could be wrong, but if someone else painted it they weren't just copying her style."

"Which would mean she's still alive."

He didn't say anything for a moment."You ever wonder how your life might've turned out different if one little thing hadn't happened?" He looked out at the snow. "I knew this guy once. He used to do dirty work for the Agency. Before he worked for them, he was half way through medical school when he got accused of raping this old woman. Ended up serving fifteen years for a rape he didn't commit. He told me that for years it drove him crazy. Thinking about how his life would've been different. You know, if it wouldn't have been for him going to prison. The difference is he knew the truth about what led him down that road. Seems I don't. I guess I deserve to know."

When Harper didn't say anything, he went on. "You know

Ray didn't really know her. He thought he did. To him, she was just another Nica with some secrets he could use. But he knew she was more than that to me. I figured that was why he stopped watching us. Thing is it might've been better if he would've kept watch.

"IIc tried to warn me off, you know. From seeing her. Said she was trouble. I'd regret it someday." He looked at Harper. "I've never asked him if he knew beforehand about what she was planning on doing. I didn't want to know." He reached for her water glass and downed it.

"I had a bad feeling about the whole thing from the get go. The thing was everybody had their goddamn secrets. Our guys, Somoza's guys, the rebels. Everybody was in bed with everybody. Half the people I knew down there survived off someone else's secrets. I tried to tell her that. Did she know they were watching her?" He shrugged. "And I know what you're thinking. Did Ray know?" He looked off towards the pool and shook his head. "I always liked to think that if Ray would've been watching that day, then maybe I would've gone to him and told him everything. Maybe he could've stopped it. But that's not the way it happened."

"What did happen?"

He looked at her for a long time without saying anything, his mind reliving that last day spent with Aminta. He would tell Harper some of it, he decided. Some he would keep for himself.

16

It took the morning and a good part of the afternoon to drive from Managua to Laguna Apoyo. The road, difficult in the best of times, proved an endless trial of military roadblocks, horse drawn carts, and potholes, some large enough to suggest rebel sabotage. Twice on the main highway to Granada they were stopped by the National Guard and asked for identification. A woman traveling alone with a *Norteamericano* aroused the suspicions of both sides, but a gringo with a State Department passport invited even more careful scrutiny.

At the second checkpoint, they waited for two of the soldiers to confer about their identity papers. As they waited, Sonny tried his best to avoid looking at a young man and a woman kneeling beside the road, both blindfolded with what appeared to be remnants of the man's shirt, their hands bound crudely behind their backs with chicken wire. Not intimidated by the soldiers, Aminta got out of the car and walked closer to study the prisoners, documenting in her mind the details of their clothes, the scattered contents of their luggage. One of the Guardsmen came over and attempted to nudge her away with the butt of his rifle. Aminta stood her ground, staring the soldier down before walking back to the car.

As they drove off, neither of them bothered to speculate on the fate of the two people kneeling in the mud. Sonny had seen enough of it first-hand. The decomposing bodies left lying in secluded ravines, the women on street corners holding up faded photographs and asking if you had seen their husband, their father, their brother.

They drove the rest of the way in uncomfortable silence. It was the end of the dry season and the smoke from the burning cane fields blanketed the plain, stinging the eyes and at times almost completely obscuring the countryside. In the valleys, the smoke clung to the bottoms in long, wispy tendrils. Occasionally, a breeze parted the haze providing a clear line of sight to the low hills just beyond the ashy fields. In spite of the midday heat, Aminta insisted they not roll down the windows, unwilling to endure the acrid odor on their clothes and hair.

Soon after they turned off the main highway toward the lake, they were forced to detour in order to avoid a village reputed to be rebel held. Sonny hid his passport under the passenger seat. He knew that if the rebels stopped them, it would only be Aminta's persuasion that would save him.

The road leading to the lake dropped from the gritty highlands outside of Granada into the bowl of an old volcanic crater that cradled the lake in a verdant bowl of forest. The unpaved road was rutted and narrow, at times no more than a cart track. Once before, they had broken an axle attempting to cross a stream bed, requiring a long trek to seek help from one of the few isolated houses in sight of the road. The condition of the road was one of several things that bothered Sonny about Aminta's plan. If her car broke down again, it would throw them off their timetable.

Halfway down into the crater, a young boy pushing a bicycle waved them down. His attention diverted, Sonny failed to notice the two men emerge from the close forest. It wasn't until Aminta tapped his leg that he saw them. One posted himself behind the car, the other stood a few feet away from the car's passenger side. Both carried carbines loosely at their side. The one next to the car had a small walkie-talkie clipped to his belt.

"*Un momento.* I must to speak to him," Aminta said, slipping out the door.

The young man waiting beside the car wore tattered, faded

fatigues. His fair skin and reddish mop of hair led Sonny to think that perhaps the man wasn't Nicaraguan. It was well known that there were Americans fighting alongside the rebels. She took the man's elbow and gestured to him to move away from the car. The man walked with an almost crablike limp, dragging his one useless leg through the thick, knee-high weeds. All the while, he kept his body rotated so as to keep Sonny in his sight. Even as Aminta spoke to him, his eyes never left Sonny. After a short conversation, Aminta reached up and stroked the man's cheek, drawing his eyes to meet hers. He nodded and turned toward the forest, gesturing for his companion to join him. The boy straddled his bike and pedaled slowly up the hill. Aminta walked back to the car, arms folded, her face intense with thought.

"Who was that?" he asked as she slid into the seat.

She looked at him for a moment and then smiled. "You are jealous, no?"

"If I'm jealous of him I might as well be jealous of half the men in Managua."

She laughed and reached over to caress Sonny's neck. "His name is Presciliano. A friend from my childhood. His father worked for us on the finca. We used to play together, the two of us. Now he is Sandinista."

"What happened to his leg?"

"The polio. What? You are still not satisfied? I have told you. I have no other lovers. Not since you and I began. I tell you this because I don't want you to think... that I use you. I ask you to do this for me because..." She shook her head. *"¿Cómo decir esto?"* She took his chin and turned his face towards her. "We are one, you and I. *¿Verdad?* Do not forget that, Sonny."

He leaned over and kissed her. She clung to him as Sonny looked over her shoulder, wondering if her friend was watching from the forest. She finally pulled away, her face again betraying some uncertainty.

"Anything wrong?" he asked.

"Nothing. Just drive."

Neither of them spoke again until they breached the steep hillside that marked the edge of her father's finca. Here the thick forest had been cleared for a small stand of banana and papaya trees. The house, a small but elegant structure of stucco and brick, looked out over the lake and the surrounding crater. In the mornings, when the air was clear, you could see the grayish smear of Lake Nicaragua beyond the crater's rim. In the dry season when the wind was just right one could even make out the vague outline of the island of Ometepe. By this time of day, the smoke and the haze from the lake obscured even the far side of the crater.

"What if he comes by helicopter? Granera and his bodyguards? Have you thought of that?" he asked, cutting the ignition.

"Ni modo. He will come. If he wants me, he will come."

She got out of the car and opened the trunk. Sonny watched her as she walked to the house, the large backpack that served as her luggage slung over her shoulder. She looked back once to see if he was coming, paused and then continued on. He sat there a while longer thinking about what they were doing. He had to stop it. But there was no sense talking her out of it. He had tried. What if he just left now? Just walked away. She might call it off. Or would she?

He got out of the car and scanned the trees that lined the steep rutted driveway and wondered if Ray had followed them this time like he had before. Was that the purpose of the two lookouts on the road? Warn them of any unexpected visitors? This is stupid. Stupid and dangerous, he thought looking back to the house. He grabbed his valise from the back seat and stood there a moment unsure of himself, of his motives, of his allegiances. She could be lying about Granera. Lied about having slept with him before. He had asked her this when she first revealed her plan. Something in her denial hinted at some half truth. He wanted more than anything to believe her. You're thinking with your dick, was what Ray had told him.

Ray had injected enough of his skepticism about Aminta that

131

Sonny was beginning to have difficulty sorting out his feelings. All that he was sure of was that their relationship had gone beyond infatuation, beyond anything carnal. He was twenty-four years old and had never met anyone like her. The women he had known in college were much like him, barely removed from adolescence and armed with just enough worldliness and self-regard to discount any sense of commitment or engagement beyond the next semester. Aminta was different, older, sophisticated, and in retrospect, calculating in her seduction of him.

Before they had met at an embassy function, he had heard the stories about her, the rumors of her reputed sympathies. On more than one occasion he had seen her in Managua in the company of men that seemed to contradict much of what he had heard. Young men of privilege. Older businessman. But never once Granera. Managua was a small town without secrets, and she lived her life in an open, reckless manner as if she were daring everyone, her family, the Somocistas, anyone, to challenge her.

It was this heedlessness that now forced Sonny to question the wisdom of his involvement in her plot. Part of him, the part Ray appealed to, entertained the possibility that Aminta was using him. His stubborn refusal to consider that possibility, along with misplaced idealism, discouraged any real understanding of how he truly felt about her. Did he love her? He wasn't sure he was even qualified to know. Up until now, his life had ill prepared him for the vagaries and complexities of the degree of emotional entanglement a woman like Aminta presented. All he knew was that when he was with her, nothing else much mattered. Was he obsessed? Undoubtedly. Did that translate into any real allegiance? At least the kind of allegiance that might get him killed? He wasn't sure. And now he was worried that Aminta's scheme might rupture the tenuous and intoxicating world they had created. He turned and stared out at the lake as if an answer might rise from its depths. When he finally walked to the house, he was as unsure as ever.

He found her leaning on the sink in the guest bedroom they

often used for their trysts, her head bowed. She had removed her blouse and bra, and in the dim light she resembled one of her paintings, her semi-nakedness a familiar erotic icon in her work. He dropped his bag on the bed and walked over to her. She shuddered at his touch, and after a brief hesitation, leaned back into him. He held her like this, cupping her breasts in his hand, waiting for her overture.

Lately, their sex had become almost choreographed, a carefully nuanced progression from embrace to consummation, a ritual meant to transport them from the world outside the walls of the small bedroom to a refuge of their own making. The candles, the perfectly placed frangipani blossoms on the pillows. An altar. La Pausa, she called it. But even here, escape eluded them.

Several weeks before, the rattle of gunfire from somewhere across the lake had interrupted their lovemaking. As it grew nearer, their efforts became more frenzied and primal, their cries of passion escalating with the crescendo of gunfire. Later that night, he awoke to a memory of a long ago hunting trip. In his mind's eye he saw himself emerging from a thick forest and stumbling upon a young buck rutting a doe. Sensing his presence, the buck turned to look at Sonny, all the while continuing its fevered assault on the trembling doe held tightly between its forelegs. As Sonny raised his rifle, the buck paused for a brief instant, only to resume its rut with renewed vigor, its eyes reflecting some wild desperation. As Sonny lay in the darkness, he wondered what his own eyes betrayed at the moment of his climax. Like the deer, he felt trapped by carnal instinct, oblivious to impending tragedy.

Now there was no gunfire, only the soft ticking of the ceiling fan, its anemic efforts barely disturbing the still, humid air. They stood this way until finally, as if in response to some subliminal message, he slipped his hands into the waistband of her skirt, his fingers grazing her pubis, searching out her moist cleft. She moaned and turned into him, her hands loosening his belt. Opening her mouth to his, she reached into his pants with a desperation that momentarily startled him. He pulled her back onto the bed, and before he was able to kick free of his pants, she began greedily devouring him.

"Wait. Aminta. *Espera!*"

He tried to pull her up to him, but she clung to him with such determination that he finally flung her to the side.

"Stop it, goddammit."

She struggled to sit up, and as he tried to pull her back, she wriggled free and stood over him.

"*¿Qué quieres?* Do you want me or not? You are being a boy, not a man. I told you, there is no one else."

"That's not it. It's about this thing tomorrow. You're sure about this? You've thought it all out? You have to know that after tomorrow they're going to know about you. I guarantee it. You're not going to be able to go on with your life the way you've been doing."

She turned and started towards the doorway.

"What about us?" She paused and turned to look at him. "You disappear into the hills. And me? What do I do? Don't you see that somebody is going to ask me about you. What I knew about this. Either my guys or theirs. They're not stupid."

She said nothing, her eyes holding his.

"Say something."

"You wish for me to give up my country for our love? You ask me to choose. *Hay algo mas a la vida que amor.*"

"There's more to life than love? Yeah, I imagine there is. Well, there's more to life than throwing it away on this hare-brained stunt of yours."

"*¿Que?* Hairy brain?"

"Harebrained. Stupid. It's idiotic."

"Then why do you help me in this? If it is so foolish."

"You know why."

"This is my country, Sonny. Not yours. You can go home. I

cannot."

She picked up her blouse from the bed and stalked off into the other room. He fell back onto the bed and stared at the ceiling. She was right about one thing. He could leave. Or could he? He realized he envied her idealism even if he couldn't understand it. Yet here he was about to risk his freedom and possibly his life for a cause he barely understood. For a country he had been in for less than a year. For a woman he had known for less than half that time. He got up from the bed, pulled up his pants and walked into the kitchen.

She stood at the sink, peeling plantains for their meal. Hearing his approach, she tossed the last of them into a pot and gathered her unbuttoned blouse around her.

"Tomorrow..." he started to say.

"There is no tomorrow. *En este momento*. Only now. Tonight. It is better if you know that."

They stood there a foot apart, silent, each holding to some imaginary boundary.

"Tell me something. How long have you been planning this? The kidnapping? Aminta," he said as she looked away.

"Eight, nine months. More, perhaps. It does not matter. It has nothing to do with you. With us. That is what you want to know, yes? Whether I use you? Whether you are the foolish one?"

She walked to him and placed her hands on his lips. He could smell the sweet green scent of the plantains on her fingers.

"You must tell Ramón that you knew nothing of this. He is *fachento*, but he is your friend. He will believe you. And then you forget. ¿*Comprendes*?" She turned away, and he pulled her back. "You remember only this," she said, her voice breaking. "*Nuestro la pausa.*"

She allowed herself to fold into his embrace as he pulled her close against him. He held her like this for a while before reaching up and slipping the blouse from her shoulders. She took his hand and led him back into the bedroom. He waited as she stepped out of her skirt and panties.

"Turn around. I want to see your back," he said.

She slowly turned, her face lifted to the ceiling. As he traced his hand down the rosary of her spine, she shivered and pushed back against him. He allowed his hand to drift down into the hot, moist declivity beneath her buttocks, his fingertips searching for her. She reached back to grasp his erection through his pants.

He began to move his fingers back and forth along her moist, slick lips. She looked back at him and began to rhythmically ride his hand. Turning his hand, his palm holding her, she thrust against the heel of it. He felt more than heard the low guttural sound she made as she twisted away. She tugged at his pants, freeing him. Hooking her leg around his thigh, she pulled him into her. He could feel her ragged breath in his ear. Covering her mouth with his, he lifted her onto him, feeding himself into her. He was lost now, captured by her heat, locked inside the grip of her hips. She made a small animal sound as they toppled back onto the bed.

He could hear them now, the thumping of the bed against the wall, the uneven sound of their breathing. He felt her tighten around him as he pounded into her, sensed her stiffen, then a sharp cry, and he emptied himself into her.

It took a moment before the pounding in his ears subsided enough to hear the small whimper of her contentment. They lay together like this, gulping air, their hips locked. He realized his pants were still around his ankles. Pulling free, he kicked them loose, then leaned down and kissed her. In the dim light, he could see her face moist with tears.

"Don't," he said, wiping them from her face.

"I am afraid."

"Don't talk."

"I do not know what will happen. What I want to happen. It is not the same. Before I only care to save my country. To do this one thing. Now I care only for us. To save us. What we have made."

He rolled onto his side and pulled her into him, cradling her head in his arm.

"Is it too late? To call it off?"

She didn't reply. After a moment, she freed herself from his arms and got up from the bed. As she stepped into her skirt, she smiled at him. *"Pollo asado con arroz. ¿Si?* I make the plantains *con pasa y ron.* You like that, no? Go to the cellar and bring us some cerveza. Your love has made me thirsty." She hummed a tune. "You know the song? I am your wood, you are my fire. No?" She turned to the kitchen, still humming.

Later, he sat at the table drinking warm beer and picking at the remnants of the grilled chicken they had bought from a street vendor in the nearby village. They hadn't bothered to start the generator for the lights. Instead, Aminta had lit dozens of candles and placed them throughout the kitchen. To Sonny's irritation, it gave the small room a funereal atmosphere.

After they had finished eating, she took the lantern and moved to a small anteroom just off the kitchen to work on a sketch of a new painting. From where he sat he could watch her as she penciled in details, erasing this part or that, and drawing with an almost manic intensity. All the while, she talked to herself, occasionally raising her voice to ask a question, not so much of Sonny but of herself as if she needed to validate in her mind some detail on the sketch pad. Sonny knew better than to speak to her, not until she would pause and look back at him.

"What do you think?" she asked finally. "You think it is too...*muy triste?* Too sad?"

Sonny leaned forward in his chair to see around her. In the white hot light of the lantern, it took a moment for the crude charcoal contours to reveal themselves into a recognizable form. The outline of a woman gradually emerged, a woman dressed in a formal gown, her lower body encircled by flowers. A halo of sorts enshrouded her head, the face itself graced only by a mouth curved in obvious amusement and the mere suggestion of eyes. In the background, loomed the smoking, conical silhouette of a volcano, Volcán Masaya. Oddly enough, the only feature that had been colored in was the gown. Aminta had used chalk to roughly tint it in an almost childlike fashion, the ruby red color bleeding beyond the margins.

"Naturaleza Muerta. A still life. *Tranquilidad.* I just want a *finca* where I can walk barefoot through the fields. Is that too much to desire?" she asked, her eyes holding his. "It will be our wish for the New Year, yes?'

"And when will you finish it? If you are hiding in the mountains," he said, not bothering to mask his bitterness. "Tell me that."

She turned and looked back at the sketch. "There will be time enough. *Más tarde.* After." She tossed the piece of chalk into a can at her feet and walked over to him. Cradling his head against her bare breasts, she held him fast against her. "For us there will be time also. This I promise you, Sonny. *Siempre.*"

17

Ray leaned back against his car and popped a Nicorette he happened to find in his shirt pocket. He squinted at his watch. Sonny was late as usual. When Sonny had called from the hotel he had said three o'clock. He was most likely still with Harper, which meant they had been talking all this time. Or not. He didn't trust her. Not her motives, not her style. None of it. Ray thought again about what she had said the night before, about being able to find Granera. Hopefully, she wasn't foolish enough to divulge that to Sonny.

He looked back at the Trapani woman's house. The bulky, mud colored adobe sat on a low hillside at the upper end of Canyon Road amidst a grove of bare aspens. A late model Audi sat in the drive. From the looks of the snow it hadn't been driven since the previous night. A thin tendril of smoke wafted up from the chimney.

He had told Sonny it might be a tactical advantage to show up unannounced. Give the woman less time to get her story straight. He had always suspected she hadn't been entirely forthright in where she acquired the paintings, and now part of him felt uneasy about what she might reveal.

He turned at the sound of a car slowly making its way up the narrow, snow packed road. A moment later a taxi edged around the small curve and rolled to a stop behind Ray's Crown Vic.

He could see Harper's profile in the back seat beside Sonny. He watched as they clambered out, Sonny holding her arm as she tried to avoid a slush filled pothole. Something about the implied intimacy of the gesture irritated Ray. Was it mere jealousy that she was Sonny's new confidante? And what exactly had they confided in each other?

"Sorry we're late," was all Sonny said as they picked their way through the snow to join him. Harper offered Ray a quick smile, one that was more smug than friendly.

"Why'd you bring her along?"

"Hey, Ray. You don't have to talk about me like I'm not here," she said.

"I want her along. Okay? Humor me. She's my perspective," Sonny said, forcing a grin.

"Suit yourself," Ray replied, picking up his cane from the hood of his car and starting up the drive.

Jeanette Trapani opened the door on the second ring. At first, she seemed surprised to find Ray on her doorstep, but then her eyes revealed a glimmer of resignation. She wore skin tight black ski pants and a turquoise colored cashmere sweater, both of which did little to hide her figure. She was tall and thin, yet hardly small busted. In the bright light reflected from the snow, Ray could now make out a few hints that she might be older then he first appreciated. It wasn't so much the few gray streaks in her long blonde hair as the wrinkles evident around her mouth and eyes.

"Mr. Cortese."

"Ms. Trapani."

"I didn't expect to see you again. I wish you would've called first. I have an appointment." She glanced at her wristwatch. "In a half hour."

"I apologize, but this won't take long. You mind if we come in?"

She shifted her gaze to Sonny and Harper, and then back at

Ray.

"I'm sorry," Ray said. "This is Mr. and Mrs. Day. They're visiting from Fort Worth and saw the painting you sold me. The first one. Anyway, they're interested in buying something by the same artist. I thought you might be able to help them."

"I'm not sure I can help you. I don't have any more of her work."

Harper stepped forward. "I know we're being forward," she said in her best Texas accent. "We just thought you might be able to help us find another piece by her. You see we have this bed room that…"

She held up her hand. "Okay. Give me a minute. I might have the name of a gallery in Houston that might know of something." She started to close the door, and then hesitated. A faint smile crossed her face. "Come in. No sense standing out in the cold."

As she stepped away from the door, she shot Ray a look of irritation. She closed the door behind them and led them into a large sitting room just off the entranceway. The room was tastefully decorated in heavy dark antique furniture set against pale rose, Venetian plastered walls. An oversize leather sofa with matching chairs faced a mammoth hearth that held the smoldering remnants of a fire. Ray recognized the large painting on the opposite wall as one he had seen earlier in her gallery, a muted, pastoral depiction of peasants toiling in a field of grain. He remembered it because the volcano looming in the smoky distance reminded him of Guatemala.

"I'd offer to make some coffee or tea but like I told you, I have an appointment," she said as she made her way over to a small liquor cabinet. Her accent betrayed her Jersey roots.

"Like my wife said, we just had some questions about the artist. And where you purchased her paintings."

"I'm not sure I can tell you anything more than what I assume Mr. Cortese has already told you," she said, her back turned. She poured herself a tumbler of what appeared to be bourbon from a crystal decanter before turning to look at them. "I never met the seller, only his agent. No name was disclosed at the seller's request," she said, sitting on the sofa. She made no effort to invite them to sit.

"You bought both of them at the same time?" Harper asked.

She took a swallow of her bourbon, hesitated, and then took another. "No. My husband bought the first one from a business acquaintance. Where he got it, I have no idea."

"You recall his name? The business partner?" Ray asked.

She shot him a hard stare. "Business acquaintance," she said firmly. "No, I don't. This was ten, no, twelve years ago. In Las Vegas. About the time I started collecting. I liked the piece. I found out what I could about the artist. Put out some feelers, and four years ago the other painting showed up at a show in Houston."

"What do you know about the artist?" Harper asked.

Jeanette Trapani smiled indulgently and nodded. "Not that much, I'm afraid. Aminta Garza Segovia. 1951 to 1979. Nicaraguan. Studied first in Rome and later received her MFA from UCLA. She had a fairly well known body of work back in her home country." She glanced at each of them in turn. "Seems she disappeared at the end of the war. I know of six of her paintings besides the two I sold to Mr. Cortese. Three are in Managua, two are in private collections in Houston, and one's in a small museum in Mexico City. All dating from the early to mid-seventies. I'm afraid that's all I know."

"Actually seems like quite a lot," Sonny said.

Trapani shrugged. "Like I said, I liked her work. I made some inquiries."

"You ever ask about what could have happened to her? I mean, if no more of her work is out there, she has to be dead or something. Right?"

She hesitated a beat, her glass halfway to her mouth. "One would assume so."

142

"That she's dead? Or something else?"Harper asked.

Trapani smiled and shook her head. "I think it's time you dropped the little charade. That shitty Texas accent."

"Ms. Trapani…" Harper started to say.

"Honey, you can't bullshit a bullshitter. I've been sizing up liars since before you were out of diapers. Besides, I know who you are. Took me a minute to place you. The name's Harris, isn't it? The gallery down the road showed some of your work last summer. So, as they say in Vegas, how's about we put all our cards on the table?"

There was a moment of awkwardness as Ray glanced over at Sonny who sat silent, his eyes fixed on Jeanette Trapani. Harper started to say something but Sonny stopped her by touching her wrist.

"Okay," Sonny said. "The truth is I knew Aminta during the war. The second painting you sold Ray had to have been done after the war was over. I know because I was there when she started it."

Trapani considered this for a moment, and then nodded. "I'm sorry but I still don't see how I can help you," she said, standing up.

"Why didn't you tell me about the second painting until three months ago?" Ray asked.

"I admired it. I didn't want to part with it."

"Now who's bullshitting," Harper said.

She looked at Harper evenly, and then sat back down. She took another swallow of her bourbon and set the glass on the coffee table. "Alright. I'll tell you what I know and then you'll leave. Agreed?"

Sonny nodded.

"I wrote a personal check to the agent in Houston. Later that evening, he shows up at my hotel and asks if I mind wiring the money to a bank in Managua instead. I thought it was a little inconvenient but in the end I agreed."

"You don't remember the name?"

"Of the bank?"

"Not the bank. Whose account it was."

"Matter of fact I do. The reason I remember is I used to have a gardener with the same first name. Rigoberto. This guy, the seller was Rigoberto…Alemán. Doctor Rigoberto Alemán. I remember that, too. A doctor. "

"You think we'd have any luck contacting the people who own some of her other paintings? Where they bought them?"

"I sort of doubt it. I tried and didn't get anywhere."

"So why did you finally sell me the second one?" Ray asked.

She smiled. I'm sure you already know a lot about me, Mr. Cortese. I heard you'd been asking around. Unlike you, I don't underestimate people. If you must know, the IRS is squeezing me. My former husband, god rest his chiseling soul, owned a casino. Therefore, I must be dirty. The Feds think I'm laundering money. They see these two people living high, not realizing for a couple of down and out kids from Atlantic City, making it was just something you did. To survive." She shook her head. "It's just nobody ever tells you when to stop. Or when you've had enough. That was my husband's problem. Never having enough of anything."She picked up her empty glass from the coffee table and set it back down.

"So are you laundering money?" Harper asked.

"You're pushing it, honey," she said, barely concealing her irritation. "I'll tell you what I told them. I do charity work. Raising money from old friends in Vegas. Most of the money ends up in Latin America. You can imagine how that must look to the assholes at DEA, but it is what it is." She made a show of looking at her watch. "And now if you'll excuse me, I have to go."

"One more thing," Harper said, pulling a brown manila envelope from her purse. She removed what Ray could see was an 8X10 photograph and handed it to Jeanette Trapani."Do you recognize him?"

Trapani took the photograph in both hands and stared at it for

144

a moment. Ray noticed her jaw tighten as she shifted her eyes away for a brief second. She handed the photo back to Harper.

"I think you're looking in places you shouldn't," she said, finishing off her drink.

"What do you mean?"

Trapani sighed and looked away. "I don't know his name. But this looks like the man who sold the first painting to my husband. He's older in this photograph of course."

Ray noticed Sonny and Harper exchange glances. Ray reached over and took the photo from Harper. The image set him back. Granera. Had to be him. Older, but he would know him anywhere. He tossed it back into Harper's lap.

"All I know is that he was Latin," Trapani continued. "And creepy. My husband was no saint, but this guy was... like he crawled out from under a rock somewhere. When I asked my husband about him, he said the less I knew about him, the better. I was happy never to have seen him again. Now if you'll excuse me."

Wait," Sonny said. "One more thing. Did this man ever tell you where he got the painting?"

She shook her head. "Like I said, this guy was a real piece of work. I remember him saying that he and the Segovia woman were lovers. I recall being a little put off by the way he seemed to brag about it. He was a creep."

Trapani stood and started for the door. Ray looked at Sonny who stood up to follow her, but seemed too lost in thought to notice the look Harper shot Ray. Ray fired back with a menacing look. He waited as Harper and Sonny started down the snow packed sidewalk before turning to Trapani who stood waiting at the open door.

"Strictly off the record," Ray said. "And I wouldn't blame you if you told me to take a hike, but you mind me asking what your husband was involved in besides casinos?"

Trapani stared at him briefly and then smiled. "You know, Mr. Cortese. I made my own inquiries about you. You've had your share of scumbag associates. Gun runners, common criminals. People I consider to be evil. You're hardly one to judge." She glanced at Sonny and Harper who stood waiting in the drive. "My late husband financed things. Things the banks wouldn't. He did well by me," she said, gesturing to the house. "And that's all I'll say. Goodbye, Mr. Cortese."

Harper and Sonny had turned and waited halfway down the drive as Ray picked his way carefully through the snow.

"When were you gonna tell me about the photo?" Ray asked, joining them.

Harper looked at Sonny and then turned to Ray. "I wanted to show it to you last night, but it didn't seem the right time."

"Where did you get it?"

Harper stared at him without replying.

"I always figured you were in bed with somebody. Who is it? The Agency? DEA?"

"Screw you."

"Have it your way. I'm just saying if I would've known about it ahead of time, I could've milked Trapani for a lot more information. Now what've we got? Alemán in Managua?"

Ray looked at Sonny who stood staring at the snow covered summit of Atalaya Mountain looming over them from across the road. "And we know our old friend Granera had some of Aminta's work. So now what?" he said, when Sonny didn't respond.

Sonny looked at him. "I guess I'm going to Managua."

"And I guess I'm going to need some clothes," Harper said.

Sonny turned and looked at her. "Mind telling me why you'd think I'd want you coming along?"

"Why not? You said you needed perspective, right? Sounds to me like you're going to need some of that."

"There's no story though. You have to promise me that."

"Agreed. I'm just along for the ride. I've got nothing else to do."

Ray stood there and watched them get into the car. Shit, Macy's gonna kill me.

146

18

PART THREE
NICARAGUA

Harper rolled down the car window, happy to smell something besides the mildew odor leaking from the anemic air conditioner. Fortunately, it was cooler up here in the hills than anywhere else she had been in the last three days, the humidity almost bearable.

"Maybe these kids know where the clinic is," Sonny said, nodding at two young boys cutting weeds at the edge of the road. They each wielded machetes in one hand and a short handled, crude rake in the other. "I'll be right back," Sonny said climbing out of the car.

She looked up and saw Ray watching her in the rear view mirror, his eyes revealing nothing. It was one of several things Harper didn't like about him. You never knew where you stood. She had to admit he seemed a lot different that night in Santa Fe when he was telling the story. She decided he wasn't the kind of person who made a habit of showing vulnerability or letting down his guard. Not that far down at least.

They sat there a moment and listened to the ticking of the hot engine.

"Her place was near here, wasn't it?" she asked.

Ray nodded and looked out the window. "You walk over there, to the edge of that bean field, and you'll see the lake. Her house was on top of the next hill over. Back then you would've been able to see the roof from here. I came back here a few years ago. Not much left of it. The house burned down."

Harper leaned forward and looked at Sonny talking with the two young boys. They had been told in Granada that the clinic was just before the village of Catarina. La Clinica de Mujeres. It was where they were told they would find Doctor Rigoberto Alemán. He ran a women and children's clinic. So far all they had seen were a few houses set far back from the road. None of them bore even a passing resemblance to a clinic. The only sign on the narrow, poorly paved road was that for Bodega Garcia, 1 km. They had twice approached the edge of the village without finding the clinic.

"You have a problem with me?" Harper asked, settling back into her seat.

Ray looked back at her again in the mirror before reaching for the pack of cigarettes. "You mean besides that you've made me take up smoking again?" He removed a cigarette from the pack with his lips and tossed the pack back on the dash. "Nothing personal, other than that I think you're playing my friend. That's what I got against you." he said, lighting the cigarette with a Bic he had retrieved from beneath the map on the dash.

"Oh, I get it. You're accusing me of being dishonest with your friend? Like you've never lied to Sonny? Come on, Ray. That's not it and you know it. No, you've got some other game going on here. I'm just not sure what it is yet."

He turned and looked at her. "You don't need to be here. I don't care what your motives are."

"You don't know anything about my motives."

"Maybe not, but I know you're using him."

"Ray, you don't know shit."

"All right. Forget it."

"And you know what I'm not going to forget, Ray? That thirty hour bus ride you made me take. You thought I'd balk at that. Counted on me ditching. Right?"

The only way Ray would agree to Harper accompanying them to Nicaragua was if she would come in the back door, in other words, sneak in some way that the Agency might overlook. That had meant her flying to Cancun, then taking an unscheduled, dead of night flight in a two seat Cessna to Bluefields on the Nicaraguan coast. From there, she had endured the grinding bus trip to Managua. Thirty hours of un-air conditioned stop and go, unwashed bodies, and the endless, smoky fields.

It was the first time she had been back in Nicaragua in twenty-six years. She hadn't seen much of the country back then. A few isolated villages in the north and a lot of night time marches to avoid the Sandinista patrols. It had mostly been two weeks of mind-numbing boredom. She had never even witnessed a firefight. She did get some great photos of the contra guerillas, along with a hefty dose of anti-Sandinista propaganda before departing from the same dark airstrip where she had arrived.

It wouldn't have been so bad, the hundred fifty mile bus trip if she had the opportunity to travel at her leisure and scrutinize the countryside and take photos. But Ray had said if she wasn't in Managua in two days they would leave without her. Sonny had offered no objection, whether out of acquiescence or his obvious state of distraction, she couldn't be sure. In the end, she had left Santa Fe without any opportunity to really talk with him.

"From your reputation, I thought a trip like that would've been a piece of cake. I told you, it was the only way we could be sure you weren't followed in. At least, not right away. It'll take 'em three, maybe four days until the word gets out. Bluefield's thick with DEA and snitches. Same with Cancun." He sucked greedily on the cigarette. "If we're lucky, we'll be out of here by the time they catch on."

"You think so? Just because it was so easy to find this Doctor Alemán? Even I know better than that. Unless you already know what we're going to find out."

149

Harper flinched at the sudden cramp in her guts and prepared herself for the queasiness and the urgent need to find a toilet that would invariably come next. She needed a toilet. A bush would do. She must've contracted something eating at the roadside snack bars the bus stopped for twice a day. Now all she could think about was how important it was to find the clinic. Or a gas station. Anywhere with toilet paper.

"You don't look that great," Ray said.

She rolled her head back on the seat. "Let's just say if Sonny doesn't hurry, we're all going to regret it."

"You're right about Alemán though. Heck, I found him before we even left Santa Fe. Thanks to the Google god. We're just lucky he was the only one in the whole country with that name. Problem is, now we're on our own. My contacts down here dried up a long time ago."

Oh, Lord," she moaned, clutching her gut.

He grinned and shook his head. "I told you to stay behind. You want me to drive you into Catarina?'

"No. I just want to hold still a while. Okay?"

"What I can't figure is why he agreed to let you tag along."

"He didn't tell you?"

"Sonny only tells me what he wants to tell me. You're screwing him, right?"

"God, you're an asshole. You think that's it? Well, you're wrong."

"Then why'd he let you come?"

She shrugged. "Your guess is as good as mine. You were there. I said I wanted to come along. He didn't say anything." She glanced over at Sonny and the two boys. "Jesus, what's taking him so long?"

"You must have some idea why he didn't stop you. I mean, the two of you talked."

"Goddammit, Ray. I could ask you the same question. Why

does he want you along? Because my guess is you've got your fair share of motivation to keep him from finding out something as inconvenient as the truth."

He took another drag of the cigarette and flicked it out the window. "I'm here to keep him from getting hurt. Pure and simple. There's no Aminta. There's no truth for him to find out."

"You're sure of that?"

"You just keep your mouth shut and we'll be out of here in no time."

"Yeah, I'll do that Ray. Oh, good. He's coming back."

Sonny got in the car and pointed back over his shoulder. "Dirt road, back maybe two hundred meters. Go in a ways and there'll be a sign. You okay?" he said, obviously noticing her discomfort.

"You think this clinic will have any Lomotil? Pepto Bismol? Something like that?"

"What took you so long?" Ray asked, swinging the car around and starting back down the road.

"Twenty questions. I did find out this Alemán's from around here. Grew up in Catarina. Med school in Estados Unidos. Houston." Sonny waved at the two boys as they passed them by. "Astros fans. Those two. They had no idea if Alemán's an art collector though."

"Screw the art. Long as he's got Lomotil," Harper said.

Ray slowed the car as they approached a dark colored Toyota Four Runner parked alongside the road. He glanced over at Sonny who also seemed to be studying the car. As they passed it, Harper cocked her head to the open window. A man in the front passenger seat of the SUV met her gaze just as his electric window eclipsed his face. She looked up and saw Ray watching the road behind them in the rear view mirror. Sonny turned and looked over his shoulder.

"You know them?" she asked.

Neither of them said anything.

"All right. Don't tell me." She gripped her stomach and slid further down into the seat.

151

19

A few moments later they spotted a simple sign made out of whitewashed plywood fastened to a fence post adorned with the faded, hand painted words *La Clinica de Mujeres y Ninos*. The sign pointed down a rutted dirt road almost hidden by a thick grove of banana trees. As they started down the track they passed several women walking alongside, all of them obviously pregnant. Ray slowed the car as he passed them. Two of them carried thin plastic shopping bags with what appeared to be fruit of some kind. One by one, they all turned to gaze with open curiosity at the car of *extranjeros*, obviously unused to outsiders traveling on the narrow, poorly maintained road.

As they passed a field of harvested corn stalks, Sonny caught a whiff of the redolent tang of the dried corn leaf. The smell tugged at some memory, undoubtedly from his childhood summers on his uncle's East Texas farm. The fleeting emotion only increased his growing ambivalence.

The end of the field revealed a clearing and a low slung, cinderblock structure, its roof a patchwork of rusted tin and palm fronds. A crude wooden porch took up one side of the building upon which sat a clutch of women watching two small boys teasing a dog with stick. The only other sign of life were a half dozen russet colored hens scratching in the dusty yard and a lone man feeding arm loads of corn stalks to a small bonfire.

Harper barely waited for Ray to turn off the ignition before throwing herself out of the car and striding up to the porch.

"Toilet. *Dónde*...a toilet?" she asked, trying not to sound too desperate.

Sonny got out of the car and leaned over the roof. "*¿Dónde está el baño, por favor?*"

One of the women pointed to what looked like a small, faded Tuff Shed on the edge of the weed lined cornfield. The low brush around it appeared littered with scraps of newspaper.

"So much for toilet paper," she muttered, hurrying over to the shed.

"*¿Dónde está el medico?*" Sonny asked, approaching the porch.

The woman nearest him clutched a small boy of two or three dressed only in a swatch of soiled cotton gauze that he wore in lieu of any shorts, the front of which was stained with what appeared to be dried blood. The boy stared at Sonny as he picked at the web of dried mucus around his mouth and nose. The woman didn't reply but gestured vaguely to an open doorway on the end of the porch. As Sonny stepped onto the porch, he caught the odiferous bouquet of disinfectant and something less benign wafting from the open window. He walked over to the edge of the porch and glanced at the man burning the corn stalks who had paused to look at them.

"Hello. *Hola!* Anyone here?"

An unintelligible response came from somewhere in the rear of the clinic, and a moment later a man appeared around the corner of the house. He was wiping his hands with a towel of startling whiteness, in sharp contrast to his wrinkled, threadbare chinos and sweat stained work shirt. Sonny had always marveled at how people living in some of the dingiest, squalid parts of the world were able to achieve such brilliantly white laundry.

"Doctor Alemán?"

The man nodded, his expression guarded. Sonny sensed he

was coolly appraising them.

"Americans?" he asked softly, glancing past Sonny at Ray who came limping up behind. The man appeared to be in his early thirties, taller than most of the local populace and lighter complected. He wore his thick, brown hair pulled back in a short pony tail, accentuating his chiseled, aquiline cheekbones and narrow nose.

Sonny nodded.

"What is it you want? If it is medical care, as you can see, I only treat women and children. There is another clinic in Catarina. If you like, I can…"

"No. We're here for something else," Ray said, stepping up beside Sonny. "My friend and I are art dealers. We understand you once sold a painting by a local artist. Aminta Garza Segovia."

Alemán shifted his gaze to the women sitting on the porch behind them in what Sonny sensed was an effort to conceal his reaction. When he looked back, his face registered mild confusion. He pointed at the women sitting on the porch. "Does this look like an art gallery, *amigo*? I am afraid someone has confused me with another person. Perhaps…"

"Un Retrado de Las Penas. You would've remembered it."

They all turned at the sound of the door slamming on the Tuff Shed. Harper walked slowly towards them, her face pinched and drawn.

"You wouldn't happen to have some Lomotil?" she asked Alemán.

Alemán smiled. "Something for diarrhea? *Si. Momentito,"* he said, disappearing around the corner of the clinic.

She looked up at Sonny, her eyes questioning something. She held the look so long that Sonny finally turned away in discomfort. He sensed her confusion. They hadn't had the opportunity to talk since she arrived in Managua the evening before. He wasn't sure of what he would say anyway. When she had said she was coming along, his initial reaction was one of mild acceptance. On the one hand, he realized he would need a buffer from Ray's murky endeavors. On the other, having Harper along might temper his own judgment. Or lack of it. Besides he was curious about what she was really after.

"I'd say he was a little too happy to change the subject," Ray said. "You see his face when you mentioned the painting? He knows something. And I figure about now he's trying to decide how much to tell us."

Sonny nodded absently and turned and looked back at the man who had been burning corn. He was nowhere to be seen.

"I don't get why he wouldn't tell you about it," Harper said, dropping onto the edge of the porch.

"Those kids said this guy was born here. Chances are his family would know Aminta's family. Or know about them. It hasn't been that long since the war. They probably still feel a little uneasy talking about their neighbors. It was that kind of war."

Alemán returned carrying a small cellophane packet in one hand, and in the other, a glass soda bottle that contained some milky green liquid. He offered them both to Harper.

"Take one of the pills twice a day for three days and you should be better. Electrolyte solution," he said in reply to her glance at the bottle he offered her.

"Thanks," Harper murmured.

He glanced at Sonny and Ray. "The painting. I remember it. It was a donation to our clinic. I sold it to purchase a machine to sterilize my instruments." He shrugged. "I have no need for art."

"There was more than one painting though, right?"

He looked at Ray in obvious surprise. "When I sold the painting..."

"The paintings. You sold at least two of them."

"No. I sold only one." He studied Ray and Sonny each in turn and then shook his head."You take me for a fool. You are no art dealers. So then I must ask myself, who are you really? Three

Yanquis who want to know about a painting I sold three, maybe four years ago. Perhaps, you can tell me a different lie. In any case, I'm afraid I can't help you."

"Okay, let's start over," Sonny said. "Who gave you the painting?"

"You know, my friend, Nicaragua is my country now. It is perhaps unfortunate that you now have to actually pay us for our bananas. And, we no longer have to accept your intimidation."

"Who's intimidating?" Ray said. "We just want to know who gave you the painting.'"

Alemán smiled, but only his mouth moved. "I cannot recall the name of the donor. Perhaps, he did not give his name. *Anónimo. Si?* An anonymous donor . I am sorry, but that is all I can tell you."

"You met him though?" Sonny asked.

Alemán shrugged noncommittally.

Sonny pulled the envelope from the back of his pants and took out the photograph. "Is this the man who gave you the paintings?" he asked, holding the photograph out to Alemán.

The doctor glanced at the photo, his eyes seeming to linger on the image longer than he wanted. He looked up at Sonny. "I don't know this person."

Sonny saw the hesitation in Alemán's eyes and sensed that he was lying.

"Did you know her family?"

"Whose family?"

"Aminta's. The artist. Her family had a home no more than a mile from here."

¿Verdad? I am afraid not. My family was poor. We knew nothing of such people. *Los rico.*"

"You mean because they were Somacistas, right?"

"I did not know them."

Alemán was lying again, Sonny thought. The same look in his eyes. Sonny held the doctor's eyes a moment before looking away. The man burning corn stalks had returned to his toil. Sonny watched him as he tossed the stalks onto the smoldering fire. The man moved in an odd way. He appeared stiff, off balance maybe.

"Where are you going?" Ray asked as Sonny stepped from the porch and started for the field.

Sonny motioned at Ray to stay put and made his way to the man burning corn stalks. As he approached, the man looked up and paused. He wore faded jeans, a dirty T-shirt and atop his head, a stained, frayed straw sombrero. He looked to be a little older than Sonny, but solidly built, no doubt from years of manual labor. He nodded at Sonny, and then took off his hat and swiped at his brow. The gray hair around the man's temples contrasted with the thin red hair plastered to his scalp. Something about the man's hands drew Sonny's attention. They were both badly misshapen, the fingers grotesquely crooked, the hands themselves scarred.

"I think I know you. *¿Te conozco, amigo?*" Sonny asked.

The man stared at Sonny for a long moment before shifting his gaze over Sonny's shoulder towards the clinic.

"¿Habla Inglés?"

"Si.Poquito," he said, shifting his eyes back.

"You were Aminta's friend? Long time ago. *¿Si?*"

He stared at Sonny, his gaze as impenetrable as if he were blind. Finally, he nodded his head an inch.

"During the war. *Durante la guerra.* Do you remember me?"

The man's face remained impassive, his eyes empty of expression.

"Have you seen her? Aminta? Since the war?"

The man frowned and cocked his head. *"Aminta es muerto."*

"You are sure? *¿Seguro?*"

The man looked back towards the clinic. Sonny turned and followed his gaze. He was looking at Alemán who stood watching them.

"*¿Lo recuerdo El Labio? Somoza's asesino?*" Sonny held up the photograph of Granera in front of the man's face."Has he been here?*¿Aqui? ¿A la clinica?*"

"*No se. No me moleste,*" the man said, leaning down to pick up an armful of corn stalks.

He had said enough. People like him knew when it was in their best interests to shut up. Sonny turned and looked back at the clinic. Alemán had disappeared, and Ray and Harper stood waiting on the porch. Sonny glanced back at the man burning stalks who now seem to redouble his efforts to make up for the time he had lost in conversation. Sonny shook his head in frustration and turned to walk to the car.

20

Ray slowed the car to allow an old man hauling a pile of brush in a donkey cart to cross the road. Here the road climbed steeply from the edge of the lake back to the headlands and the main highway. The air held the cool, dank smell of the lake, an almost welcome respite from the occasional veils of smoke from the burning fields. The three of them had talked little since leaving the clinic, their disappointments competing with fatigue, Harper's intestinal malady, and the uncertainty of their next move. To Ray's irritation, Harper started to bring up again the ineptness of their cover story about being art dealers.

"That Trapani woman wasn't fooled either. Don't you guys ever consider just telling the truth?" she asked.

"The truth? God, I never thought of that," Ray replied as he stomped on the accelerator, urging the small compact up the hill. "Like the truth ever gets you anywhere. A little persuasion is what's needed here. Our doctor friend may wake up tomorrow and find me sitting beside his bed and I'll do some persuading. Least we might get his truth."

"Forget it," Sonny said. "All you'll get is his version. Besides, I'm starting to think I'm done with this."

"Already? We just got here. Hold it. What's this?" Ray said, nodding at the road ahead.

They had come around a sharp curve in the road only to find

it had been partially blocked by a pair of patrol cars at the crest of the hill. Ray slowed the car, his eyes scanning the edges of the road for any exits.

"Fifty bucks says this isn't just some routine traffic check," Sonny said.

"Maybe," Ray said, glancing in the rear view mirror. "They look like Policia Nacional types. But I'm not quite so sure about the jokers behind us in the Four Runner. Same guys we saw before."

Sonny turned and looked at what Ray was referring to. He glanced at Harper. "Think you can play up the 'woman about to crap in her pants' routine?"

"Shouldn't be much of a problem," Harper said, forcing a smile.

Ray stopped the car a few meters in front of the patrol cars and waited as two of the policeman got out of their vehicles and walked up on either side of the car. The one approaching Ray's side made a show of noting the license plate before approaching Ray's window.

"Pasaporte, por favor."

Ray reached carefully into his pants pocket and handed the patrolman his passport.

"Su amigos, también."

The cop waited as Sonny and Harper retrieved their passports and handed them forward. He gave each of the documents a cursory glance, looked at each of them in turn and then walked back to the patrol cars. The policeman reached into the window of his patrol car and retrieved his radio handset. He looked down the road towards the SUV as he appeared to read from the passports.

"Not exactly subtle, are they," Sonny said, looking back again at the SUV parked fifty or so yards behind them. The heavily tinted windshield prevented them from seeing who was inside. "What do you think?" Sonny asked.

"My guess would be DID."

"What's DID?" Harper asked.

"Dirección de Información para la Defensa. Secret police."

"Great. What did we do to deserve this?"

"I already noticed them when we checked into the hotel this afternoon," Ray said. "For all I know they could've even picked us up at the airport in Managua. Stepping on toes already."

"Question is, whose toes?"

"Alemán maybe," Ray replied. "We haven't been here long enough to piss anybody else off."

"So how do you want to play this?"

"We could always try Harper's way. Tell 'em the truth. That way they don't have to beat it out of us."

"I don't think I care as long as they have a decent toilet," Harper said.

Ray watched in the mirror as someone stepped out of the Four Runner's passenger side. The man wore plainclothes. Even from this distance Ray could see his suit was rumpled and fit him badly. The man stood there for a long moment before turning to speak to his driver. He then unzipped his pants and began urinating on the roadway.

A moment later, the policeman tossed his handset back into his patrol car and walked back to their car. He handed Ray their passports. *"Continuar,"* he said, stepping away from their car and waving them on.

"What do you think? Sonny asked.

"I figure they already had me and Sonny's number. Guess now they know about you," Ray said, glancing back at Harper. "Now we wait and see. Just like the good old days. Right, Sonny?"

"If I recall, in the old days we'd wait it out in some hotel bar. Out of the sun. So what the hell. Let's go to the hotel," Sonny replied.

21

"Any idea what the occasion is?" Harper asked. Sonny looked at her, his mind obviously preoccupied with something other than the scene unfolding around them. They were sitting on the terrace of the Hotel Alhambra across from the Parque Central, drinking mojitos and watching a procession of young girls dressed in brightly colored pinafores twirling and dancing down the cobblestone street. A brass band composed of boys of similar age marched somberly behind them, their musical production an annoying hybrid of salsa and John Phillip Sousa. An old pickup truck rumbled slowly behind them, its bed displaying placards presumably attesting to President Ortega's myriad accomplishments. The crowd, a mixture of locals and camera laden tourists, cheered and applauded with exaggerated exuberance. The parade had come out of nowhere, the din disrupting what a moment before had been the solitude of the approaching dusk. The two of them had been drinking and silently watching the façade of the cathedral across the park gradually turn from bright yellow to umber with the fading light.

"You want to tell me what you're thinking?" she asked, in response to his silence.

Sonny drained his glass and shook his head. She sensed his irritation. They had spent the day visiting as many art galleries in Granada as they could in search of Aminta's work or at least someone who knew of her. To Sonny's bewilderment no one knew her, or if they did they wouldn't say. Only one elderly man in a small shop off the plaza that sold cheap local landscapes meant for the tourist trade admitted to knowing her work. Still, all the old guy was willing to impart was that Aminta had disappeared at the end of the war along with most of her work.

"I guess it's just strange being here is all. After all this time. That and I keep wondering what kind of trouble Ray's getting us into."

"You sure he's just not up in his room avoiding me? If you haven't noticed, he and I aren't exactly *simpático*."

Sonny looked at her before draining his mojito. "You want another?" he asked, waving the waiter over.

Whatever medicine it was that Alemán had given her, it had seemed to fight her dysentery to a tenuous draw. Another mojito might turn the course of the battle. Exactly in whose favor she wasn't sure.

"Why not?" she said, leaning back into her chair and looking out at the park. The procession had moved on, and the tourists now began haggling with the drivers of the flower bedecked horse drawn carriages that lined the street across from the hotel. From somewhere inside the hotel, music had begun to play. The slow, mournful melody coupled with the soft evening air and rum buzz elicited an odd mixture of melancholy and contentment.

"Dos Gardenias," Sonny murmured. "Ibrahim Ferrer. He's the vocalist. The Cuban Sinatra."

She cocked her head and listened. "It's beautiful. Sounds sad. What's it about?"

"He's singing about love and betrayal. When the gardenias die, he knows his lover has betrayed him for another."

"She done her man wrong. Cuban country western."

Sonny shot her a grin. "There was this guy I knew once."

"Spare me another 'guy I knew once' story. Who are we talking about? You or Ray?"

Sonny smiled and looked away.

"Start with Ray."

Sonny stared at her a moment before saying anything. "You may find this hard to believe, but I really don't know much about Ray. At least from before we first met up. He's never talked about his family, or growing up. I have read his files though."

"You saw his files?"

"Once. The usual Agency pedigree. He stumbled around and busted up lots of things before ending up in the army. Military intelligence for god knows what reason. Maybe they knew a duplicitous son of a bitch when they saw one. Never was a good match though. Ray never was one to do what he was told unless he could do it his way." He hesitated a moment before going on. "Ray and the Agency finally parted ways when this journalist, a woman with Reuters, leaked something she shouldn't have. Ray had this informant in the Venezuelan military that was going to be a big time asset. The guy gets outed, disappears and most likely killed, and Ray ends up the Agency's scapegoat."

"What did he do after he left the Agency? I get the feeling the restaurant's a relatively new line of work."

He looked at her as if gauging what he should reveal. "He did things for people. Found out things. Sold information you might say. Did some personal security."

"You mean like a bodyguard?"

Sonny didn't say anything. The waiter brought them their drinks. Sonny took a sip before going on. "He took a pretty bad beating down in Mexico a few years back. He was working as a go between on a kidnapping. Cartel guys were holding the son of a Matamoros businessmen. Turns out these guys had already killed him. When Ray shows up to negotiate, it got ugly. Macy read him the riot act after that. He's gone straight since then."

"Sounds to me like he should be sitting this out."

"Maybe we all should. Those guys this afternoon, the ones back on the highway. They weren't just playing around. Things might get dicey in a hurry. Especially if Ray is stirring things up. Unfortunately, that's what he does best."

"And what about you?

"What about me?"

"Did you ever work for the Agency?"

"Let's just say I never took their money."

"But you did things for them."

"You're asking if I was a spy or something? No, not really. All I ever did was pass on information when I had something. To Ray mostly. And never anything that ever kept me awake at night."

Harper took a swallow of her drink. "You said something to me that night in your tent. You asked me something like 'that wasn't the first time, was it? I thought maybe you could tell."

"Tell what?"

She hesitated, gauging what to say next. Maybe she should've stopped with the first mojito.

"I guess what I mean is that it wasn't the first time that I was in a...situation like that." She paused and looked away. "I guess what I'm trying to say is don't worry about me. I've been around." She looked back at him. "Some people it maybe makes more cautious. Like they've used up their chances or something. Some people just anesthetize themselves. That or maybe after awhile you come to realize that no place is ever that safe."

Neither of them said anything for a long moment.

Why not tell him, she thought. What had he said that night? Something about having to share it to make it real. Pillow talk.

"There was this one time in Croatia. My driver and I got stopped at a roadblock. Some militia types. I'm not even sure whose side they were on. Middle of the night. Middle of nowhere. Let's just say we shouldn't have been out driving around past curfew." She hesitated as her mind slipped back. She met his eyes and stared at him before going on. "They took us out

165

into the forest. I was lucky that…"

"Harper. You don't have to tell me this."

"They killed my driver. It was my fault. I should've known better. I mean…"

"Stop."

Something in his voice made her want to ignore his request, to reveal every ugly truth about herself whether he wanted to hear it or not. *Your usual feeble attempt to sabotage any real intimacy,* her therapist had told her. *You tell him about your rape. Tell him the bullshit about how it was your fault. Show him all the scars. Scare him away.*

They sat there for what seemed a minute, listening to the sounds of the traffic, the muted music from the bar inside, the wail of a distant siren sinking back into the night.

"I'm sorry," she said. "You must think I tell that story to just anyone. More like never. I'm embarrassed."

"Don't be. It's just that…you don't have to prove anything."

"Why did you let me come along?" she asked.

"Why did you want to?"

"It would be easy to say I was just bored. And I wouldn't be lying entirely. But it was more than that. I agreed I wasn't going to do a story, but there is a story here. And just because I can't write about it later doesn't mean I don't want to know about how it all ends. Does that answer satisfy you?"

Sonny grinned. "Ray thinks we're sleeping together."

"Let him think what he wants. So are you going to tell me why you let me come along?" she asked when he fell silent.

He looked over at the last hem of sky to the west and shook his head. "The God's honest truth? I thought you might be some kind of messenger."

"Like the stealth nun?"

He laughed. "Yeah, like that nun in the work boots. When you showed up at Ray's that night, it was like…God, where's this going? You see, I like to think there's a purpose to things. I'm still not sure why you're here. Maybe it is just that perspective thing. Maybe I need someone to tell me when to leave well enough alone. So, tell me. Should I leave it alone?"

"I don't know, Sonny. Myself, I like endings. Even if they're not so neat. And I think I know you well enough by now to know you're not going to rest until you find some answers."

"See. Perspective. That's all I needed."

"You still think she's alive?

"I don't know anymore."

She measured what she was about to say. "You believe Ray? That she died in that jail?"

He downed the last of his mojito and glanced out at the park. "Her and I stayed at this hotel once. A couple of weeks or so before it all ended. I remember this terrace being different back then. Screened in, I think. I remember the trees. And the carriages. Funny thing is I don't remember much of anything else about that evening. Or maybe I don't want to. I don't know." He fell silent, his face revealing nothing. He lowered his gaze and looked over at her. "I think I'll turn in. I'll see you at breakfast," he said, standing abruptly and walking off.

She watched him disappear into the hotel, half-wanting to go after him. She wanted to be with him, the reasons for which seemed as muddled as ever. She glanced down at her drink. It's only the rum talking. Give it a rest. The waiter appeared at her elbow.

"¿Comida, sénorita?"

"What the hell? Might as well live dangerously. Do you have fish? Uh, ¿Pescado?"

"¿La plancha?"

"Whatever. And una mas mojito. Doble.."

22

Sonny waited at the antiquated elevator for what seemed an eternity before finally deciding on the stairs. On the second landing, he glanced up and a flood of memory washed over him as he stared up at the painting in the hallway. He remembered now that evening with Aminta. In a fit of impatient ardor, they had also taken the stairs. And now, just like that evening thirty years ago, he stood there transfixed by the painting. Not so much by the painting itself as the emotion of seeing it again after all these years. In itself, the painting was far from memorable. A faded portrait of a young woman in an evening gown. The style of the gown and the young woman's hair style suggested late-nineteenth century. The woman cradled a small white lap dog in her arms. Behind her was a muted bucolic vista of orchards and mountains. Her smile hinted at some small satisfaction.

"*Presumido*," Aminta had murmured upon seeing the painting. "I forget how you say this in English. Proud? No, not *exactamente*. Smug? That is the word. *¿Si?* This woman. They had a good life in those days. The rich ones. The privileged. *La vida tranquilo.* I still see these women. At the parties. The wives of the generals. The mistresses. *Presumido.*"

He stood now looking at the painting, recalling in his mind the contempt in her voice. He remembered how they went up to their room and made love. Frenzied, almost violently. He wondered how much of that intensity reflected some self-loathing on her part; a revulsion of her own class and upbringing. As well as a certain envy. A longing for what she called a still life. *La vida tranquilo,* she called it. A life seemingly out of her reach.

The sudden vibration of the cell phone in his shirt pocket startled him. It was the first time the cell phone had rang since Ray had given it to him when they first arrived in Managua. He fished it from his pocket and dropped onto the bench below the painting.

"Listen, I've been asking around about our friend Alemán," Ray said before Sonny could even answer. "Seems he's not exactly popular with Ortega's bunch. Political activist of sorts. Ties to the opposition down here. Wouldn't surprise me he's the reason we're getting the attention."

"Then I guess you better be careful where you stick your nose. Why don't you call it a night and let's rethink this over breakfast?"

"One more stop to make. A guy I used to know in Guatemala. He's privy to a lot of rumors. Used to be that people would tell him things they might not tell anyone else. Figure it's worth a try."

"Okay, but don't push it."

Sonny snapped the phone shut. He sat there a moment, struggling to sort out his feelings. Was it despair or simple ambivalence? Acknowledge your feelings, a therapist had once told him. The therapist eventually became his lover. He always found her advice suspiciously self-serving.

Why was he doing this? Hadn't he made the conscious decision to move on? The past was the past. Nothing could change it. He could easily go back to the States tomorrow. Go legit. Come out of the cold and use his real name. Spain wasn't likely to extradite him. He had enough money. He could start over. There was only one thing not within his reach. A connection to something. Face it. That was the only reason he was here. And that connection was most likely long gone and buried. Time to move on.

He thought about Harper. What was she? Just a distraction? Or a different direction? He sat there a moment longer before getting up and going downstairs. Harper watched him approach, her expression revealing no sense of surprise. She had ordered another drink and a small salad rested by her elbow.

"Care to join me for dinner?" she asked when he made no effort to sit.

"What are you having?"

"Not sure. Some fish. *La plancha,* whatever that means. I could use an interpreter. But I've got mojito doble down pretty good though."

"You mind we start over?"

She looked at him as if she were measuring him for something.

"I imagine it's worth a try," she said.

"I thought we could talk about something besides me. Besides all this. I realized I don't know much about you other than some of your work. I imagine there's more."

"You'd think. Lately, I'm not sure."

They stared at each other for a long moment before each of them broke into a smile. She remembered the first time he had smiled in that tent in the Sudan. This smile was different this time, less guarded maybe.

"Have I ever told you about my mother?" she asked.

"Your mother?"

"You're right. Too much information. Okay, how about the time I had to pass myself off as a prostitute to get my pictures? Was in Bangkok. Not a lot of hookers of color there. What's that look?"

Sonny smiled. "It's just that I'm trying to wrap my mind around you in heels and fishnet stockings. Okay, you've got my interest."

"Maybe we ought to talk about my mother first," she said,

picking up her drink. "We can talk about the heels and fishnet later."

Later that night, he experienced the same dream as always. A speeding car careening recklessly down narrow streets filled with children on bikes and produce vendors. It always took a moment to realize he was the driver. As pedestrians hurled themselves from his path, he found himself struggling to read a crumpled sheet of paper clutched in his hand. No matter how many times he tried to decipher it, the scrawl remained unreadable. He looks up suddenly. Some instinct? A premonition. And always a moment too late. A young woman frozen in the street, her eyes meeting his for an instant. He swerves to avoid her. She is replaced by an old man stepping from the curb, his face registering first surprise, followed an instant later by what Sonny always felt was acceptance. Then the windshield exploding into a prism. Blinding light. Someone slamming their fists on the roof of the car. He feels hands on his chest, clutching him, and again the slamming on the roof.

"Sonny."

He came fully awake with a start, gasping for breath, his sudden panic the only evidence he had been dreaming.

"Someone's at the door," Harper whispered.

Someone was pounding on the door. Pulling himself from Harper's arms, he sat up on the side of the bed and squinted around the dim room.

"Abierto! Venga!"

"Stay here," he said, grabbing his pants from the chair and hurriedly slipping them on. He picked his way through the darkness toward the thin edge of light escaping from beneath the door. As he started to flip the dead bolt, a sudden sense of déjà vu made him hesitate. A memory of a door. Was it from the dream? He turned the deadbolt and opened the door.

"Senór Bass? You will come with us."

The man standing in the doorway was a heavy set, dark complexioned young man with an acne-pitted face. He wore a white guayabera over pair of faded jeans. Behind him, stood two older men dressed in police uniforms. Sonny could see one of them held a large revolver against his leg. Before Sonny could react, the young man in the guayabera pushed past him into the hotel room.

"Wait! *Espera!*" Sonny said as he made a feeble effort to stop him. Out of the corner of his eye, he saw Harper slip into the bathroom.

"You friend. She comes also," the young man said, flipping on the light switch. He took a moment to survey the room before picking up Sonny's shirt from the chair and tossing it to him.

"Where are we going?"

"*Silencio!* You will dress and come with us. *Vamos!*"

Sonny put on his shirt and walked over to the bathroom and opened the door. Harper turned from the sink and looked at him. She had put on her bra and panties but nothing else.

"Don't worry," he said, shaking his head in feigned amusement. "I'm sure Ray's got this all figured out."

23

Ray glanced up at the pair of stained glass windows above the old priest's head. There was just enough light from the bodega across the street to illuminate the usual vignette of mutilated, beheaded martyrs. And always the usual clutch of stricken followers huddled at their feet. He took another drag from his cigarette and looked back at the priest.

"What's the bullshit percentage here? You know as well as I do that people tell you a lot of stuff in the confessional. Make up things to keep it interesting. You know what my favorite sin was? When I couldn't think of anything else to confess to? Not that I was ever all that hard up for sins. But my fall back was always 'I had impure thoughts about my friend Bobby's mother. Ten times, Father. Maybe more.' That always got me two Our Fathers and a dozen Hail Mary's."

The priest's braying laugh echoed through the small chapel, setting off a fit of a squealing from some unseen denizen of the bell tower above their heads. Bats. Or maybe some belfry loving rodent.

"The lad's mother, you say?" the priest replied in his heavy Irish brogue. "Yes, I think I have heard a version of that more than a time or two. A universal story, I dare say. Here in Latin America though the object of desire is more often their friend's sister. Mothers? *No está permitido.*"

Ray waited as the priest considered whatever it was he was considering.

"You want to know if what I tell you is really true. You know yourself, that more times than not there is always some truth to these stories. Especially the most scandalous ones."

The priest was right about there always being some kernel of truth. Over the years, the information the old Irishman had supplied him had been right more often than not. Ray had cultivated his relationship with him while posted in Guatemala City. The priest ran a free clinic that also served as clandestine gathering spot for what remained of the left-wing underground. He had been exiled once by Somoza in the mid-seventies, then again by the Sandinistas a decade later. He had only been allowed back into Nicaragua on the condition he abstain from agitating amongst the poor. Ortega himself had supposedly come to see him to make the point that the poor were the sole purview of the Sandinista Party.

"I can tell you this. There is still a great deal of bitterness in this country regarding the war. That is why you must be very careful about who you ask questions of. Granada is a small town. And I am not the only one with large ears."

"I'll take that under advisement. So what can you tell me about her?"

The priest didn't say anything for a moment before allowing himself a brief sigh. Ray wished the darkness wasn't concealing the old priest's face for he had never been an accomplished liar.

"I only know what everyone else does. She is dead. Forgotten."

"So why do I get the feeling there's something more you're not telling me?"

"That was what? Thirty years ago? Ancient history. The kind people like to forget. There are quite enough reminders of those times without resurrecting up the dead."

They both fell silent for a moment, the only sound the muted riff of music from the bodega.

"I better go," Ray said, pushing to his feet. He picked up his cane and reached for the priest's extended hand. It felt like a claw, cold and scabrous.

"Be careful. I am afraid no good can come of this," the priest said.

No good will come of this. Where had he heard that before? As he turned down the aisle, Ray glanced once more at the windows. One of the martyrs, a woman, had been bound to a tree and pierced with arrows. In his mind's eye, he flashed on the image of the painting in his cellar. Time to end this, he decided. Sonny or no Sonny.

No sooner had he stepped out into the humid night then he sensed the presence of the men waiting in the shadows on either side of the door. He braced himself, half-expecting what would come next. But instead of a blow, he felt his cane ripped from his grasp, and then someone grabbing his arms from behind.

"You come with us," the voice said.

"Who's us?"

"*Callate!*"

Ray turned to look at the speaker, a slim man dressed in black. Before he could react, one of his other assailants slung him against the wall. He felt a revolver pressed into his ribs. A second later, one of them slipped a rough sack cloth over Ray's head.

"*Vamos!*" someone said, grabbing him by the shirt.

The ride in the back of what he sensed was a windowless van took no more than perhaps ten minutes, the last five over what seemed an unpaved road, devoid of traffic or other noises. By the time they finally stopped, Ray was drenched in sweat. His head still cloaked, his captors hustled him along a graveled walkway and through a series of doors. They left him standing for perhaps a minute before roughly shoving him onto a chair. Only then did they remove the sack from his head.

He found himself in a small, eight by ten space that was

clad in cheap particle board and crudely painted a watery blue. A small ceiling fan ticked away, barely circulating the dank air that smelled of sweat, unwashed bodies and what Ray had always imagined was overworked adrenals. Something on the floor, a coiled bright green garden hose, caught his attention before he looked up at the two men standing in front of him. He recognized the older of the two as the guy in the Four Runner who had pissed beside the road. He looked to be about Ray's age, with a goatish head, long and sloping, and a smile that tugged at some memory. The smile vanished as quick as a cat's paw as he took the thin manila folder he had folded beneath one arm and tossed it onto a huge wooden cable spool that served as a table. His companion Ray recognized as the man who had abducted him at the church. He looked at Ray for a moment before taking up a position somewhere behind Ray.

"I am Colonel Jasique Blanco," the older man said, dropping his bulky frame onto the chair opposite Ray.

Ray searched his memory for the name but came up empty. Still, the head that looked like a coffin and the man's face seemed familiar.

"You are trying to remember, yes? Where you might know me from?" Blanco shrugged and fingered the file on the table before him. "You knew me by a different name back then. Come, Ramón," he said almost affectionately. "You can't have forgotten me so easily. But then, I was much younger. With more hair," he said, making a show of rubbing his hand across his balding head. He smiled again, reaching into his coat pocket and removing a thin cigarillo. He lit it with a Bic, puffing several times before looking back at Ray. He had the kind of face that one imagined at one time had been quite handsome, but now was lined and sagging with the gravity of a life most likely spent in serious pursuits.

"Would it help if I told you I was once on your payroll? *El confidente.* One of your most trusted informants." He offered up another smile from what Ray guessed was a large repertoire as varied as a vending machine.

"Yeah, I think I remember you now," Ray said, nodding. "One of the guys at the university. Wait. Give me a second. Benito, right? You always had some dirt to tell me about this one professor. Let's see, what was his name? Maximillian? Something like that."

"Máximo. Yes. You might be interested to know I personally shot him after the war. He played too many sides."

"Seems to me we all did," Ray said. "Okay if I smoke?" he asked, reaching into his shirt pocket. Blanco nodded and slid his Bic across the splintered table. "Your English is better," Ray said after he lit his cigarette.

"Tulane. Bachelors in Psychology. 1981."

Ray shook his head in amusement. It seemed like everyone they ran into down here had gone to school in the States. Aminta. Alemán. Even Granera. Now this guy.

"Psychology, huh? That must come in handy."

Blanco shrugged and opened the file folder and removed what looked like Ray's passport. There appeared to be nothing else in the file except for a blank sheet of paper.

"A new passport. A shame. I am sure it would be amusing to see where you have traveled lately." He paused to write something on the blank paper with a pencil retrieved from his shirt pocket. "Do you still work for your government?"

"Not in quite a while, but I'm sure you already know that. You see, I got tired of all the bullshit games. Same kinda bullshit games you're playing. No difference. Same tree, different monkeys. Let me ask you something, Benito…or Jasique or whatever you go by these days. Do you ever get tired of it? Parroting all that crap. The fucking party line. Take your Presidente Ortega. I figure he's just as full of shit as our guys."

Blanco laughed, and then glanced self-consciously over Ray's shoulder at his companion before looking back at Ray. "I remember you always had a mouth on you. *Boca grande.* Quick with the joke. I always thought it was your arrogance. But maybe it's just…how do you say? Façade? A disguise. For your fear, perhaps."

"Don't waste your Psych 101 bullshit on me, Blanco. Just tell me why I'm here."

Blanco started to reply but hesitated when someone tapped on the door. Blanco's companion hurried to answer it. He conferred for a few seconds with someone in the hallway before returning and handing Blanco what Ray could see were two passports.

"It seems your friends have at last arrived. Perhaps, now we can save some time and I can still see *mi esposa* for breakfast. Should we make that our objective, Ramón? I see my wife in the light of day and you get to leave here."

"Along with my friends?"

"Perhaps. It depends on what we discuss here." He picked up one of the passports and studied it. "But this one." He held the passport out to him, the pages splayed to show Harper's image. "I think we'll keep her a bit longer. Show her our hospitality, so to speak. She has no immigration stamp. That is curious, and for her not a good thing. We have very open borders. A simple tourist hasn't the need to sneak into my country. A drug smuggler. Or a spy. That is a different matter."

"Come on, Blanco. If Langley sent her, don't you think they would've at least supplied her with an immigration stamp?"

Blanco smiled."Of course, you are right. She's no spy. There must be another explanation. Maybe one that I should know about." He leaned back in the chair and looked at Ray quizzically. "Let me see. I have an ex-CIA agent. A woman who entered my country illegally, and…" He picked up Sonny's passport and made a show of studying it. "Your friend has not been to Latin America. At least not on this passport. Who is he?"

Sonny stared at Blanco for a long moment before replying. "Okay. She came in through Bluefields because she's on some State Department watch list. She's a journalist and they think she's subversive. She thought she'd get hassled later if they found out she was down here. "

Blanco hissed in derision. "And Senór Bass?" When Ray didn't reply, he leaned over and said, not unkindly, "Come, Ramón. You must know we have many informants. No different than you in those days." Blanco leaned back and glanced up at the fan. "It seems you and your friends have been asking about a certain person. A person of interest."

"Who might that be?"

"Stop with the foolish games. You know...."

"Games? Aminta was one of yours, Benito," Ray replied tightly. "Or do you sanctimonious revolutionary types forget that fast? I would've thought *La Revolución* needed martyrs. They're always helpful when you rewrite history."

Blanco scribbled something again on the paper before lifting his eyes to meet Ray's. "Why are you interested in her?"

"My friends and I are art lovers."

"Don't waste my time, my friend. Toying with me has consequences. You of all people should know that. You tell me the truth or..." He shrugged.

"Or what?"

"Your woman friend might have a problem. You see, no one has a record of her entering our country. She could be in Mexico. I hear that women disappear in Cancun all the time. She could disappear anywhere for that matter."

The two men held each other's gaze for a long moment before Ray spoke. "I knew Aminta. During the war. And I know all about what supposedly happened to her. Everyone says she's dead. But I've got reason to think she's not. I just want to know what happened to her."

Blanco smiled but only his mouth moved. "And Bass? What is his interest?" He held up his hand to stop Ray from replying. "Answer carefully, my friend. No more lies. Don't underestimate me. Let yourself imagine the... skills one must acquire to achieve my position." He nodded and smiled. "Enough lies."

Ray ground out his cigarette in the upturned jar lid that served as an ashtray. "My friend worked here during the war, too. With USAID. Small business development liaison. He wasn't one of ours."

Blanco puffed on his cigarillo a couple of times before saying anything. "Let me guess. He also knew Aminta. And Bass is not his real name." He shook his head in frustration. "His real name escapes me now." He slipped into silence as if he were unreeling some film clip in his mind. "Back then I heard things about her. Rumors about her and her American lover. She was a *machista*. She liked Americans. That's why no one trusted her."

"Listen, all we want to know is if she might still be alive."

"I can save you a great deal of time then. She is dead."

"You have proof?'

"Come. You know what happened to the people they murdered. There is no grave if that is what you are seeking. Do you not think it is strange that no one speaks of her? That there are no monuments or boulevards named after? I am sorry but all I can offer is my assurance. My word. What? You don't believe me?"

"It's hard believing people who make a living out of lying."

"I too, heard the stories of what happened to her," Blanco said quietly. "You think I did not interrogate certain people?" He regarded Ray silently for a moment. "You also ask about El Labio."

Ray looked at him, hoping his surprise was not obvious.

"Oh yes, the old priest. He talks too much, doesn't he? You should know better than to trust men like him."

"We're not interested in Granera."

Blanco nodded. "They say he killed her. But then who knows?"

Ray held to his silence.

Blanco leaned across the table. "I am not the only person who lies for a living, yes? So I have difficulty believing you when you say that you have no interest in finding our friend

Granera. I suspect you have reasons. Personal reasons."

Ray struggled to keep his face from revealing anything. How could Blanco know? He couldn't.

Blanco sat back in his chair. He seemed to be considering something for he fell silent for a moment. He finally looked up, his eyes fixed on Ray's. "He is an enemy of my country. Yet, there are reasons that my office does not interfere with him. Some practical. Some shall we say…diplomatic?" Blanco waved his hand in a gesture of uncertainty. "However, that does not mean that his fate is of no interest to my government. Or to me," he added.

They stared at each other for a long moment before Blanco tore off a piece of the paper he had been scribbling on, wrote something on it, and placed it on top of their stacked passports. "Aminta is dead. She disappeared like so many of our comrades. That's all you need to know, my friend. That is enough, yes? You are free to go," he said, pushing the passports across the rough hewn table top. "You have my permission to visit and enjoy my country. For several more days. No more. And don't worry, we have stamped the woman's passport. To facilitate her timely departure," he said, rising to his feet.

Ray scooped up their passports and Blanco's note. He glanced quickly at what Blanco had written and started towards the door. Blanco's sideman handed Ray back his cane. Ray turned and looked back at Blanco.

"Tell me something. Whose side were you really on back then? As I recall, you came to us because some Sandinista killed your father."

"Oh yes, that was true. He was killed by a Sandinista." He took a long pull on his cigarillo and exhaled out of the side of his mouth. "I just never told you that I was that Sandinista," he said, smiling. "Don't feel bad, my friend. *El fue un bastardo.* And an enemy of *La Revolución.*"

Ray started to walk off.

"One more thing, Ramón. I am curious. What will you tell

your friend? About Alemán? Yes, that old fool of a priest was very talkative. It's what keeps him in wine and whores. "

Ray turned and looked at him. "I guess you're not willing to tell me if what he told me was true or just some crap you wanted him to feed me."

Blanco shrugged and cocked his head in comic bemusement. "The truth is always difficult to know, is it not? Nevertheless, we should perhaps talk again. I think you will find we have mutual interests."

Ray looked at him for a moment before turning for the door. He passed through a crude anteroom that opened up to a yard enclosed with the familiar cinder block wall topped with razor wire and broken bottles. Sonny stood waiting at the gate, waiting in the yellow light coming from a bare spotlight suspended from the razor wire. In the dim light just beyond, the Four Runner stood idling, its doors flung open. Harper was nowhere to be seen.

"Where is she? Ray asked.

"She asked if she could use their facilities. I told her it wasn't that kind of place. She told me to go fuck myself, quote, unquote." Sonny smiled. "You have to admit she's ballsy. You should give her a chance."

"I already have." He turned and looked back at the door. "All in all, I'd say that went rather well," Ray replied. "You okay?"

"Peachy. I was sort of expecting rubber hoses and battery cables clipped to my nuts. So what's the deal?"

Ray handed Sonny the two passports. Ray fingered Blanco's note for a moment before slipping it into his shirt pocket.

"Granera's in Puerto Lempira. Goes by the name of Mireles now."

"I thought they were the ones supposed to be getting information out of us. What gives?"

"Let's say we traded information."

"So where's Puerto Lempira? Seems I've heard of it before."

182

"It's just across the border in Honduras. On the Rio Coco. Back in the eighties, our guys used it for a staging area for supplying the contras. Did you ever make it down to Ciudad del Este in Paraguay? The Triple Border? No? Well Puerto Lempira's the low rent version. I'm sure the Agency still has ears on the ground there. Middle of bumfuck nowhere and out of sight. Makes it a perfect stopover for the cartel boys. And probably the kind of place someone like Granera would likely go to ground."

"You trust the guy who told you this?"

"What's not to trust? Sure he could be playing us. I guess."

"You guess?"

"What I mean is I'm pretty sure he's got his own agenda. So what do you wanna do?"

Sonny looked away, muttering something under his breath. "Hell, I don't know anymore," he said finally. "I need some time to think about it."

"While you're thinking about it, I'm going back to Santa Fe. If you change your mind, you know where to find me."

"Fair enough. You really didn't have to come anyway. I mean, this has nothing to do with you."

Like hell it doesn't, Ray thought glancing over his shoulder at the waiting Four Runner.

"Anybody that you talked to know about Aminta?"

"No," he said, turning back. "Everyone says she died. End of story."

"What about Alemán?"

"What about him?"

"You find out anything else?"

He shifted his eyes for the briefest of instants and wondered if Sonny was still any good at reading faces. "Nothing more than what I already told you. Seems Alemán's what they call a *tercerista*. Hates Ortega, and is no friend of the opposition either. A third way advocate. Whatever that means these days. If you

183

recall there were lot of them back during the war. Didn't trust either side."

They turned at the sound of the door slamming and watched as Harper came walking towards them, pulling at her skirt. She had a faint smile on her face.

"The facilities were Four Star, I take it," Sonny said.

"I've seen worse. I just got a proposal for dinner from some Colonel. I told him I'd take a rain check. He said he fixed my passport. I guess he thought he deserved something in return." She sidled up against Sonny. "Guys, I have to say it's been an interesting evening. Now what?"

Ray looked at Sonny. He hoped he had the good sense not to mention Puerto Lempira. It was crazy enough bringing her this far.

"Seems someone just told us where to find Granera," Sonny said. "Only question is whether we're stupid enough to go looking for him." He started for the Four Runner.

Harper looked at Ray. "Is that right? You found Granera?"

"If you check your passport, you'll find you're legal now. I'd take advantage of that and go home."

"Not until Sonny tells me to."

"And I'll bet you've made it easy for him to keep you around."

"You're a shit, Ray."

"Listen to me. I just saved your ass from some jail time. You don't want to be in their jails. People still disappear in these places. They had you. No visa, no records." Ray stabbed his finger in her face. "So you owe me one."

Harper looked at him without saying anything.

Ray started to walk away, and then turned back. "Okay, Harper. If you really care about Sonny, then you take him away from all this. Make him forget. Fuck his brains out. Lie to him. Whatever it takes, just make him walk away."

He turned and made his way to the Four Runner. Make him forget. Just for a little while. A week maybe. All it would take. Just keep him out of the way.

He pulled himself into the back seat next to Sonny. He would have to think this through. He looked back at the darkened doorway of the crude building where they had been detained. It seemed clear enough what Blanco really wanted, he just couldn't come straight out and say it. Too many ears, he figured. And if he took Blanco up on it, he'd need help. There was only one person he could think of that might be able to help him. And to sign him on, he would have to pull in some favors. And some cash. In the end, it might be the only way he could get to Granera first.

24

PART FOUR
PUERTO LEMPIRA, HONDURAS
One Week Later

Harper plucked at her damp blouse and blew at the sweat trickling down between her breasts. The suffocating, late afternoon heat and humidity hung over everything like a wet blanket. Even the low hanging cloud cover offered little relief. She looked over at Sonny who lay sprawled in the spare grass at the edge of the landing strip, his head propped against his carry on, his face hidden by a baseball cap, the single word Cancun gilded across its bill. It was a landing strip not a runway had been their first argument of the day. It wasn't a runway, she had said. Runways were supposed to be paved.

She tilted back the bottle of lukewarm orange Fanta and looked in either direction at the deserted airstrip. It consisted of little more than a graded red dirt scar with the occasional outbuilding and a line of trees sketching its boundaries in gauzy green. Room size potholes, many still filled with muddy water from the last rain, pockmarked its length.

"I'm going to keep asking you, you know," she said, tossing the bottle into a nearby bush littered with several dozen identical bottles. When he didn't reply, she dropped down beside him. "There's still a flight later this evening to San Pedro de Sula.

186

This woman I met on the beach said the ruins at Copán were a must. She even gave me the name..."

"Hold it, Harper," he said, tilting his cap just enough to meet her eyes. "Didn't I tell you to stay in Cancun?"

"Yeah, you did. But you didn't give me any options. You know. The option of coming along. I would've thought by now you'd know women my age don't take orders very well. And they like options. Options and goddamn estrogen are what drive our decision making process."

"Shit. I told you already. Ray's here. And I just want to know what he found out."

"Yeah, and you had to track him down to find that out," she said, hiking up her skirt to her thighs. "What does that tell you? If Macy hadn't let us know, we'd still be in Cancun. Jesus," she said, allowing herself a smile, "I can't imagine the six kinds of hell Ray's going to catch when he gets back to Santa Fe."

"He would've told me in due time."

"Told you what? Sonny, none of this feels right. Let's just say Ray found him. Then what?"

Sonny pulled his cap down further and said nothing.

She hadn't been privy to their conversation, and she could only guess at the reasons Ray gave Sonny for not telling him where he was. She had her suspicions. What had Ray told her that last night in Granada? Make him forget. Keep him occupied. Is that what he had really meant? To keep him away? She felt at least a little guilt over the fact that she had done her best to do just that.

The two of them had hung around Granada another day, going through the motions of asking about Aminta, all the while dodging the obvious surveillance by the same three men who had taken them in the night from their hotel. Sensing Sonny's growing restlessness, she threw out the suggestion they fly to Cancun. To her surprise, he agreed with only minor resistance.

Once there, they played the scripted role of tourists. Mornings, they lounged on the beach and swam, retreating at lunch to drink beer and eat shrimp in the hotel bar. Afternoons, they spent in their over air conditioned hotel room, probing each other's sexual defenses. Sonny was a skilled lover but still his efforts seemed both dispassionate and almost desperate. At times it felt as if she was fulfilling some doomed prisoner's last request.

His post-coital banter on the balcony proved to be just as tenuous and unrevealing. He seemed honestly interested in her life, her background, her career. That and his keen knowledge of photography had sustained them for two nights. But by the third night, their conversation gave way to long silences punctuated by small talk that seemed carefully crafted to forestall any revelations on his part.

It wasn't until the fourth day, his tongue loosened by prodigious amounts of tequila, that he began regaling her with stories of his life as a bureaucrat in DC. That led to a handful of abbreviated travelogues and concluded with a protracted anecdote about being trapped in rush hour traffic in Lima during an earthquake. Yet in all these vignettes, he seemed like a bit character; off stage, distant , careful to stay concealed. He reminded her of a half completed, abandoned picture puzzle, the missing pieces providing the barest suggestion of the puzzle's intended likeness.

Sonny's lack of transparency only added to her growing irritation with herself. To her dismay, she realized she was doing Ray's bidding after all. She was keeping Sonny occupied. Keeping him away. From what and for how long was the question. And even though she felt she was making progress in forming some deeper connection with him, she found herself asking how long their awkward dance of seduction would last before one of them lost interest. There would be the usual hasty progression to the finale of promises to call, missed connections, and finally, the nostalgia brought on by an evening alone, a memory she would drag out like one might a favorite scarf you never remember to wear.

"Problem is you don't know yourself why we're here. Do

you?" she asked again, risking his irritation.

He lifted his ball cap, not in response to her question but at the sound of a vehicle approaching along the edge of the muddy runway.

"Shit," she muttered as a mud-dappled Jeep Cherokee lumbered up in front of them. The tinted window on the passenger side lowered revealing Ray's smiling visage.

"You kids been having fun in the sun?" he said, leaning over to open the door.

They grabbed their bags and flung them in the back and climbed in, Sonny in the front. The Jeep smelled of kerosene and over ripe fruit. Neither of them said anything as Ray accelerated and turned down a small dirt track leading away from the strip.

"So, like I told you on the phone," Ray said after a minute. "I wanted to do some recon. In case you changed your mind."

"I'm that predictable?" Sonny said with what seemed genuine curiosity.

"You know how I like to plan things. Be prepared. And I also figured we might need some help. I've got this Honduran guy with me. I know him from back in Santa Fe. Freddie. He knows people here. People we might need." When Sonny didn't say anything, he went on.

"This guy, Freddie's *Mara*. A gang banger. You've heard of Mara Salvatrucha, haven't you? Well, down here these guys are like the Elks or the Rotary. Every two bit village has a freaking chapter. They even have like this meeting hall. You should see it. It's like something out of a Tarantino movie."

"And we're supposed to trust these guys? Drug dealing gang bangers? I mean, what's to keep them from selling us out?"

Ray grinned and shook his head. "Honor among thieves, maybe. I don't know. Don't worry. Freddy's made his deal with the devil and he won't renege. Besides these guys have a hard on for Granera's people. Turns out they're sorta like competitors."

"So what's this place like?" Sonny asked.

"About what you'd expect. Peaceful little town on the surface, but turn over a rock and there's the usual bunch of *narcotraficantes* and lowlifes. Columbians and Mexicans mostly. Then there's the narcs passing themselves off as missionaries. You see a gringo and you have to figure he's either DEA or southern Baptist. And knowing those assholes, most likely both. I even heard a rumor that some Al-Qaeda types were hiding out here. Everybody's got the hairy eyeball. You know what I mean? No different than the old days. But if we keep our heads down, we'll be all right. But just in case," he said, popping open the glove compartment to reveal what looked to Harper as the butt of an automatic hidden beneath some papers and a carton of cigarettes.

"God, I already feel safer," she said.

Ray looked at her in the mirror and smirked, acknowledging her for the first time.

"You still having an intimate relationship with the porcelain?" he asked.

"I missed you, too Ray. I guess I should look at this as good background color for a story," she went on. "My editor will eat this up. Just promise me we're not going to get dragged into another midnight interrogation."

"So what have you found out?" Sonny asked.

"The name this guy Blanco gave me, Jaime Mireles? Managed to find out there's a business license registered in that name. Fiberglass panel assembly. Has a warehouse with a pier out on the lagoon. Lots of new security fences, round the clock guards, surveillance cameras. So far that's it. We've been watching but haven't seen anyone going in or out other than the guards and the occasional delivery van. No truckloads of fiberglass either. And no sight of him. At least not yet," Ray said, turning down a dirt road on the edge of town.

The road led through a series of overgrown pastures studded with cactus and the large, leafy trees that Sonny had called *guanacaste*. A few scrawny cattle foraged along the fence line, each with a desultory egret perched on their backs. The crude fence posts separating the road from the pasture sprouted what appeared to be new growths of small leafy branches. She remembered a similar fence she had slept beside once in Pakistan.

Ray slowed the Jeep and pulled onto another road that was narrower with deep ruts marking its path. A clearing opened up to reveal a low slung wooden building perched on short stilts. It resembled a surplus military barracks. On one end of the rusted tin roof, an outlandishly large satellite dish festooned with colored streamers perched like some freakish tropical bird. Through a clearing on the side of the structure, the flat gray expanse of the lagoon stretched to the equally gray horizon.

They pulled up beside a muddy pond in which a trio of young children were wading and slinging rocks at a pair of ducks. A man and a young woman nursing an infant sat in the shade of a nearby beach umbrella. Harper noticed the young man had his hand on a rifle propped against his chair. As Ray cut the ignition, the man released his grip and nodded his head. Behind him, another man appeared at the corner of the house. He cradled some kind of small machine gun loosely in his hands.

"I take it this isn't our hotel," she said.

"We're meeting Freddie here. He called and said he's got some new intel." Ray climbed out of the Jeep and gestured with his head for them to follow him. "Don't worry," he said, sensing Harper's hesitation. "They're just like this pack of feral dogs used to hang out in my neighborhood when I was a kid. After a while they'd recognize me. These guys, they know me now. And if you're with me, you're okay. Just remember you're in their yard."

A generator rumbled from somewhere in the woods, barely audible over the pounding rhythms coming from a lone speaker propped in the notch of a nearby tree. Harper vaguely recognized the song. Some female singer. Shakira, maybe.

"*¿Dónde es Freddie?*"

"*Atrás,*" the guy leaning against the corner said, gesturing with his head for them to follow. He led them around back to a muddy clearing beneath the canopy of a huge tree festooned with hundreds of grenade sized, purple-green fruit. Guava, Harper guessed. Beyond the trees, she could make out more of the lagoon and a short sweep of its coastline. Two men sat at a card table in the center of the clearing, drinking beer and playing cards. One of them, upon seeing them, looked up from his cards to watch them approach. His companion, his gaze still focused on his cards, said something that led the other man to drop his cards, pick up a large revolver from the table and walk inside the house.

The man that had remained seating looked up, his eyes taking in Sonny and then lingering on Harper. If it wasn't for the inviting and curious eyes, Harper would have found the man menacing. He seemed older than the others, fortyish maybe, but still had the youthful look of a neighborhood tough gracefully passing into middle age. A patch of white stubble on his shaved head further betrayed his age. His white sleeveless T-shirt revealed a well muscled torso covered in the requisite tattoos of the Virgin Mary and hearts bound in barbed wire. The insincere smile he offered Harper reminded her of an old high school boyfriend.

"¿Cómo está, amigo?" Ray said, dropping into one of the empty chairs. "My friends. Sonny and Harper. Freddie Ascensión."

Mucho gusto," Freddie said, reaching to shake Sonny's hand. He nodded at Harper.*"¿Cerveza?"* he said, reaching into the ice chest by his feet. He placed three bottles of Heineken on the table. "You wan something to eat? *¿Barbacoa?"*

Harper caught the smell of grilled meat coming from somewhere inside the house.

"Maybe later," Ray said. "Tell us first what you found out."

Freddie opened the bottles with the edge of a switch blade knife that lay next to a plate of limes and handed one to each of them. Harper rolled the bottle across her forehead and down her neck before taking a sip.

"Your guy, Mireles, he live in *apartamento* on top of the warehouse. They say he never leaves."

"Who says?"

"One of the guards. *El es un tío.* Uncle, yes? The uncle of one of these guys," he said, tilting his chin towards the house behind them. "He never sees him, this Mireles. The uncle, they only let him guard the gate. But he hears the other guards talk about this man. *Este viejo.* They say he *es* maybe... *loco. ¿Como se dice? Excéntrico?* They say he sleeps all day, awake all night." Freddie laughed. "The guards are like women. *Tienen miedos de él.¿Comprendes?"* he said, looking at Sonny. "They are afraid of him. They say he has the smile of the devil."

"So how do we get in?" Ray asked, taking a long draw of his beer.

"No problema. I cut a hole in the fence. In the back of warehouse there is a big tree. I cut the hole there. I wait. No alarms. No guards."

"You see anything that looked like surveillance cameras?"

Freddie shrugged. "No one come. They don't see *nada."*

"And say we get in," Ray said, picking some lime from the stubble on his chin. "There's got to be other guards besides the ones at the gate, right?"

"Mebbe. I think you only gotta worry about one guy. How you say in English? *Guardaespaldas?"*

"Bodyguard."

"Si. El es muy malo. Un asesino. He with this Mireles all the time. *Un Americano,* like you."

Ray considered this for a moment before saying anything. "That's it? Mireles is upstairs above the warehouse. He's got a bodyguard. Maybe some more guards, maybe not. Shit, Freddie. I told you before. I don't want to go in shooting."

Freddie looked at Ray slyly for a moment and nodded his head. *"Hokay.* You say we need better plan. No *problema."*

"You at least know what the bodyguard carries?"

Freddie shrugged. *"No se."*"

"Wait," Sonny said. "This is beginning to sound more and more like some kind of half-ass black ops thing. If he's here, I want to talk to him. For that I need him alive."

Ray didn't say anything but took a long swallow of his beer, his eyes never leaving Sonny's. Harper glanced at Freddie who had been absently carving something on the table with his switch blade. Now he looked up at Ray, a barely perceptible shift in his features flickering across his face. Freddie shifted his gaze appraisingly first at Sonny and then Harper.

"Why don't we talk about it later," Ray said, getting to his feet. "You say there's *barbacoa* inside? What do you say we go eat?"

"Maybe later," Sonny said.

Harper glanced up at Ray and shook her head. Ray hesitated as if expecting at least Freddie would follow him. He looked at Freddie for a moment and then turned toward the house.

Harper looked over at Freddie. "Are you really *Mara*...what is it? Salsa *trupa*?"

Sonny grinned and shook his head in amusement.

Freddie stared at her impassively."Mebbe you tell me. What you are. *La* DEA? Or CIA? Ramón says you are guys that will pay him to kill this man, Mireles, no? *¿Y qué?* You change your mine? Now you wan jus talk to this *pendejo?*"

Sonny and Harper looked at each other. "Maybe," he said, looking back at Ascensión."So tell me, Freddie. Where's this warehouse?"

Freddie looked toward the house. "You still pay me, yes?"

Sonny nodded. "Sure."

"Es by *la laguna.* Six, mebbe eight kilometers that way," he said, pointing with his chin. "You see *un signo* say Taverna Perro Rojo. You go right, then to end of the road. I tell you, *es*

not easy to go there and nobody see you. Much better we wait." Freddie looked up at the sky. "Pretty soon goin' to be dark. Then we go."

Sonny nodded, got to his feet and walked off a short ways before turning to look to see if Harper would follow him.

"It's too bad I don't have my camera, Freddie," Harper said, pushing her chair from the table. "Has anybody ever told you that you're very photogenic?" She smiled and walked over to join Sonny.

"Come on. Let's go," Sonny said, casually taking her by the arm and leading her to the side of the house. "I just remembered where I've seen Freddie before. Which knowing Ray, means they've got some kind of deal going on."

"Where are we going?"

"I noticed Ray left the keys in the ignition. And from what I can see the Jeep's the only vehicle here. I'm guessing if we go now, I'll have some time."

"Time for what?"

"I decided I'm going to go see Granera on my own."

"You really think that's such a good idea?"

"All I know is I don't want to do it Ray's way."

"What's he up to anyway? I saw the look on your face when Freddie said that thing about someone paying them to kill this Mireles…Granera. If that's who he really is."

"Like I said, Ray's playing his usual games. It's just how he operates. I just don't want to play."

"It's still crazy."

"You said you liked options. So here's the deal. Stay here or come along. I was just thinking I might need someone to call the cavalry if it comes to that."

"I'm not going to be able to talk you out of this, am I?"

"So are you coming or not?"

Harper glanced back at Freddie who was talking to someone on his cell phone, not paying them any heed. God, Ascensión would make a great subject for a lead in to a story, she thought. She already had the title. 'The Dark Underbelly of the Central American Diaspora.' What she wouldn't give for an afternoon here with her camera. Maybe later. If there was a later, she thought grimly. She looked at Sonny and shook her head.

"Let's go then."

Ray dropped the greasy rib onto his plate and cocked his head and listened. He wasn't sure what it was he was hearing. It almost sounded like the thump of a vehicle bottoming out on the rutted road. Maybe someone was coming, he thought. He grabbed his cane and walked over to the doorway to look.

"Goddammit!"

He slammed the cane against the wall as he watched the Jeep disappear through the trees. He hobbled as quickly as he could to the back door, brushing aside the two young women smoking in the kitchen.

"Freddie!" he yelled. "Where's the other *troca*?"

Freddie looked up at him, the cell phone still against his ear. *"Más tarde,"* he said into the phone before tossing the phone onto the table. "One of the girls take this morning. *¿Por qué?"*

"What did you tell Sonny?"

Ascensión shrugged and smiled. "Your friend say he want to talk to Mireles. So what? I tell them where he is. He don seemed worried. Why should you? We still kill him later. Your friend Sonny say he still pay."

Ray took his cell phone from his pocket and punched in a number. "Come on, come on. Pick up." He took a deep breath and glanced around him. They're gonna get themselves killed for sure. "Is there anybody around here you know with a car?" he asked Freddie. "We need to get to that warehouse."

Freddie nodded his head and smiled. "No car but something

mebbe better. Pepito," he yelled towards the house. "*Vamos!*
Prisa!' He looked back at Ray. "Pepito, he has boat. *Muy* better
than *un troca. ¿Si?*"

Ray turned his back and stared out at the lagoon, the phone on
his ear."Sonny. If you get this message call me back, you hear?
Don't do this." Ray paused and added, "I know. I should've told
you." He snapped the phone shut and looked at Freddie. "Alright. Get the boat. But hurry it up." He thought of something
else. "And I need another gun."

25

Sonny cut the headlights and slipped the Jeep into neutral, coasting around a slight curve in the road. He could just make out the warehouse enclosure through the thick trees, its silhouette framed by the thin hem of the dusk above the lagoon. He pulled off the road into the tree line and cut the ignition. The trilling of hundreds of insects momentarily filled the oppressive stillness. They sat there without speaking for perhaps a minute before Harper said something.

"What changed your mind? I mean last week you said you didn't care anymore."

"Last week was different. You were…" He shook his head.

"What? A nice diversion?"

"That's not what I was going to say." He felt her gaze and turned and looked at her. "He's fifty yards away and you think I'm not going to go ask him about her?"

She didn't say anything but instead turned to the window.

Sonny took the cell phone from his pants pocket and flipped it open to check it. Ray had left a message. "Looks like we get reception here. Ray's number is in here. If I'm not out of there in a couple of hours, you call him."

"And if I can't reach him?"

"You go find him." He reached into the glove compartment

and pulled out the automatic. He checked the clip and thought for a moment. "You ever used one of these?"

"Sonny," she said, grabbing his arm. "Don't do this. It can be over. You tell yourself enough times and it does get easier. I swear it does."

Does it? He thought back to the wrinkled prayer card he had paper clipped onto the last page of his passport. Straight as an arrow to the point of completion. Completion. The end of it. The death of the old German had shaken him, almost made him give it up. He had thought he was done. So what had changed? The painting is what had changed. The chance that part of his life had been based on a lie. And now he knew that it wasn't over. Not until he knew for sure.

"Take it." He handed her the gun. "You never know. You might need it. And I'm better off without it." He reached up and turned off the overhead dome light, and opened the door. He hesitated a moment before climbing out. "Tell me something, Harper. Have you ever seen something through your view finder, a shot you know you were just meant to take? Like it was something predetermined. You know, you're at this one place at this one exact moment. Light's just right. Composition's just right. You tell yourself that being here, at this moment, is just supposed to happen. You understand what I'm trying to say?" He leaned his head inside to look at her. "And if I'm supposed to be back here in two hours, then I'll be back."

"Sonny."

He strained to see her face in the darkness. He reached over, found her outstretched hand and held it for a moment before slipping out of the Jeep. He carefully closed the door and set out down the darkened road.

It took him a good fifteen minutes to find Freddie's hole in the fence. He waited in the darkness for several minutes, watching for a roaming guard or maybe dogs. Satisfied he hadn't been seen, he slipped through the hole and sprinted to the rear of the warehouse. Again he waited for several moments before making his way to a half open, dimly lit doorway. The entrance opened onto a stairwell illuminated by a single bank of flickering florescent lights at the next landing. He started to climb the stairs and then stopped in midstride, sensing too late that someone was behind him.

"Hold it right there."

Sonny felt the hard steel pressing against the back of his neck. He could smell the guy holding the gun. Sweat overlaid with a whiff of cheap cologne.

"Where's the woman?"

"I don't know what you're talking about." Sonny almost tripped as his unseen assailant shoved him against the wall, the gun barrel hard against his head.

"Don't fuck with me. Hands up and against the wall."

Southern accent. And jacked up on something Sonny guessed from the tension in his voice.

He carefully frisked Sonny, removing his passport and small roll of dollars. In the ensuing silence, Sonny sensed he was inspecting his passport.

"So who do we have here? Mr. Samuel Bass. You're the one that goes by Sonny, right? Goddammit, I told you face front. Yeah, I can guess what you're thinking, 'how does this guy know my name? And how do I know about your lady friend?" He took the gun from Sonny's neck. "Okay, you can turn around."

The man standing in front of him was short and well built, dressed in camouflage pants and a sweat stained, sleeveless black T-shirt. Not old, not young. Shaved head but with a ginger colored goatee. Sonny had a hard time deciding what was harder to look at. The barrel of the automatic staring him in the face or the man's misshapen nose. His eyes, cold, gray and close set, were the tie breaker.

"So you come to talk to him? You give up on the idea of doing him? How come?"When Sonny didn't reply, the man lowered the automatic a few inches and smiled. "I'm gonna find her. Mark my word. So here's the deal. You tell me where she is and you'll make it easier on both of you."

Sonny suddenly thought Ray should've known better than to trust Freddie.

"Yeah, you just figured it out, didn't you? Your man Freddie. He's a businessman, that guy. Knows when to look out for himself and make an extra buck. Afraid it's not gonna be as profitable for your friend Ray. So you gonna say something or not?" he said, leveling the gun in Sonny's face.

"I'm only talking to him. No one else."

The man cocked his arm as if he were going to hit Sonny with the gun, and then stopped himself.

"We'll see about that. Now get up there," he said, grabbing Sonny's arm and shoving him up the stairs.

At the top of the stairs was a heavy, reinforced metal door. The bodyguard grabbed Sonny by the shirt collar and jerked him to a halt, opened the door and pushed him inside. The first thing Sonny became aware of in the dim room was the mechanical chatter of a window air conditioning unit. Overlaying this noise was a throaty hiss, a sound like gas escaping. It came from somewhere in the center of the room. In the time it took for his eyes to adjust to the dim light coming from an adjoining room, he placed the sound. A nebulizer machine. His mother had been asthmatic and had used one several times a day for the last few years of her life. Whenever he would visit her, he would listen to her through the thin walls of her bedroom as she drew in the vapor that allowed her to carry on a conversation of more than six words.

At first, he could only make out a vague shape of someone sitting in a chair and the faint light coming from the nebulizer's control panel. As the seconds passed, the figure sitting there slowly came into focus.

"So, Slater. What have you brought me? One of my would be assassins, I assume."

Then he was suddenly there, his hand still on the lamp switch, the light jarringly bright. They looked at each other in silence for a long moment before Granera looked past Sonny to the bodyguard.

"You say there is a woman? Then bring her to me. It is always more interesting to bargain with women. Go on. He will not be giving me any trouble," Granera said, placing his right hand on a small chrome plated revolver that sat atop what appeared to be a large metal chest of some sort. A cluster of small brown bottles, medicines from the appearance of the labels, had been placed in a careful row on the box's edge. The room held the smell of unwashed linen and something medicinal.

Slater pushed Sonny down onto a chair, and then produced a roll of duct tape which he used to bind Sonny's hands and feet to the chair. When he was done, he handed Sonny's passport to Granera and hurried out. Granera picked up a thin green loop of oxygen tubing from his lap and looped it over his face, meticulously affixing the prongs to his nostrils.

He looked frail, ravaged, yet there remained a vestige of the almost benign menace Sonny remembered. The corrupt cruelty of his mouth, a lifetime of it seemed etched there. He wore his gray hair long and tied in a knot at the crown of his head. The sunken cheeks and several days growth of beard made him appear even more sclerotic. One of his eyelids appeared to droop. He wore a pair of threadbare, piss colored silk pajamas that looked badly in need of a washing.

"Do I know you…Señor, Bass?" he asked, examining the passport in the light of the lamp. "I've been told you have come here to kill me. You will have to excuse me if I am not impressed. I have made more enemies in my life than I can remember."

"You really don't remember me? How about Aminta Garza Segovia? You remember her, don't you?"

Granera's eyes seemed to slip out of focus, his eyelids fluttering as if he were about to faint. He opened his eyes and looked off to the side before turning his gaze back at Sonny. He smiled and nodded.

"Ah, yes. So it is you. The American. From Madrid? You

have finally come." Granera pushed himself from the chair, gun in hand, and tottered over to Sonny's chair. He pointed the revolver at Sonny's chest and leaned forward to study him, his face so close that Sonny could see the fine mist of droplets left by the nebulizer's vapor on Granera's thin beard.

"I had given up on seeing you again. But here you are. You look different." He glanced down at Sonny's hand where he was missing the finger, before backing away, almost stumbling before he dropped back in his chair. "I remember now. You and your friend. The CIA errand boy. I forget his name. You must excuse my memory. As you can see, I'm not well. But Aminta I remember well. How could I forget someone as beautiful as her? *Ella fue una fruta muy deliciosa.*"

Sonny suddenly felt foolish. He should've listened to Ray. Let Ray take care of him.

"You're the same old evil shit you've always been."

Granera smiled. "Yes. Someone like me cannot change. I cannot ignore my appetites. Or my abilities. I realized long ago to accept who I am. And what I am. There is no reason to struggle against one's own nature, is there? Especially now that I have such little time. So I enjoy my few simple pleasures. The occasional woman. Rum and a good whore can almost make me forget my circumstance. There is a saying in my country. You may buy the nights, but never the mornings. Sadly enough, there are no more mornings."

He reached down beside him and retrieved a bottle of brown liquor and a small tumbler. He poured himself a drink and tilted the glass to Sonny in a salute before downing it in one swallow. "I am sorry I don't have another glass or I would offer you a final drink. A toast to Aminta perhaps. But then your hands are not free." He seemed to stare again at Sonny's hand. "She was as stubborn as she was beautiful, was she not? A worthy trophy," he said, his voice empty of intonation. He dragged up some phlegm and coughed into his sleeve. For a moment, he struggled to catch his breath, gasping like a fish out of water.

"I just want to know what happened to her," Sonny said. "If

she's really dead."

Granera glanced up at Sonny, the hardness seeming to have left his eyes. "It has been a long time, my friend. What is the point? If she is dead…" He shrugged. "And if she is alive, she has long ago forgotten you." He smiled. "I can assure you of that. It would be best if you released yourself from your vanity."

"I hope your death is unpleasant."

Granera closed his eyes, his forehead wrinkled as if in deep contemplation. "You are a very stupid man," he said, finally. He poured himself another drink and looked at Sonny. "It was not me who killed her." He began to cough convulsively, spilling his drink. "He did," he whispered after catching his breath. "Your friend. He killed her."

Sonny stared at Granera, the old man's words washing over him, past him. It took a moment before the meaning of what he had said began to register.

"What do you mean my friend killed her?"

Granera smiled weakly. "Ah, it delights me that you do not know this. I had always hoped I would be the one to inform you of this one thing. How does it feel to know your bitterness has been misplaced? *Es muy cómico. ¿Si?*"

"You're lying."

Granera pushed himself to his feet and shuffled over and leaned down to look in Sonny's eyes.

"Am I? It will be amusing to watch you ask him. If things go as planned, he will join us very soon."

Sonny looked away, not wanting Granera to see what his face undoubtedly revealed. The sudden awareness of what Granera was intimating filled him with an overpowering sense of loss that quickly turned into a white hot knot in his chest. Now he understood Ray's initial reticence to look for Granera. And why he had meant to kill him before Sonny could find him. He felt utterly deflated, suffocated by the realization that the engine that had driven most of his life had been false. The decades of enmity built on a deception. He looked at Granera.

"I've changed my mind. I would like to kill you."

Granera smashed the revolver against Sonny's face. It was a feeble effort but still held enough rage to bloody Sonny's lip. Granera reached for a strip of duct tape Slater had left on the back of the chair.

"Enough of your talk," he said, pressing the tape over Sonny's mouth. He stood over him a moment before stumbling back to his chair. "Perhaps later," he said, obviously out of breath. "When you have more things to say."

He pushed the prongs of the nasal cannula back into his nostrils and sat there with his eyes closed for a moment before reaching for one of the medicine bottles. He twisted off the cap and took a long swallow.

"It seems your woman has arrived," he said, his attention suddenly attracted by something behind Sonny. "We will see if she proves to be as entertaining as Aminta."

Sonny twisted his head to see what Granera was looking at. A television monitor on the wall beside the door displayed a grainy image of a brightly lit room. In the center of the room, Slater leaned over a kneeling Harper. He grasped a handful of her hair with his one hand, in the other he held a coil of what appeared to be thin rope.

"What is the word? Déjà vu? Does it not seem so?" Granera smiled and reached for a different medicine bottle. "The one wonderful thing about being old. The memories. They are like a fine wine. They must be savored, yes?"

26

Ray cursed as he tried to stretch out his bad leg in the small boat. A pile of fishing net and some extra gas cans allowed him little room to maneuver, forcing him to finally drape his leg over the side. He cursed again when the wash from Freddie's paddle sloshed over his shoe. The three of them, Ray, Freddie and Pepito, had waited until just after dark to set out across the lagoon to Granera's warehouse. Freddie had assured Ray that the element of surprise would negate the need for more manpower other than Pepito, a scrawny young man who looked barely out of adolescence. The oversized T-shirt and baggy shorts he wore made him appear even more benign and childlike.

To conceal their approach, Pepito had cut the outboard motor a hundred or so yards from shore, and now he and Freddie were paddling the skiff towards the lights that marked the warehouse. The darkness and low cloud cover made it difficult to make out the shoreline. The only sound was that of the muted slap of the paddles and the occasional fish breaching the calm water. The small boat smelled of fish and stagnant water, the odor made worse by the lack of any breeze.

Ray had tried calling Sonny's cell phone several more times, each time leaving a message more desperate than the last. With each passing minute, his mood was more one of regret for ever coming here. The money Blanco had offered him, the chance of revenge against Granera - none of it meant anything if something happened to Sonny. It was stupid of him to think it would be easy or risk free. Maybe if Sonny hadn't shown up. And if he would've had the time to devise some kind of plan. Instead, he was about to stir up who knew what kind of trouble, stumbling headfirst into a situation he knew nothing about with only a couple of unpredictable gangbangers for backup. He thought of Macy and Sadie and wondered at what misguided vanity led him to risk losing them.

He could now make out a low dock protruding out into the lagoon a short distance in front of them. To his surprise, it was unlit. Freddie and Pepito stopped paddling, allowing the boat to drift slowly towards the pier. What appeared to be a small cabin cruiser sat docked on the other side, the silhouette of its flying bridge barely visible against the sky.

"You're sure there aren't any guards here?" Ray asked, softly.

Freddie didn't reply but instead rose to his knees to brace himself as he grabbed hold of the edge of the dock. In the faint light coming from the warehouse Ray could see Pepito had already leaped onto the pier and had started securing the boat to the dock.

"No guards," Freddie said matter of factly.

"How can you be sure?"

Freddie looked at him, his face concealed in the darkness.

"Remember, what I told you, Freddie. No shooting unless we have to. You brought me a gun, didn't you?"

Freddie seemed to hesitate a moment before reaching down into the boat and picking something up. Ray could see that Freddie had picked up what looked like a Mac-10 and was casually pointing it in his direction. He still couldn't make out Freddie's face.

"Shit," Ray muttered. The sudden realization made his stomach roll.

"Lo siento mucho, amigo. Es business. They pay me lot of

money. And I need money. *Por mi familia.* To start again. *¿Comprendes?"* he said, pulling himself up onto the dock."Come now. We get this thing done. *Es mejor."*

Ray wondered if he could knock the machine gun from Freddie's hand with his cane. Freddie must have read his mind for he backed away from the edge of the pier. Ray looked over at Pepito. Even in the dim light he could see Pepito had pulled a large pistol from his waistband and was pointing it at him.

"How much money you want?" Ray asked, tossing his cane onto the dock.

Freddie kicked the cane into the water and gestured with the MAC-10 for Ray to get out of the boat.

"Besa mi culo, Freddie."

"Your knife. You have?"

Ray shook his head.

"Muy bien. Hokay. Vamos."

Ray pulled himself onto the dock and started towards the warehouse, the two Hondurans on either side of him. As they approached, a lone figure appeared in the half lit doorway. The man was dressed like a weekend warrior in camouflage pants and a black T-shirt. He held a large automatic loosely in his one hand.

"You're late," the man said.

Freddie grunted and nudged Ray toward the doorway.

"So, Freddie. Is this the guy you said was a pussy?" Ray said. "About the only thing you weren't lying about. He's ugly, too."

"I think I'm going to enjoy doing you," the man said, smiling. He looked past Ray at Freddie. "You and your little bitch can get lost."

"You owe me money," Freddie said.

The man pointed his gun at Freddie. "I told you. You'll get your money when I feel like it. So, get lost." He looked at

Ray and smiled. "Goddamn beaners. Always got their hands out for more dinero. Okay," he said, motioning to Ray with his gun."Upstairs."

Ray turned and glanced at Freddie who quickly looked away.

"So you're his bodyguard? Let me guess," Ray said stepping into the doorway. "Ex-jarhead, right? And you figure this is a lot easier than getting shot at by the mujuhideen. I used to know plenty of your kind. On the other hand, maybe you're just some white bone cracker too dumb to sack groceries."

Ray collapsed in pain as the man kicked Ray's bad leg out from under him.

"You mother fucker!"

"Get up, shit-head, before I put one in your ass." He grabbed Ray by the arm and shoved him towards the stairs. "Your buddy's waiting for you. And if you're wondering about your lady friend. The mocha gal. She's waitin' for me. Yeah, she can't wait to see old Slater again."

Ray cursed under his breath as he struggled up the stairs, his one leg almost useless. The door at the top of the stairwell was slightly ajar. Slater pushed him through it. Ray stumbled forward, his gaze on the floor, not wanting to see, not wanting to remember the images that scrolled through his mind.

"Ah, finally. Our guests are all present," Granera said.

Ray looked up at the figure standing before him. He recognized the voice, but still it took some effort to assimilate the frail old man leaning on the walker with the memory of the man he had last seen in that dingy prison hallway thirty years ago.

"It has been a long time, my friend. But I must tell you, Ramón. That is your name, yes? You have become fat and old. And very stupid."

Ray looked over at Sonny who sat slumped over in a chair, his hands and feet bound with tape. His mouth had also been taped, but thin stream of blood and mucus dripped from his nose.

"Sonny."

Sonny seemed to lift his gaze slightly, but otherwise offered no other acknowledgment. Ray glanced around the room, but saw no sign of Harper.

"In the chair," Slater said.

Ray slumped down into the chair, too dejected to resist. Slater began taping Ray's hands to the arms of the chair.

"I have just told your friend how you shot Aminta. He seems...how shall we say? Disappointed? His friend killed the woman he loved. Is amusing, yes? Your secret is no more. And this time you will not be able to bargain for your friend's life." Granera sat back into his chair, whipping his oxygen tubing to the side. "On second thought, perhaps I should make you an offer. Maybe you kill the woman, and I let your friend go. Something you know how to do. ¿*Qué*? That is not a generous offer?"

Granera poured himself a drink from a bottle of brown liquor he had retrieved from the floor beside his feet. He took a swallow, spilling a good part of it on the front of his pajamas. He closed his eyes for a moment, his head dropping momentarily onto his chest.

"It darkens the soul, doesn't it? The knowledge that you are about to die."

Granera slowly pulled himself back to his feet and shuffled his way over to Sonny. With the barrel of the gun, he lifted Sonny's chin up so he could look in his face. "Because of you, Aminta denied me. You understand?" He pressed the barrel hard against Sonny's cheek."Only one thing makes your death more sweet, my friend." He started to laugh but quickly ran out of air, forcing a fit of coughing. "I must tell you this," he said finally, his voice barely a whisper. "The truth. She is not dead. And, I am sorry to tell you, you will never see her."

Ray could see Sonny was shaking with rage.

"You see your friend did not kill her. His bullet merely... How do you say? Grazed her? I did not let her die. Or perhaps she refused to die. Although I would have thought she would very much wish for death. After what my men did to her. After what I did to her. Oh yes. Now you wish to kill me. Yes? I see it in your eyes."

Granera turned and reached for his walker, almost stumbling in the effort. Once he had found it, he stood there breathing heavily before dropping back into his chair. Sonny shot Ray a quick glance, meeting his eyes for the first time. There was not so much rage in his eyes as confusion.

"I kept her alive out of my affection for her. Yes. Affection for what had been a possibility. You of all people should understand," he said, turning to Sonny. "And yes, I hoped she would prove useful when things ended. *¿Como se dice?* A bargaining chip? It was unfortunate that when the time came, no one cared. Not her Sandinista comrades. Not her family. She was already dead to them. *Muy desgraciado, si?"*

Granera lifted his eyes to the ceiling for a long moment as if lost in thought. Ray took the opportunity to look around the room, searching for anything that might be useful as a weapon. A heavy alabaster lamp sat on an end table several feet to Granera's right. He noticed that the window air conditioner had a good four feet of electrical cord. The room behind Granera looked like it might be a kitchen. Plenty of things there, he thought. Not that any of it would be of any help unless he could free himself.

"I was not sure what to do with her. Kill her? Leave her for the communista Ortega and his criminals to find her? Every day it became more dangerous to stay. But then I find out something." He spread his hands theatrically."The old woman whom I had entrusted to keep Aminta alive. She tells me. Aminta *es embarazada.* Yes. Pregnant. Aminta knew this also. *Es* like *un telenova.* Yes? "

Sonny cried as if he were in pain. Granera started to laugh but instead began coughing for what seemed a minute before he was able to stop. He panted as he looked at Sonny. When he finally caught his breath, he offered up a thin smile. "I have always wondered whose child it was."

Ray suddenly remembered what the old priest in Granada had told him. About the rumors of Granera having a son.

"There were so many guards."

"I'll kill you," Ray shouted. "You're dead!"

Slater grabbed Ray by the hair and quickly stuffed a rag into his mouth. Granera turned his eyes back to Sonny who had slumped forward in his chair.

"I imagine there is always the possibility the child is mine. Who knows? Do you suppose it is possible you are the father of this boy? Yes, she bore a son. I heard later it was a very difficult labor." He laughed without really making any sound.

"And now you die knowing this. My revenge... *es* absolute." Granera glanced up at Slater." They are yours now. *¿Comprendes?* I am finished with them." He waved his hand in dismissal and reached again for his drink.

"You betcha your sweet ass they're mine," Slater said as he cut Sonny loose from the chair. He just as quickly grasped Sonny's hands and retaped them behind his back. As he pulled Sonny from the room, Sonny looked down at Ray and shook his head in what? Resignation? Defiance? Ray wasn't sure.

Granera waited until they were gone before leaning forward in his chair. "I tell you something else. I know who sent you here. *¿Ese bastardo Blanco, si?* If it were not for that little *pinche* Honduran friend of yours, you might have succeeded. Blanco has interfered with me too many times. Denied me what is mine. He will pay. In time. But now, it is your time."

Ray looked back at Granera. He felt suffocated, as much by his emotions as the rag in his mouth. Granera gazed back at him with a look as impenetrable as if he were blind. In the minutes it took for Slater to return, Ray never took his eyes off Granera, focusing his rage, as if the strength of his will could kill the adversary sitting across from him. His fury made him feel oddly disconnected. Almost as if he were observing this was occurring to someone else. He hardly felt his hands being taped behind his back, the pain in his leg as he was dragged roughly to his feet. He caught one final glimpse of Granera as Slater shoved him through the doorway. It would be the last image he would have of the demon that had haunted him for so long.

27

Harper slumped to her knees, too exhausted to stand any longer. Standing had at least relieved the tension on the rope that bound her hands to the length of rebar mounted in the ceiling above her. Now the hard, uneven stone floor and the thin rope biting into her wrists forced her to reconsider. But she feared that if she stood up again, she would faint. The stifling heat and oppressive odor of mildew in the small, windowless cell had already made it difficult for her to stay alert.

The pain in her knees and hands at least momentarily heightened her senses enough for her to reassess her situation. It had taken a while for her eyes to adjust to the dim light, the only illumination a rhomboid of pallid light leaking through a crude grated window at the bottom of the wooden door. The room was empty except for a pair of wooden chairs she had seen when the man who had abducted her had briefly turned on the large overhead light so he could tie the rope to the rebar. In that brief moment of terror she had also seen what looked like a small surveillance camera mounted in the corner of the ceiling next to the door.

For perhaps the twentieth time, she gave the rope a hopeful but unsuccessful tug in the hope it might give. She shook her head in frustration. She should've shot the bastard as soon as he appeared at the Jeep's window. He had surprised her, and for an instant she had mistaken his smile as one of benevolence. Her hesitation had allowed him to reach in and grab her wrist. And now here she was, confident her situation would not end well. Her assailant had in fact promised her as much as he looped the rope over the rebar and jerked it tight. She clung to the faint hope that Sonny's absence might mean he still was out there somewhere. That or perhaps Ray and Freddie might show up to rescue her.

No longer able to stand the pain in her knees, she rose to a squatting position and realized it allowed just enough slack in the rope to regain some circulation in her wrists. She glanced up at the ceiling above her and immediately gagged on a clot of blood dislodged from her nose. He had slapped her hard, not once, but twice. Once when he dragged her from the Jeep and again after he had secured the rope to the rebar. She had kicked at him, her feckless attempt earning a laugh and a promise that he would return soon so the two of them could get acquainted. Slater he had called himself. She and Slater were going to have some fun, he had said before slamming the door and leaving her in the darkness.

She fought the urge to vomit as she struggled back onto her feet. Wiping her mouth on her sleeve, she tried to guess how long she had been here. An hour maybe. Maybe less. She started to tug at the rope again when she heard someone approaching the door. A second later, she heard the bolt being thrown open. The door swung open and the cell was suddenly bathed in harsh light. Sonny stumbled through the doorway, his hands and mouth bound with duct tape, the man who called himself Slater behind him. Sonny looked at her, his eyes revealing some emotion she couldn't readily decipher.

"I imagine the two of you have lots to talk about," Slater said, ripping the tape off Sonny's mouth. "But don't take too long on the farewells 'cause I'll be back real soon," he said, slamming the door behind him and sliding the bolt.

Harper saw that Sonny's lip was swollen and bloody and there was a red welt on his left cheek just below his scar. Sonny started to say something, but instead looked around the small chamber.

"Too bad if you're waiting for me to come up with one of those snarky one liners they use in the movies," she said after a moment.

"Help me here," Sonny replied, still looking around the room. "You see anything sharp? Have to cut this tape."

He looked up at the surveillance camera mounted in the corner of the ceiling, then dropped his gaze back down at the two wooden chairs. He kicked one of them onto its side and leaned over to examine the bottom.

"They're going to kill us, aren't they?" Harper asked.

He brought his foot down hard on one of the chair legs. He looked at her. "I'm sorry, Harper. I should've never let you come," he said, stomping on the chair, fracturing one of the legs supports.

"If you remember you never gave me the option. Come or leave. It would've been that simple." No, it wouldn't have. It was beyond that now.

He looked at her again, and then dropped to his knees, his back to the broken chair. She could see he was trying to cut the tape with the splintered end of the wooden dowel.

"Sonny. I wish...God. I can't believe this." She fought to hold back the tears.

Sonny leaned back, forcing the dowel between his wrists. With each effort, the chair kept sliding away.

"Not gonna work," he muttered, struggling to his feet. "Think you can bite through this tape?"

"Are you serious?" she asked, laughing through her tears.

Before Sonny could reply they heard someone opening the door again. Slater stepped through the doorway, dragging Ray behind him. He shoved Ray onto his back, then reached down and removed the gag from Ray's mouth.

"Talk amongst yourselves, assholes," Slater said, grinning.

"I'll be back in no time at all. And then we're all going on a boat ride." He whistled something as he walked out the door, locking it behind him.

Sonny and Ray looked at each other.

"I should've told you," Ray said.

"Yeah, well, doesn't seem to matter much now, does it?" Sonny glanced up at the surveillance camera. "Got any of those well thought out plans of yours?"

"No, I don't. I think we're fucked." Ray craned his neck to look over at Harper, then back at Sonny. "I should've told you two to stay away. Let me deal with it."

"You're imagining some other outcome?"

"Maybe not," Ray said struggling to a seated position. "But I bet I would've put the hurt on at least one of these sorry bastards." He shifted his body, his bound hands beneath him. "We still have some time between here and the boat. And maybe even later." He started rubbing his wrists against something on the rough concrete floor.

Sonny looked over at Harper. "Let me see if I can get to your hands," he said. "You have to get down as low as you can."

She eased herself down, grimacing at the pain in her wrists. She could smell him behind her, the musty pheromones seeping through his clothes. She turned and placed her head against his stomach. They both stood there like this for a long moment before he slowly turned his back to her.

"I need to get to your hands, Harper. Give 'em to me. Please."

She placed her hands in his, both their fingers desperately seeking anchor. And then he began working at the knot with one finger.

"Sonny…"

"Knot's too tight." He turned and looked at her and smiled more with his eyes than his mouth. "I need to say something. And there might not be time later. This past week…I started to remember who I used to be. You made me remember. I'm grateful for that. And I'm sorry if that's not worth much to you. But it's all I've got."He glanced at the surveillance camera before looking back at her. "I never should've looked you up in New York. All this wouldn't have happened. I'm sorry."

She looked away, not wanting to see his eyes. "Come on, Sonny. I thought you were into kharma. That stuff that happened in Sudan. All this…" She looked around the cell. "You sure had me convinced. It's all kharma." She looked back at him. "Things happen. Sometimes for a reason."

"You'd think so, wouldn't you? Doesn't always make those reasons right though."

He turned toward the door and a moment later Harper heard the door bolt slide open. Slater stepped inside wearing a grin on his face and holding a fishnet diving bag that appeared to contain a bottle of liquor and a box of Ritz crackers. A large hunting knife hung from a sheath on his belt.

"Talky time's over. Time to party." He glanced down at Ray. He pulled his leg back as if he were about to kick Ray. In that instant of hesitation, Harper saw a figure appear in the doorway behind Slater. The deafening sound of the gunshot reverberated on the bare concrete walls. She saw the muzzle flash of a second shot, and then watched as Slater in almost slow motion, pitched forward, his head twisted to the side, his face distorted.

Harper looked at the figure in the doorway. If it wasn't for the size of the revolver extended out in front of him, the shooter looked like some kid pointing a cap gun. The sideways L.A. Laker's cap and baggy shorts made him appear almost comical.

He said something to Ray that Harper couldn't make out over the ringing in her ears. She heard also what sounded like Sonny yelling something. Ray scuttled away from Slater's body and the widening pool of blood coming from the bodyguard's head. She could now barely make out some of what Ray was saying. Something about Freddie. It sounded like *Donde* Freddie?

The kid looked down at Ray as he shoved the revolver into his waistband. He produced a switchblade from his pocket and leaned down and proceeded to cut the duct tape from Ray's wrist.

"Goddammit! *Cuidado*! You cut my goddamn hand, you little asshole!" Ray pulled his hands free and held up a bloody hand to show the boy who merely shrugged and looked over at Sonny who had already turned his back to offer his bound hands to the boy.

"Who is this guy?" Sonny asked Ray who had stumbled backwards and was struggling to get up onto his knees.

"Freddie's sidekick. Name's Pepito. *El sicario, si?*"

Pepito deftly cut Sonny's tape, this time without drawing blood and then walked over to Harper and began slicing away at the rope above her head. Once freed, Harper dropped her arms to her waist, too weak to extend her hands. Pepito took his time working at the knots that bound her wrists. He said something over his shoulder to Ray in Spanish, and gestured with his head to something above them.

"What'd he say about Freddie?" she heard Sonny ask Ray

"Seems Freddie changed his mind. Least that's what Pepito here's saying. He's up there. With Granera," Ray replied, wrapping the discarded gag around his bleeding hand.

"Why?" Sonny asked louder than was necessary.

Ray looked up at him. "Why do you think? Gonna waste his ass, most likely."

Sonny started for the door. Harper hesitated a second and went after him.

"It doesn't matter, Sonny," she yelled as he started up the stairs.

"The hell it doesn't," he said, without turning.

She ran after him. They both reached the first landing when she heard what sounded like a muffled gunshot from somewhere above. She saw Sonny pause for an instant, then hurl himself up the stairs. By the time she reached the top of the stairs, Sonny had disappeared into the open doorway. She struggled to catch her breath as she glanced through the partially open door. Over

Sonny's shoulder she saw Freddie, his arm extended toward Sonny, a revolver pointed at him. Freddie shifted his eyes to Harper, smiled and lowered the gun.

Harper stepped inside the room and stood beside Sonny. It was only then that she saw the old man sitting slumped over in the chair; his head thrown back, his eyes wide open and empty. His chest was heaving as he gasped for breath. His one hand clutched the widening stain of blood on the front of his pajamas.

"You have money for me, yes?" Freddie said to Sonny.

Sonny leaned over the chair and stared at Granera. The old man shuddered and expelled a final guttural sigh. In the silence that followed, the only sound was the soft hiss of the oxygen tubing bubbling through the bloody mess of the old man's chest.

"God. Why did you have to shoot him?" Sonny asked, shaking his head.

"He was goin to shoot me. But I shoot him first," Freddie said. "*Es* what you want, yes? What you pay me to do. *¿Donde es Ramón?* He *hokay?*"

Sonny looked up at him and nodded. "Yeah, he's okay. And you can ask that bastard to pay you your damn money."

"I bet this *pendejo* have some money here," Freddie said, reaching for the metal box next to Granera's chair.

"*Momentito,*" Sonny said, kneeling beside the box and prying the lid open. "I at least get to have a look."

The box was more like a small trunk. Harper watched Sonny lift a tray off the top that held a dozen or so neatly wrapped piles of what looked like U.S. currency. He handed the tray to Freddie before removing the next one. It held an assortment of medicine bottles and several Spanish language paperbacks. He dropped it on the floor beside him and looked back into the trunk. He stared at something inside, his open hands suspended above the open box. Harper moved up behind him and looked over his shoulder.

Resting inside the tray was a carefully folded royal blue military tunic of some kind. The left breast displayed an array of ribbons and medals. Sonny knelt there motionless. She could only assume he might be reliving some memory. After a moment, he pulled out the uniform and tossed it roughly aside.

Sonny rifled through the underlying layer of starched, neatly folded white shirts, and then paused, his attention caught by something on the bottom of the chest. A brown manila envelope. He picked it up, opened the clasp and let the contents slide out into his hand. Several folded pieces of paper fell out, along with what appeared to be a small piece of cardboard. Sonny held the cardboard up to the light. Harper could see then that it was a mounted, black and white photograph of something. Sonny stared at it for a moment before turning it over. Something was scrawled on the back in heavy blue ink. He raised his head as if in thought, then reached down and picked up one of the medicine bottles from the floor beside him. He stared at the label a moment and then shook his head.

"What is it?" she asked.

He handed her the bottle. She tilted it to the light of the floor lamp and squinted at the writing on the label. There were some instructions written in Spanish followed by the name of a doctor.

She looked at him, her mind reeling as she tried to make sense of it.

He handed her the photograph. It showed the image of a boy of eight or ten standing in a cobblestoned courtyard. Above his right shoulder was what appeared to be a small bell tower and behind him a whitewashed building, a chapel or small church from the looks of it. Something about the boy's face seemed vaguely familiar. Harper turned it over. A date scrawled in thin blue ink. 1988. And a single word. Berto.

Sonny stood and glanced at Freddie who emerged from one of the backrooms with what looked like an entire stereo sound system tucked under one arm.

"*Gracias, amigo,*" Sonny said, plucking the photograph from her hand. "Take what you want. And then burn this place down." He started to turn away, but instead reached down and picked up one of the medicine bottles and slipped it into his pocket. He looked down at Granera one last time.

"Do you understand what's going on?" Harper asked.

"No, but I plan on finding out," he said and walked out the door.

She looked back at Freddie who was busy rifling through the drawers of a night stand.

"Thanks," she said. He looked up and shrugged. She started to walk away when she noticed the thin sheaf of papers on the floor. They had fallen out of the same envelope that held the photograph. She picked them up and studied the first one, then quickly glanced at the rest of them. She thought for a moment before stuffing them into her blouse and hurrying out of the room.

28

CATARINA, NICARAGUA
The Next Day

The rain had turned the road leading to the clinic into a muddy wallow littered with jutting rocks and puddles the size of a bath tub. Sonny suddenly felt grateful that a four wheel drive Jeep was the only vehicle the rental agent in Managua could offer on such short notice. He grabbed the dash to steady him and turned to glance out the rear window. All he could make out though the mud splattered glass was the brown arc of road as it disappeared into the muddled green veil of trees.

"Don't worry, Blanco's boys aren't gonna follow us," Ray said, glancing in the mirror. "My guess is they already know where we're going."

"How so?"

"I'm sure they knew about us before we even landed. Knew what car we were driving before we left the rental lot. It's not like the old days. You have to realize that even the Third World is wired up. Hard to hide from the goddamn computers."

Sonny started to turn back around but instead glanced at Harper. She met his gaze with indifference and looked back out the window. She had a large bruise on the right side of her face and her lower lip was swollen and scabbed where it had split.

There had been little conversation between the three of them on the drive down from Managua. There had been even less on the flight from Bilwi. The truth of the matter was none of them had much to say ever since leaving on the hastily arranged dead of night flight from Puerto Lempira.

Freddie's *mara* friends just happened to know a young Miskito with a plane for hire. For two hundred dollars and a tank of gas he would fly them to Bilwi on the coast just across the border into Nicaragua. Fortunately, the young Indian had proven to be more skillful at flying a plane than bargaining, for the flight had been a roller coast ride of abrupt banks and white knuckle plunges as he maneuvered the small plane through and around a string of thunderstorms. They arrived in Bilwi with just enough time to catch the morning's return La Costeña flight to Managua.

The events of the night before combined with their fatigue created a fog of palpable tension between the three of them that none of them seemed willing or able to breach. Even the hastily devoured breakfast of huevos y gallo pinto at the airport lounge had been interrupted by only the most rudimentary dialogue. Sonny couldn't blame Harper for her sullenness. Twice now he had almost gotten her killed. Still it didn't surprise him when she told them she was accompanying them to Catarina.

"I wouldn't miss it for the world," she had murmured solemnly through her swollen lips.

He waited a moment in vain to see if she would say something before turning back in his seat. Ray slowed the Jeep as the gray silhouette of the clinic appeared between the feeble swipes of the windshield wipers. He drove the Jeep up into the yard before cutting the ignition.

"There's something I forgot to tell you," Ray said, his voice almost lost in the drumming of the rain on the Jeep's roof.

"Why does that not surprise me?" Sonny said.

"So I don't always tell you everything. Get over it. What I was gonna tell you is that Blanco and Granera had some kind of connection. I get the feeling it was some old score that never was settled. Granera told me something last night. Something about Blanco interfering with him. Denying him something is how he put it."

"Let me guess. Now that we've done his dirty work, you figure he's going to have to sit down with us. See what we know."

"You got it. And it won't surprise me that he'll be waiting for us out on the road."

Ray opened the door and struggled for a moment before propelling himself out into the downpour. It was obvious he was in a great deal of pain from where Slater had kicked him, a condition aggravated by the loss of his cane. Sonny hesitated a moment before swinging open his door and stepping out into the driving rain. By the time he made his way through the mud and onto the porch, Harper had joined Ray beneath the porch's leaking canopy. Sonny walked past them and opened the screen door leading into the clinic.

The doorway opened into what appeared to be a small waiting room. A badly dented bucket sat in the center of the floor to catch the steady drip of water from the leaking roof. A poster on one of the unpainted sheetrock walls proclaimed the many benefits of condoms. Other than a pair of crude wooden benches and a soggy pile of discarded magazines, the room sat empty.

"*Hola!*" Ray yelled out. Not bothering to wait for a reply, Sonny brushed past him and walked into the next room.

Alemán sat at the far end of a long wooden table, his attention focused on whatever he was doing between the splayed legs of a young woman who lie stretched out on her back before him. Her simple muslin dress had been hiked up to her mid thighs, revealing her mud smeared calves. She craned her neck to look up at them, her expression reflecting nothing more than mild curiosity.

Alemán glanced up at them briefly, and then tossed a pair of long forceps onto a metal tray beside him. He stripped off his surgical gloves and dropped them into a wastebasket at his feet, all the while his eyes on Sonny. "*Momentitio*, señora," he said as he delicately pulled the woman' dress up over her knees. He turned his gaze to Harper and then to Ray, his eyes finally settling on Ray's bandaged hand. "It appears your inquiries did not go well," he said.

"Actually things went better than expected," Sonny said, reaching into shirt and pulling out the manila envelope. He removed the photograph and held it out to Alemán.

Alemán used the back of his hand to nudge his glasses higher on his nose and gave the photo a cursory glance.

"You know where I got this?" Sonny asked.

Alemán looked up at Sonny and cocked his head. "I should know this child?"

"Cut the bullshit, Alemán. I took it from your father. I got this from him, too," Sonny said, tossing him the medicine bottle.

Alemán caught the bottle in both hands. He didn't bother to study it, but instead set it on the table in front of him. He stared at Sonny, his face expressionless, before finally looking at Harper. "I have a request, Miss....?"

"Call me Harper."

"Harper. I could use your assistance. It seems my nurse has been detained by the storm."

Harper nodded and walked over and stood beside the doctor. Alemán leaned closer and inspected her face. "You have cleaned your wounds well I hope. In this climate, they tend to fester. When we are done here you must allow me to clean them properly. As for the two of you, please wait outside. Then we will talk," he added when Sonny made no effort to leave.

While they had been inside the downpour had slowed, the rain now only a soft patter on the clinic's tin roof. Sonny waited for Ray to join him on the porch before dropping onto the bench. Ray stood there awkwardly for a moment before lowering himself beside Sonny. Neither of them said anything for a moment.

"As soon as this is over I'm going back to Santa Fe," Ray

225

said finally. "Seems my work here is done," he said with a smirk.

"You mean your work where you fuck up everything you touch?"

"*Exactamente.*"

Sonny smiled and shook his head. They again fell into silence, each seemingly content to stare out at the rain. Ray grimaced as he stretched out his bad leg in front of him.

"I realized something last night," he said. "Something I don't care to admit." He paused before going on. "That asshole, Slater. There was a time when I was a lot like him."

Sonny looked at him. "I doubt you were ever like Slater."

Ray didn't reply at first. "You don't know half the stuff I did. I crossed a lot of lines. Macy made me step away from that," he said, glancing out at the empty corn field. "It's no excuse for some of what I've done, but what happened to Aminta, and you…I don't think I ever really faced up to it." He looked back at Sonny. "You deserve to know the truth about all that happened."

"I think I've already heard enough. Let it go, Ray. I have."

Ray nodded and fell silent. "You have to do something for me," he said finally. "If you find her, you tell her…" He shook his head and started over. "You just tell her I'm sorry."

Sonny clapped his hand on Ray's thigh. "Let's not be getting all touchy feely, okay? Doesn't become you."

Ray snorted and looked away. "Do you have this figured out yet?" he said after a while.

"You mean about Alemán being Granera's son? What else am I supposed to think? This photo. The medicine bottles with his name on them." He looked at Ray who sat staring silently at the floor. "Unless there's something else you're not telling me."

"He's the right age, isn't he? Alemán?"

Sonny looked away. He guessed at what Ray was intimating. It was obvious, wasn't it? Aminta's son. Granera's son. Made sense. Maybe. Unless… He couldn't bring himself to consider the other possibility.

"I told you I talked to this old priest. This informant of mine from the old days. He said there was a rumor that Alemán is… or was Granera's kid. As far as who was Alemán's mother… *No se.* He wasn't telling or he didn't really know. Not that I believed him."

The screen door opened and the young woman Alemán had been ministering to stepped out onto the porch, Harper at her side. Harper held the woman's elbow as she slowly made her way to the edge of the porch, her muddy sandals scraping across the porch's rough wood planking. The woman hesitated at the edge, then carefully stepped down into the mud and started off.

Harper turned and looked at Sonny. "Shouldn't we drive her home?"

Before Sonny could say anything, Alemán appeared at the door carrying what appeared to be a coffee pot and four mismatched tin cups. "She would not accept your offer," he said. "Besides, her home is only three kilometers from here."

"Three kilometers?" Harper said, shaking her head.

Alemán handed them each a cup and then filled them with café con leche. The smell of the coffee along with that of the wet mud elicited in Sonny some vague ennui; a fleeting sense of comfort that just as quickly was replaced by an unnamed dread.

"I knew her father," Alemán said, squatting peasant style at the edge of the porch. "He lost his arm in the war, yet he worked in the fields every day up until the day before he died. These people, they endure much and ask for little." He took a swallow of his coffee and looked at Sonny. "The photograph. May I see?"

Sonny picked it up from the bench beside him and handed it to Alemán. The doctor examined both sides carefully before handing it back. "I suppose you wish to know if Granera was my father, yes?"

"Among other things," Sonny replied.

Alemán took another swallow of coffee before replying. "He is dead?"

"Yeah, he's dead."

Alemán nodded. "I think he believed that he was my father. At one time, I believed that also."

"What about your mother? She never told you?"

"So you know? About my mother?"

"Your mother was Aminta Garza-Segovia. Right?"

Alemán shrugged and looked away. Sonny could tell he was trying to decide how to answer. "My mother," he said after a moment had passed. "She..." He hesitated and started over. "My earliest memories of her are of her painting. Night and day she painted. I remember lying in her bed, watching her as she worked at her canvases. Many years later, I found out she had burned every one of them. This was after he took me from her."

He fell silent for a long moment, his eyes fixed on something in the near distance, as if he were replaying some film in his mind. "I still remember the day. *Dia de los Difuntos.* The Day of the Dead," he said, looking back at them. "That night there was a festival in the village. A bonfire. Music. And then I woke up and he is standing over my bed. My mother hit him with a pot, but he pushed her away. He hit her then many times. I must have been five or six. Too young to stop him."

He looked back at Sonny. "He took me to Guatemala. To El Salvador. He kept me close. We lived in many places. And I came to know him as my father. I never forgot her though."

"And Granera raised you? As his son?"

"Yes, he raised me as if I was his son. He sent me to the finest schools. To medical school even. You are curious about the medicines? He was here. A year ago. But this time he did not ask about her. He merely wanted my help. I could see he was dying. I gave him medicines. That is all."

He looked at Sonny. "It is complicated. It is true he was not my father. And yes, he was not a good man. But I helped him.

Or so he thought. I knew the medicines would not save him. Perhaps I wanted him to have false hope."

"I need to know what happened after the war," Sonny said. "What happened to your mother?"

He gestured with his chin in the direction of the lake. "We lived in the house by the lake. You know Presciliano? The man you spoke to in the field? He freed my mother. After Granera had fled. He brought her here. Protected her. Or tried to."

He fell silent for a moment. "After Granera took me, my mother disappeared. Many people thought she had died. Others said she had gone away. To Mexico. To Costa Rica. They said only Presciliano knew the truth. And when Granera came back again to look for her, he found only Presciliano. So Granera and some men took him away. You saw Presciliano's hands? They did that. But he never told them anything. My mother was gone."

"But she's alive, isn't she?"

It was obvious from the look on Alemán's face that Sonny's question caused some private pain for he quickly turned away. "I came back to Catarina," he said after a moment."I came back because I wanted to know the truth about my mother."

"And you found her?"

"No. She was gone. The house was no more. Burned." He looked out at the cornfield."But Presciliano was here, living in the ruins. There was nothing left of her. Nothing but the one painting. The one I sold. Presciliano had hidden it all those years."

"Are you saying she's dead?"

Alemán shook his head, the bitterness again obvious in his face. "No," he muttered.

"Then where is she?"

Alemán downed the last of his coffee and dropped the cup at his feet. "Presciliano warned me you would come back. That you would want to know things. He says nothing good can come of knowing. You see, in my country, too many of us are at war with our memories. The memories often win. These memories, they are often *muy tragico."*

"Goddammit! Where is she?"

"You are not my father," Alemán said, his anger visible. "Isn't that what you really want to know?"

Sonny shook his head in frustration. "Look, I just want to see her."

"It is not possible."

"What do you mean it's not possible? She's alive, isn't she?"

"It is not possible. No one can. No one but me. And Jasique."

"Jasique?" Ray asked. "Blanco? What's he got to do with her?"

Alemán shook his head. *"Madre. Perdón."* He mumbled something unintelligible. "He has protected her. Protected me. All these years. He still protects us. It was… *una deuda.* A debt. It was what he said. Blanco owed her a debt."

Sonny looked at Ray, his own bewilderment mirrored in Ray's face.

"What kind of debt?"

"That is not for me to say."

"To hell with Blanco. Just tell me where she is," Sonny said.

Alemán held Ray's gaze for a long moment before replying. "You must understand. My mother…she is *enclaustrada.* I forget how you say the word in English."

"Means something like closed up, doesn't it?" Ray asked.

"En convento. My mother, she is in a convent."

"Cloistered? Where no one can see her? Is that what you mean?" Harper asked.

"Yes. There she is safe. Safe from the past. Safe from everyone. From you."

"You've seen her though?" Sonny asked.

Alemán hesitated. "Yes, I have seen her. I visit the convent often. I serve as their physician. Now if you will excuse me, I have work to do," he said, getting to his feet.

Sonny stared out at the approaching dusk, too stunned to say anything. "How long?" he said after a moment. "How long has she been there?"

Alemán paused as he started to open the screen door. He glanced down at the floor, his back to Sonny. "A very long time. Almost twenty three years," he said quietly and disappeared inside.

Harper moved from where she had been standing next to the door and sat beside Sonny. He looked at her and shook his head. "Seems you've got your story," he said.

"There isn't a story until there's an ending."

"I thought we just heard it."

"Not quite," Ray said, nodding with his chin towards the road. "Didn't I tell you he'd be along soon enough?"

A black Toyota Four Runner edged its way slowly through the trees, stopping just short of where the road ended at the edge of the cornfield. Because of the heavily tinted windows and the approaching dusk it was impossible to see who was inside. It sat idling there for a minute or so before resuming its careful track across the muddy yard towards the clinic's porch and coming to a stop beside their Jeep. Another minute seemed to pass before the front passenger door opened and Blanco emerged. He paused for a moment to remove his white linen jacket and toss it into the front seat before picking his way through the thick, ankle deep red mud. He stopped at the edge of the porch to scrape the mud from his shoes, and then looked up at them.

"My wife. She will be disappointed," he said, gesturing at his mud stained pants legs. "Your arrival has been inconvenient. We had dinner plans." He tugged at the strap of his shoulder holster and smiled. "I believe we have not yet met," he said to Sonny, extending his hand.

Sonny made no effort to rise from the bench but merely

stared at Blanco.

Blanco dropped his hand to his side and looked at Ray. "I assume your trip to Honduras went well?"

"Granera's dead, if that's what you're asking. Now you owe us some answers," Ray said.

Blanco looked away for a moment before turning to Sonny. "I must also assume Rigoberto has told you certain things. Things you must find difficult to understand."

"Like why you locked Aminta up in a convent for twenty three years," Sonny said.

"It was her decision. Not mine."

"Alemán said you owed her some kind of debt. What debt?"

Blanco raised his hand to his mouth and closed his eyes as if carefully deliberating his reply. When he opened them, they revealed what Sonny could only guess was an immense sorrow. And possibly also relief for he sighed deeply as if some crushing weight had been lifted from his soul. He looked at Sonny and what passed for a smile seemed to restore some semblance of composure to his face.

"My debt? I owed Aminta a life. You see, it was I who betrayed her. It was because of me that she fell into his hands. Yes, I owed her a life."

29

Ray gaped at Blanco, too stunned at first to react. Blanco's revelation had apparently affected Sonny in the same way, for Ray saw his friend slump down as if the air had been sucked out of him. No one spoke for several moments, the silence filled by the slow drumming of the rain and the undulating chorus of the frogs.

"You son of a bitch," Ray muttered as he pushed himself up and launched himself unsteadily at Blanco.

"Careful, my friend," Blanco said, stepping back. "Don't be foolish." He looked over at Sonny. "You deserve answers. Unfortunately, that is all I can offer you."

"I just want to know why," Ray said. "Why any of this? Why did you send us after Granera?"

"I sent you because it was convenient," Blanco said, his voice rising in unexpected anger. "What is the word your government likes to use? Deniability, yes? I wanted Granera dead. But this was something I could not do myself. Why not? Because there are members of my government who forbade me from interfering with him or his business. Yes, you were convenient."

He walked over to Sonny and leaned down to meet his eyes. "What happened to Aminta deserved justice. Retribution."

Sonny looked up at Blanco. "She deserved more than that,"

he said.

Blanco nodded, and then turned and dragged one of the benches and placed it across from Sonny. "Sit, my friend," he said, gesturing to Ray. "You must realize certain things," he said once Ray had joined him. "It was not my decision to place her in the convent. At least not entirely. You see…" He paused to gather his thoughts. "She had lost too many things. Her friends. Her family. A lover," he said, looking at Sonny. "And her son. She had paid too high a price."

Ray glanced over at the doorway and saw that Alemán had quietly joined them on the porch. In the approaching dusk, it was difficult to clearly see his face.

"Granera taking Rigoberto from her was the final blow. Here we call it *el dolor.* Grief. I believe there is a term in your language. Post-Traumatic Stress Disorder. Yes? She was… lost. She wanted nothing more than to leave this world. I believe she considered taking her life, but she could not. Suicide, even insanity, were not options for her. Not for someone as strong as her."

He sighed deeply before going on.

"That was how I found her. You see, I too thought she was dead. After the war ended, I looked for her. By then, I had many eyes and ears at my disposal. I heard many rumors. But found nothing. Finally, I came here. To Catarina. I found her living in the ruins of her house like an animal."

He paused again before going on. "I brought her to the convent out of desperation. I knew Granera would not find her there. Life would not find her there. Do you understand this?" he asked, touching Sonny's arm.

"You said you betrayed her," Sonny said. "What happened?"

Blanco glanced at Ray. "Your friend here, he of all people should understand what I am about to tell you. The treachery of those times. A treachery we all shared in."

"Speak for yourself, Blanco," Ray said.

Blanco shrugged in assent. "Several days before, I was detained by Somoza's police. I happened to be at the wrong place, with the wrong people when it happened. You know what they did to people near the end. The torture. I meant to save myself. So I gave them your name," he said, looking at Ray. "I told them I was one of your informants. A spy for your government.

"One of your men, an agent of the CIA, was there with my interrogators. I never knew his name, but I recognized him. It seems Granera already knew of Aminta's plan. Someone had talked. In the end, they released me."

He lowered his head and murmured something unintelligible. When he looked up, Ray sensed that Blanco was on the verge of sobbing. Blanco wiped his mouth with the back of his hand. "I did not warn her. For that I am guilty."

"Why? You must've known what would happen to her," Sonny said.

"Why? Because it was necessary for me to…How do you say? Ingratiate myself, yes? To make them think I was working for them. Aminta was to be sacrificed. To play a bigger game. It is what my superiors ordered me to do. I followed orders. You may think this…*escéptico*. Cynical, yes? "

"You knew they would kill her," Sonny said, his voice trembling with emotion.

"*Claro*. Of course," Blanco said, his own voice now breaking. He lowered his head into his hands. *"Así, mi deuda.* My debt, my sin." It sounded almost poetic coming from a man like Blanco.

"You said something about justice for Aminta. How about you? What price have you paid?" Sonny asked bitterly.

"I have lived with my sin for over two decades. It is often in my mind as I fall asleep at night. If I sleep. My punishment may have not been so severe, but I assure you, I have honored my guilt."

No one spoke for a moment."I still want to talk her," Sonny said, finally.

"As I said, that is not possible. Perhaps if you wish to see the convent. That can be arranged. But only on one condition. You must promise to never again ask to see her. Agreed?"

Sonny didn't reply at first. "No," he said after a moment. "I can't agree to that."

"Then I am afraid…"

"I will bring you there," Alemán said. "To see her."

They all turned and looked at Alemán.

"Rigo, I made a promise to her," Blanco said.

"Yes, Jasique. You did. You made a promise to protect her. This man, I suspect, he also once made that promise." Alemán looked at Sonny. "Tomorrow, we will go. You may see her only. Nothing more," he said and turned and walked inside.

30

Blanco picked them up at their hotel before dawn in what appeared to be a brand new Ford Expedition with the requisite blacked out windows. The streets were mostly empty, save for small dark knots of people on their way to work or perhaps to the large market located several blocks away from the Parque Central. Even though the air felt cool and damp, Blanco ran the air conditioner at full throttle, fogging the windows and forcing Harper to move closer to Sonny in the back seat in an effort to stay warm.

When they checked into their hotel after leaving Aleman's clinic, Harper had requested her own room. She didn't offer Sonny an explanation, all the while avoiding his gaze. Whether her reticence to engage him was some form of emotional sanctuary, or some misguided attempt to spare Sonny any confusion over allegiances, he wasn't sure. Regardless of the reason, he sensed her distance. He half-expected her to knock on his door later that night, but it wasn't until they met in the lobby as they waited for Ray, that she seemed willing to convey anything.

"The big day, huh?" she said, offering a faint smile.

"You don't have to do this."

"I thought you knew me better than that by now," she replied, her voice betraying a hint of bitterness.

"I thought you liked options."

"I do. So what are ours?"

"Harper…"

"I mean, what happens tomorrow?"

He shrugged. "To be honest, about three o'clock this morning I was half-considering taking a cab to Managua and flying… somewhere. I'm lost here, Harper. I'm sorry if I'm no help, but that's all there is."

"You mean to us? That's all there is to us?"

"No, that's not what I said. I meant that's all there is to me. Now. Today. Tomorrow? Who knows? You have to understand. I'm…opening up this door that someone shut on me thirty years ago. And I don't know what's going to happen."

She fell silent. "I get it," she said, finally. "I really do. It's what I would do."

"What do mean what you would do?"

"Never mind," she said. "Here's Ray," she said, nodding at the elevator.

He reached for her hand but she slid from his grasp.

Now they sat huddled in the back seat as Blanco maneuvered through the narrow streets on the outskirts of Granada on their way to pick up Alemán, who they had arranged to meet that morning. The cobblestoned streets had given way to muddy, irregular roadway studded with rocks and flooded potholes. Most of the houses were cinder block structures, but here and there were what appeared to be hastily thrown together affairs of plywood and discarded corrugated metal. To his surprise, many, even the crudest of them, sported television antennas. Sonny rolled down the window as the first rays of sunlight pierced the cloak of thin fog. The air carried the smell of wood smoke and the cloyingly sweet bouquet of burnt sugar so common to Central America.

They found Alemán leaning against an ancient Toyota pickup truck beneath a huge amate tree beside a deserted gas station. He held what appeared to be a doctor's bag in one hand, in the other a large thermos with a ring of small tin cups attached by a string to the thermos' handle. He joined Harper and Sonny in the back seat, offering them each a slight nod and nothing more.

"*Cafecito*," he said, lifting the thermos.

Blanco murmured something in Spanish about not ruining his new seats. Alemán grunted in obvious irritation, and then painstakingly began filling them each a cup of the steaming coffee. Blanco didn't refuse his, but instead slurped the coffee noisily as he did his best to guide the SUV through the rough, uneven streets.

"How far do we have to go?" Sonny asked.

"An hour, perhaps. No more," Alemán replied. "It depends if the road is passable. The rain…"

They drove in silence as the road beyond the barrio opened onto scrubby woodland that still held patches of thick fog in the arroyos. After a while, the road began to wind its way up into thickly forested headland. Patches of paving block covered many of the low lying stretches, but for the most part, the road was unpaved. Here, the fog was thicker, obscuring everything but the dense curtain of dripping forest on either side of them. Only a thin hint of sunlight penetrated the shroud of drifting mist and drizzle. They drove like this for perhaps a half hour before the roadway again opened onto rolling hills and pastureland.

"What's the name of this place?" Ray asked.

"*Convento de la Concepción Inmaculado,*" Alemán replied. "It is quite small. Perhaps, fifty nuns. Not many young women choose this life anymore." He shrugged. "I am not devout by any means, but I believe religion serves a purpose. If it were not for religion, the poor in my country would rise up and kill the rich."

"Wasn't that what the revolution was all about?" Ray asked.

Blanco laughed. "Yes, in theory. I often wonder what has really changed."

"So how do you reconcile a view like that with your job?" Harper interjected.

239

Blanco shrugged. "Someone must do this. Better me than others, yes?"

A few moments later, a simple wooden sign beside the road announced the convent ahead. A faded canvas banner draped from the trees above the sign proclaimed *"Madre de Heros y Matires Ruega por Nosotros"*.

"Mother of Heroes and Martyrs Pray for Us," Sonny said in response to Harper's questioning look.

The road ended in a small clearing, its far boundary marked by a high, adobe wall. Just beyond the wall, they could make out what looked like a small chapel, and beyond that, the façade of a two story stucco structure. Blanco pulled up in front of the gate and cut the engine.

"You must wait here," Alemán said, exiting the SUV. He picked up his bag and disappeared through the gate as Blanco also got out and walked a short distance away. They could see he was talking on his cell phone.

"You really trust him?" Sonny asked.

"Who? Blanco? Do we have a choice anymore? I have to get out. My legs are killing me," Ray said as he climbed out of the SUV.

Sonny looked at Harper. "About this morning…"

"Forget it," Harper said almost too quickly. "I understand. I really do."

"It's just that…I don't want to confuse what I'm feeling with what all that's happened. Am I making sense?"

"Perfect sense. I've been there. Letting feelings get ahead of me. Why don't we just take it as it comes?"

Alemán stepped through the gate and walked over to Blanco. The two men spoke for a moment before Alemán turned and walked back inside. Blanco motioned for Ray to join him and they walked over to the SUV. Sonny lowered his window.

"If you wish to see her, then you must follow me," Blanco said. He gestured with his head to the top of a hillside that backed up to the convent grounds.

"Count me out," Ray said.

"Muy bien. Come," Blanco said as he reached inside the SUV and retrieved a pair of binoculars from the console.

The trail up the hillside led through thick stands of Caribbean pine. Here, the air held the musky, chlorine-like smell of decay and wet mud. As they hiked, their movements stirred up flocks of motmots and seedeaters inhabiting the verdant undergrowth. Sonny regretted not choosing better footwear, for he and Harper slipped and fell several times on the steep, slippery trail. Even Blanco, who wore boots, appeared to have difficulty negotiating the slope.

By the time they reached the summit, their clothes were soaked through from the rainy mist and the effort of the climb. Blanco walked to the edge of a small outcropping and motioned for them to join him. From this vantage point, they could see the grounds of the convent, and beyond that in the distance, the dim silhouette of Volcán Masaya. Behind the two story building, a field had been cleared of trees and appeared to have been cultivated with rows of corn, fruit trees and what he guessed were vegetables of some kind. A few figures were visible amongst the rows of plants, their backs bent in toil.

"So she's supposed to be down there somewhere?" Sonny asked.

"Wait," Blanco replied.

After several minutes, a man, Alemán from the figure's appearance, emerged from the building and walked over to one of the nuns standing amongst the rows of corn. He appeared to converse with the nun for several minutes. After a while, Alemán turned and walked back inside. The nun started to follow, and then hesitated and turned towards the hillside and looked up. Blanco handed Sonny the binoculars without comment.

Sonny raised the binoculars to his face and adjusted the focus for a moment before he was able to make out the figure. She wore a habit that obscured most of her face. But he could clearly see that she was staring in his direction. Other than the vague visage of her face, the only other visible parts of her body were her hands which she held folded in front of her. They both stood like this, frozen in...What? Memory? Regret? He would never know what she was thinking. Or what she felt after all this time had passed.

After a long moment, she lifted her one arm in some vague, tenuous gesture. Then she nodded and turned and walked back towards the convent. Sonny watched her until she disappeared behind a wall.

"That's all?" Sonny asked Blanco, lowering the binoculars.

"I am afraid so, my friend. Come," he said, turning to leave.

All this time had passed. The remorse, the self-recrimination. For this? He felt deflated, disappointed. But at the same time he felt an indefinable feeling that something had passed. Was it merely closure? He somehow realized that he might not fully know for a long time, if ever. He looked at Harper who returned his gaze with a mixture of puzzlement and sympathy.

"I'm sorry," was all she managed to say. She shook her head and started after Blanco.

Sonny hesitated and glanced once more down at the field of corn before joining them.

Ray climbed out of the SUV as he saw them approach. "So?" he asked.

"I saw her. Or I guess I did. It was hard to tell."

"And that's it?"

Sonny shrugged.

They all turned at the sound of the gate opening and watched as Alemán walked towards them. He held a large burlap sack that appeared to hold something oblong and thin. He walked up to Sonny and handed him the burlap sack.

"She wanted me to give you this."

"What did she say?"

"Only that you would understand."

"That was all?"

"You must realize she has taken a vow of silence. Her words are never many. I am sorry. You expected more I'm sure."

Sonny walked over to Blanco's truck and propped the package carefully against the fender. He stared at it a moment, guessing at its contents from its heft and feel, before slowly slipping off the burlap shroud. The painting had been done in what appeared to be inexpensive acrylics laid down on a thin sheet of sanded plywood. His eyes were at first drawn to the words scrawled boldly in gold leaf at the bottom. *'Naturaleza Muerta en un Vestido Rojo.'* AGS. There was no date. He considered the words a moment before lifting his gaze to the image above.

It depicted a likeness of a young woman standing alone in a field of waist high sunflowers. She wore an elegant red evening gown, her bare shoulders just visible beneath her long red tresses. Her attention seemed to be focused on something just slightly offstage, the eyes holding a hint of amusement. Her smile was serene but vaguely wistful, the full lips slightly open. In her one hand she held a spray of red roses, in the other, a pair of artist's paint brushes. In the far background, loomed the iconic outline of the volcano turned crimson and gold in the reflected light of the setting sun.

Sonny pulled his eyes away, his anguish suddenly too great to endure looking at the image any longer. It was only when he looked at it again that he noticed the two small figures standing at the edge of the field of sunflowers. A man holding a small child, his arm raised in greeting. He stared at it a moment longer before placing it on the hood and turning away.

"What does that writing on the bottom say?" he heard Harper ask.

"It says 'Still Life in a Red Dress'," Ray said after a moment.

Sonny walked over to the gate and placed both his hands on its roughly hewn surface. It took everything he had to keep himself from pushing it aside and walking in. He knew it wasn't the answer. Or what she wanted. He lowered his forehead against its surface and stayed there a moment before finally turning away and joining his friends. Blanco and Alemán had already gotten back into the SUV.

He picked up the painting and slipped it back into its burlap sleeve. "I want you to take this back with you," he said, handing it to Ray. "Hang on to it for me. Maybe, come summer, I'll make it back to Santa Fe. And you might want to show it to Macy," he said as an afterthought. "Maybe she'll understand. Who knows? She might even go a little easier on you."

Ray nodded and smiled."I can always hope."

"Sonny," Harper said. "There's something I should've shown you." She lowered her eyes as she looked away. She cleared her throat and looked back at him. "There was this," she said, removing a sheaf of papers from her handbag. "If you remember, they were with the photograph. You left them on the floor at Granera's." She held them out to him.

He looked at them without taking them. "What are they?"

"There's a copy of Rigoberto's birth certificate. I thought you might want to see it."

He stared at the papers before lifting his eyes to meet hers.

"There's no name listed for the father, but there's something else. The hospital report. About the delivery. I had the clerk at the hotel translate it for me. It says the term of gestation was thirty nine weeks. He was born in August. Doesn't that mean Alemán could be your son?"

"Or Granera's. Or anyone of…"He shook his head, not wanting to consider the other possibilities.

"There are ways to know for sure. DNA testing. Sonny…" she said when he looked away.

"And what if it isn't me? I don't want to know that. Don't you understand?"

He took the papers from her and held them without looking

at them. "It doesn't make any difference," he said. "It doesn't change anything."

He watched her face react in bewilderment as he slowly tore the pages in half. Then he tore them again and again until they were only small crumpled squares. He dropped them into the puddle of muddy rainwater at his feet.

"Sonny..." Her eyes were wet.

He looked at the convent. "Maybe Aminta had a point to make. About a still life. It's all she ever really wanted, you know. Maybe I'm realizing we all deserve that." He looked back at her. "I think I'm going to stay down here a while. Alemán can probably use some help. Maybe I'll put a new roof on the clinic. Add on to his waiting room."

Harper smiled."Okay. You want some company?"

He reached over and stroked her cheek. "I'm not sure a still life is compatible with a woman in need of lots of options. At least not yet. Give me some time. I'm not going anywhere."

"In that case, I'll hang on to this." She reached into her handbag and brought out a key chain with a single key attached.

"What's that?"

"A key to a storage locker in Brooklyn. Your Cuban records. Consider it collateral. I expect you to call me from the airport some cold snowy night and maybe I'll let you buy me dinner and redeem them."

He smiled and nodded. "I'll hold you to that."

They turned to go, but Sonny hesitated and glanced once more at the convent. One of the upper story windows lay open. For just a moment, he thought he saw a figure standing in the shadow. He watched for a moment, and then raised his hand in a vague gesture of farewell and turned away.

AUTHOR'S NOTES

I suspect, for many Americans, the Nicaraguan Civil War that took place in the late 1970's is a distant, vague memory. For a generation of younger Americans, that war, along with the subsequent Contra War and the Iran-Contra scandal, most likely fail to even register on the radar. As for me, that particular Central American conflict still manages to resonate in my consciousness. Perhaps it is only my leftist leanings or the fact that I am a junkie for current events that explains my fascination for that time and locale. And it probably explains why an obscure article in a long since misplaced newspaper or magazine caught my attention.

The article in question related a little known incident that took place during that conflict, the subject of which was a woman by the name of Nora Astorga. I suspect the article may have appeared on the anniversary of her death in 1988, but I can't really be sure of the timing or the circumstance that led me to delve further into her story. I invite the reader to Google her biography for more details of her life.

Her story, a fascinating tale of intrigue and bravery, is worthy of Hollywood treatment. Subsequently, reading about her stirred my creative juices. But the idea sat on the back burner of my imagination for years waiting to evolve into a story line I might use in a fictional work. When I undertook writing *STILL LIFE IN A RED DRESS*, I had only the vaguest idea of weaving her story into my novel. The story line finally evolved with its usual false starts and dead ends.

This story is a work of fiction. The characters and circumstances arise from my imagination. Only the central germ of Ms. Astorga's experience serves as the central plot device. Instead of an attorney, the Nicaraguan woman in my story is an artist- a painter. Her lover, a young American working for the US Agency for International Development, is also imagined, as is his friend in the CIA. Only the details of the pivotal episode that vaulted Ms. Astorga into the annals of history are borrowed for the central drama of this story.

The heroine of my story, and by extension Nora Astorga, may seem iconic on some level. By that I mean her story serves as a reminder that it is only through great courage and struggle that circumstances change, that worlds move and a different future can be realized. On the other hand, her saga should not be taken as some leftist anthem to an idealistic revolution, for the political and social progress that has been made in Nicaragua is uneven and is a work in progress at the very least. Patriotism has many faces, some that present a countenance we might find unsettling. Still, her story is a universal one of heroism and sacrifice. I hope you enjoy it.

Santa Fe, New Mexico
January, 2012